Louise Allen has been immersing herself in history for as long as she can remember, finding landscapes and places that evoke powerful images of the past. Venice, Burgundy and the Greek islands are favourites. Louise lives on the Norfolk coast and spends her spare time gardening, researching family history or travelling. Please visit Louise's website, www.louiseallenregency.com, her blog, www.janeaustenslondon.com, or find her on Twitter @LouiseRegency and Facebook.

Also by Louise Allen

Marrying His Cinderella Countess
The Earl's Practical Marriage
A Lady in Need of an Heir
Convenient Christmas Brides
'The Viscount's Yuletide Bride'
Contracted as His Countess

Liberated Ladies miniseries

Least Likely to Marry a Duke
The Earl's Marriage Bargain
A Marquis in Want of a Wife
The Earl's Reluctant Proposal
A Proposal to Risk Their Friendship

Discover more at millsandboon.co.uk.

THE DUKE'S
COUNTERFEIT WIFE

Louise Allen

MILLS & BOON

First published in Great Britain 2021
by Mills & Boon, an imprint of HarperCollins*Publishers* Ltd,
1 London Bridge Street, London, SE1 9GF

www.harpercollins.co.uk

HarperCollins*Publishers*
1st Floor, Watermarque Building,
Ringsend Road, Dublin 4, Ireland

Large Print edition 2022

The Duke's Counterfeit Wife © 2021 Melanie Hilton

ISBN: 978-0-263-29594-8

03/22

MIX
Paper from
responsible sources
FSC™ C007454

This book is produced from independently certified FSC™ paper to ensure responsible forest management. For more information visit www.harpercollins.co.uk/green.

Printed and Bound in the UK using 100% Renewable Electricity at CPI Group (UK) Ltd, Croydon, CR0 4YY

Chapter One

June 1st 1819, a London quayside at dawn

'I do wish you would reconsider and travel by the Mail, or even take the stagecoach, Miss Parrish,' Mrs Walgrave lamented. 'You would be in Great Yarmouth in twelve hours and with snug inns along the way.' She looked around at the grimy dockside in the early morning light, her sniff of disapproval eloquent.

The housekeeper's hasty sidestep as a porter rushed by, pushing a loaded barrow, somewhat diminished her dignity.

'*Snug* is not the word I would use to describe most of the inns I have encountered in my travels,' Sarah said, reaching out to steady her. 'I always become hideously queasy on the stage—and as for the Mail, why those springs are even worse than they are on a post-chaise. I enjoy travelling by sea and I do not suffer from seasickness—it must be all that fresh air. And it is half the price, into the bargain.' Which was always a consideration.

'Even so, goodness knows what insults and inconveniences might befall an unaccompanied young lady. All those rough sailors!' The Tower of London, looming on the horizon through the early morning mist, added melodramatic emphasis to the warning.

'Millie is with me and we will have a cabin to ourselves,' Sarah soothed the housekeeper. 'And Captain Barlow used to be one of Papa's bosuns and Papa was always exceedingly careful about the men he employed.'

'Yes, but goodness knows what depths the man has sunk to since your poor father's sad demise.'

'I cannot imagine why he should have *sunk*,' Sarah said briskly, refusing to contemplate the reference to the bankruptcy of her late father's shipping company and his subsequent suicide. 'After all, Mr Barlow has been promoted to captain, has he not? He will look after me well, I am certain. Now, dear Mrs Walgrave, the ship is just around this corner. Let us say goodbye here, for I know you must get back to Golden Square before Mr Cardew arrives to take possession, and time is getting on.'

'Oh, goodness, yes. I have to say, Miss Parrish, that I fear he is not going to prove to be an easy employer, so unlike our dear Miss Trotter.'

If Sarah needed evidence of that, then she had received it in the exceedingly curt note informing Miss Parrish that, as her employer was deceased, he, her nephew and heir, had no need for the services of a lady's companion and she would oblige him by quitting the premises before his arrival in one week's time.

She managed a cheerful smile. 'Mr Cardew is certain to recognise exemplary housekeeping, Mrs Walgrave. Now, thank you again, for all your kindnesses to me. Goodbye!'

'Goodbye, Miss Parrish, dear. You will write?'

It was clear that she was going to have to make a determined effort to leave, Sarah thought, or the anxious housekeeper was going to be standing here wringing her hands until the ship sailed. She leant forward, kissed the older woman warmly on the cheek. 'Come along, Millie.'

Her maid, who had been standing patiently throughout the prolonged farewell, picked up two of their valises and Sarah took the others, one in each hand. The thump as she turned away, only to run straight into something immovably solid, jolted her off balance. A large hand gripped her forearm as she teetered.

'I beg your pardon, ma'am,' the immovable object said coldly, revealing itself to be tall, dark, male and irritated. Behind them Mrs Walgrave gave an anxious squeak.

'It was entirely my fault, sir,' Sarah said, returning chill for chill. 'I was in haste to join my ship.' He was still holding her arm and she glanced down pointedly at the gloved hand.

'The *Yarmouth Gannet*?' the man enquired. 'I believe that is the only vessel moored at this end of the dock.'

'Yes, it is. Come along, Millie. Sir!'

He released her arm only to wrest the bags from her hands before striding off towards the corner of the warehouse.

'*Sir.*' She hurried after him. 'I can perfectly well manage— Oh! I have hurt your leg.' She must have trodden on his toes, or kicked him when she walked into him, because he was limping.

'No, you have not. Here is the ship. Allow me to go first, the gangplank is steep.'

Sarah told herself that the collision had been her fault and that if this rude man had an existing injury to his leg it was doubtless frustrating

to have people comment on the fact. He was behaving like a gentleman—albeit a very boorish
one—by helping her, she supposed.

She followed meekly up the gangplank, took
his proffered hand at the top and jumped down
to the deck. When she turned back to see if
Millie was managing all right she found that a
youthful manservant was helping her aboard.
Presumably he was in attendance on the dour
gentleman.

'Morning, ma'am. Sir. Captain Lockhart.' A
stocky, middle-aged man with teeth yellowed by
chewing tobacco and lank brown hair tied back
into a straggling queue came forward, gesturing to a sailor to take their bags. 'Miss Parrish
and Mr Smith, is it?'

He eyed them quizzically and Sarah realised
her hand was still resting on a sleeve of fine
broadcloth. She snatched it away. 'I am Miss
Parrish, yes. And this is my maid.'

'And I am Smith.' The gentleman gestured to
the silently waiting servant. 'My man.'

*Mr Smith? And I am the Duchess of Devon-
shire. I refuse to believe anyone with that accent,
that arrogance and that nose is called Smith.*

'Where is Captain Barlow?' Sarah asked,
averting her gaze from that haughty profile.

'You knew him, ma'am? Then you'll be grieved to hear he's dead. Fell off the dock here late last night. Drink taken, I fear. Very sad. Duncan, show Miss Parrish to her cabin.'

The sailor picked up two of the bags and she followed him, Millie close on her heels. They negotiated a steep companionway—her nautical jargon was coming back to her—and went a short way along a low, dark and odorous passageway. He opened a door, dumped the bags inside and jerked his thumb towards the stern of the ship.

'Saloon's along that way if you wants anything. Cook'll have some coffee on the stove. Breakfast after we sail.' He walked away, his bare feet slapping on the planks.

'Rude bu— Er…bloke,' Millie said. She was one of Sarah's late employer's charity girls, rescued from the local workhouse and given respectable jobs in the kitchen or as housemaids.

Once Sarah had managed to dissuade her from the worst of her colourful language she had proved to be bright and capable and eager for promotion to lady's maid. And, fortunately, she had been more than willing to accompany Sarah to her new post rather than risk the unknown quantity of Mr Cardew. 'We're getting our share of 'em this morning, miss.'

'We are,' Sarah said, trying to sound amused about it. The sailor was an uneducated man in a tough world. His lack of address was easily understood and overlooked. But as for Mr Smith... For some reason the memory of a pair of blue-black eyes would not be erased. They had not been as cold as the rest of him...

She gave herself a little shake: it was wrong to allow one overbearing male to assume more importance in her mind than the death of poor Captain Barlow. She had known the sailor only by name, but nothing could erase the anxiety that perhaps his drinking, which must have led to the accident, had been a result of the collapse of Parrish Shipping.

'I do not think we need go to the trouble of unpacking anything but the bedding.' She gave the cabin a critical survey. Two bunks, one above the other, furnished with thin straw-filled palliasses, a stool, some nails banged into the bulkheads and a dubious-looking pail in the corner comprised the furnishings and, eyeing what passed for bedlinen, she was glad she had packed sheets.

'If we hang this from those nails,' she said,

twitching the covering off the lower bunk, 'we can place that bucket behind it.'

'Yes, miss.' Millie shook out clean sheets. 'I thought sailors were supposed to scrub everything white. They could do with some well-trained housemaids around here.'

'You are thinking of holystoning, and the top deck looked clean enough. Never mind. It must surely be better than being cooped up in a stagecoach with people whose acquaintance with soap and water is minimal and whose idea of a sustaining snack is a large onion as happened to me once,' Sarah said.

'Shall we see what this saloon is like?' she suggested when they had finished their minimal unpacking. 'I expect it is nothing more than a space with benches and tables that drop down on chains, but it might be more interesting than this cabin for our meals and there may be other passengers.' Hopefully more congenial ones than Mr Smith. 'Then we will go on deck: they will be casting off soon.'

They encountered the taciturn gentleman surveying the common room with an expression of distaste. He bowed slightly and continued his inspection. Two burly men who looked as though they might be traders of some kind were deep in discussion in one corner. They half rose at the sight of a lady, then sat again and continued their conversation.

'Let us go on deck,' Sarah said and turned back in the direction of the companionway.

A hatch had been opened halfway along the passage and a large crate or box, about three feet square and wrapped in canvas, was being man-handled down by a gang of sailors.

There was a volley of instructions from on deck. 'Watch yourselves, you clumsy lubbers!'

Sarah put out a hand and drew Millie back into the slight protection of a cabin doorway as the box thudded to the deck, twisting slightly as it landed. A corner of the canvas caught on one of the iron brackets for holding lanterns and tore the stitches free along the length of one side.

The language from above increased in violence and Sarah slapped her hands over her ears, even as she peered at the damage, unashamedly curious. It was a well-made crate under the canvas, good wood tightly jointed with, on the top edge, a small branded mark made with a hot iron. *R. B. & R.*, she thought, squinting at it. And was that odd lumpy thing a crown?

When the canvas was wrestled back in place,

the men hoisted up the crate and made off down the passageway away from her, shuffling like crabs to move their burden in the narrow space.

Once their way was clear the two women went up on deck, found a small clear space by the rail and wrapped their cloaks firmly around them. Ropes were being cast off and sailors in a large rowing boat struggled to get the *Gannet*'s prow out into the flow. There was always something to look at on the river, Sarah thought, an almost forgotten contentment stealing over her.

'The tide's with us and will carry us down until there is wind for the sails,' she said, half to herself as she inhaled deeply. The familiar smells of tarred rope and bilge water mingled with the scents wafting from the warehouses—the exotic perfume of spices and tobacco, the greasy smell of wool, the clean scent of sawn timber. Her father would have been able to tell exactly where they were along the length of the docks, simply from the air around the warehouses.

She had stood like this too many times to recall, close against her father's side as one of his ships had slipped into the Thames and made its way to the ocean. He had taken her aboard when she was only a week old, he had told her on her sixteenth birthday. 'The business will be yours one day, Sally girl.'

Her mother had died at her birth and Papa had never seemed to have the heart to consider marrying again, even though it meant he had no son to inherit the business.

On her seventeenth birthday they came to tell her that he had shot himself at the firm's offices, just minutes before the bailiffs arrived, and that his business manager, Josiah Wilton, had vanished, taking their best ship, sending orders that diverted the rest of the little fleet to goodness knows where. All the cash and bonds in the safe went with him. Sarah had been on her own then. No family, no money, only debts. Everything had been sold to meet them: their home, the warehouse, Mama's pearls…

Sarah blinked away the tears that were blurring the view of the crowded riverbanks sliding past. She had survived then, found respectable employment as companion to a very distant relative, and now, five years later, almost to the day, she was bound for a new position, one that Cousin Eliza had arranged when she had realised that her heart was failing her. She could survive again. No, more than that: she would thrive because now she was older, more confident, more certain of herself.

Norfolk would be a stimulating change of scene and Mrs Gladman was, by the evidence of her letter, a busy person, the widow of a small landowner in Acle, a village not far from Great Yarmouth where she took, so she wrote, a great interest in parish affairs. She was very fortunate, Sarah reminded herself, yet again. She would not repine and she would enjoy her new life. Of course she would.

'I'd say that gentleman looks like someone who's lost a crown and found a farthing,' Millie whispered as Mr Smith walked past. The slight halt in his gait did not appear to hamper his balance as the little ship danced across the wake of one of the new steam tugs that bustled noisily through the choppy water of the Pool of London. 'But he's so top-lofty I reckon he wouldn't even know what a farthing was.'

'Hush now,' Sarah warned. 'He's coming back.'

Nick paced back along the deck, resenting the nagging ache in his thigh and cursing the likelihood that two days at sea would probably make it a lot worse. But he had the need to see for himself just what the passenger accommodation was like on these coastal vessels. The answer appeared to be that it was appalling, if this one was any indication. At least the experience was helping him clarify his thoughts.

'Miss Parrish.' He stopped next to the women. 'I strongly recommend that you move away from the side. The motion of the vessel can only become more marked the closer we get to the estuary. This is not some Ramsgate pleasure steamer designed for passengers.'

The foolish female had perched actually *on* the rail, one hand carelessly holding a rope that descended from the mast to a fixing on the side of the ship.

Not rope. Shrouds—that was it. An appropriate name under the circumstances.

'Thank you, Mr... Smith.' She spoke coolly and did not stir, merely regarded him with eyes the colour of good sherry. 'My sea legs are very good. I have been on the deck of smaller craft than this in a storm.'

'Parrish,' he said, suddenly struck by why the name had seemed familiar. 'Your father—'

He got no further. Miss Parrish stood up. 'My father is dead, sir. Come, Millie, we will walk a little so you can learn to keep your balance before we reach the sea.'

And that put me firmly in my place. It was a novel experience and one he did not enjoy, Nick realised. The fact that he had been abrupt and intrusive and fully deserved a snub was no help to his mood. Was Miss Parrish indeed the daughter of Richard Parrish, whose career he had recently reviewed along with other merchant fleet owners? It seemed she was, to judge by her reaction. If so, she had every excuse for not wishing to discuss her father. He had been either the innocent dupe of a dishonest employee or an inept fraudster, depending on who you asked.

He remained on deck, leaning against some of the cargo stowed under tarpaulins at the stern while the *Gannet* turned her prow into the wide waters of the estuary. The morning light glinted on the mudflats of Canvey Island on the port side. Here the clean tang of salt was dominant, the stinks of the Pool of London left far behind them.

At last Miss Parrish and her maid walked back from the prow. He heard her mention the Isle of Grain and Sheerness and then remark, with a gurgle of laughter, that it was time to sample the delights of whatever was on offer for breakfast.

A handsome young woman, if one appreciated that kind of tall, self-assured directness, very unsuited to her single status. She had a straight nose, apparently designed for looking down, and arched brows, one shade darker than the coiled hair that showed under the plain and unflattering bonnet. His fingers twitched with the urge to pull it off her head and toss it into the water. And then there were those assessing sherry-coloured eyes: definitely her finest feature.

He gave the women a minute's start, then followed them down to the deck below and along to the grandly named saloon, pausing to bang on the door of his cabin as he passed. Pendell, his valet, had expressed some concern about seasickness and was doubtless flat on his back with his eyes closed, but Nick suspected that a full belly would help the young man more than lying braced for the first twinge of nausea to strike would.

The saloon appeared no more inviting on the second inspection. Essentially this deck had simply been divided up into boxlike cabins, leaving a virtually bare open space for communal use. Nick nodded to the two other passengers, the men he had assessed as merchants, and took a place at the end of the board at which they were seated. The two women were at the other board, heads together in quiet conversation, and did not look up when he sat, but the maid glanced up when Pendell entered, gave him a saucy smile, then looked away, a healthy colour in her cheeks.

'You appear to have made a conquest,' Nick said drily.

Pendell wrinkled his freckled nose. 'She's a silly young chit, sir.'

'Not so much younger than you,' Nick observed. Pendell's uncle had been his valet until a heart attack had led to the man's retirement. He had recommended his nephew to replace him and Nick was still deciding whether to be amused or irritated by the young man's attempts to appear twenty years older than his true age.

A pewter jug was banged down on the board in front of them along with two thick china mugs and two tin plates. A scrawny lad of about ten followed the sailor, dumping handfuls of knives, forks and spoons, all of them slightly bent. The sailor returned balancing three larger plates, one for each pair, and deposited those, then he and the boy vanished into whatever hole they had emerged from.

Pendell peered at the food. 'What is it, sir?'

'Herring,' Nick diagnosed. 'And bacon—I

hope that is what it is—with some kind of beans and either a piece of the deck or possibly bread. Get it down you, your stomach will thank you for it.'

It was more likely to come straight back up again, but he speared a rasher of the bacon, slapped it on the bread and took a bite. It took a while to chew. *'Probably* bacon. Go on, eat.'

'Sir.' Pendell chewed valiantly and eventually remarked, 'The herring tastes better than it smells.'

'One can only pray for bread and cheese at midday,' Nick said, braving what he could only assume was supposed to be coffee.

There was a muttered, 'Amen,' beside him.

Chapter Two

The day passed slowly, relieved at noon by some mousetrap cheddar and more of the hard bread as the *Gannet* butted her way through the choppy waters and into the Blackwater Estuary with a stiff breeze behind her.

'Why are we anchoring?' Nick asked the captain.

'To take on some more hands,' the man said, shifting the wad of tobacco in his mouth and spitting over the side before nodding towards a rowing boat that was coming out to meet them.

Eyeing the unprepossessing pair who scrambled up the rope dropped down to them, he could only assume that the small ship needed more hands than his calculations had led him to expect. From the frown between Miss Parrish's dark brows he suspected that she was thinking the same thing.

'We'll be where we're due at first light tomorrow,' the captain said, perhaps feeling some explanation was due a paying passenger. 'It won't delay us.' He grinned, not a reassuring sight. 'We're right on schedule, Mr Smith. Right on time.'

Sarah woke to see a glimmer of light through the salt-encrusted glass of the porthole and knocked on the wooden slats of the bunk above her. 'Wake up, Millie. It's dawn.'

A pair of braids appeared over the side, followed by the maid's face, disconcertingly upside down. 'Do you reckon we can get any hot water, miss?'

'I doubt it. My plan is to take a room at the Golden Plover inn for a couple of hours so we can bathe, have breakfast and tidy ourselves before we seek out the carriage Mrs Gladman promised to send to meet us. I told her that I expected that we would dock at about eleven o'clock, in order to allow us plenty of time at the inn.'

Millie clambered down, flannel nightgown billowing, disappeared behind the makeshift screen and then emerged to scramble into her clothes. When Sarah repeated the process her maid helped her into her gown, then went to peer through the thick glass.

'We've stopped, miss. But we're still out at sea.'

'They won't sail into the mouth of the River Yare until it is fully light. I recall Papa telling me once that it is quite a tricky entrance.' Sarah glanced at the porthole. 'But the visibility seems good now, so I wonder why we aren't moving. Shall we go up on deck and have a look at what's happening to cause the delay before we risk the cook's coffee?'

They pinned up their hair, found their cloaks and climbed up to the deck. Sarah stopped on the top step and looked around her, confused. They were close inshore and the little ship bobbed at anchor, the sails half furled, but there was no sign of the entrance to the Yare, no other shipping and no buildings on the low shoreline.

There was a huddle of men further forward by the main mast and several of them were holding belaying pins in their hands.

'I don't know what is happening,' she said and found she was whispering.

Behind her, several steps down, Millie said, 'Oh, sorry, sir. We're just going up.'

There was a press of bodies and Sarah stumbled onto the deck.

'My apologies.' Mr Smith was by her side. He took her arm as she caught her balance. 'What is going on?' He, too, kept his voice low.

'I have no idea,' Sarah began.

Behind them the hatch cover over the companionway thudded closed and, as though the sound triggered the violence, two of the sailors by the main mast raised their belaying pins in their hands and struck down. Two figures fell to the deck.

'That's those other passengers,' she gasped.

Beside her Mr Smith swore under his breath. 'Get below. Now.'

He pulled her around and they found themselves facing a sailor across the closed hatch. In his hand he held an unpleasantly large pistol. Sarah realised with sickening clarity that it was pointed right at her midriff.

'My God!' That was the valet. They swivelled back as both unconscious men were heaved over the side and the sailors, their captain at their head, turned to face them.

'You will have the goodness to tell me exactly what, besides cold-blooded murder, is going on here,' Mr Smith said. His voice was authoritative, perfectly controlled, but through the hand grasping her upper arm Sarah could feel the shiver of tension running through him.

This wasn't a man quaking with fear, she realised. This was someone poised to move, to attack.

'Now you are making the ladies all of a flutter,' Captain Lockhart said. 'I was hoping to deal with you all nice and quiet in your cabins, the swells being known for lying abed in the morning.' He raised his hand and she saw he was holding a pistol as large as the crewman's. 'You take the lad, Bill.' His grin was horrible. 'Gents first, I think. We might have a use for the women.'

'You are not interested in money, then,' Mr Smith said, his voice almost covering the double click of hammers being cocked and the leering snigger of one of the sailors.

'What? We'll have what's in your cabins, right enough. Now—'

'Ransom,' Smith said calmly. 'How much do you think a duke is worth? A duke and a duchess and their valued servants? A tidy fortune, wouldn't you say?'

'You're no duke.'

'No? Would you care to see my card? I have

it here in the breast of my coat.' He released Sarah's arm. The barrel of the pistol lifted until Sarah was staring, mesmerised, into its sinister black eye. 'No, do not be hasty. I have no weapon here, as you can see.'

She thought for a moment that it was a trick, that he had, despite his words, got a gun or a knife concealed, but instead he took out a slim gold card case and offered it to the nearest sailor, who snatched it and passed it to the captain.

Lockhart took out a rectangle of pasteboard and stared at it, lips moving soundlessly as he read. Then he repeated it out loud. 'Nicholas Terrell, Duke of Severton. Severton Hall, Gloucester. Hanover Square, London,' he said slowly. 'Well, well, well. Yes, I think we might have a business proposition here, Your Lordship.'

'Your Grace,' the valet blurted out. 'You call a duke Your Grace.'

'I'll call him what I damn well please and you shut your mummer if you don't want to end up as fish food,' Lockhart snarled. 'Now, where's this duchess?'

'Here, naturally.' Mr Smith—no, *the Duke*—drew Sarah close to his side.

'Dukes and duchesses don't travel on coasting vessels—what's your game?'

'An elopement,' the Duke said, convincingly disdainful at discussing his private business. 'The lady was promised to another. I wanted her, we married at St Magnus the Martyr two days ago and I thought it prudent to give Lord… the unhappy suitor a false trail to follow.' He smiled down at her, the blue eyes sending her messages far removed from the tenderness of the smile. 'Really, one does not wish to spend one's honeymoon fighting duels.'

'Oh, Nicholas,' she gasped, clutching hold of his arm with both hands and burying her face against his shoulder. 'I have a clasp knife in my reticule, but it is in the cabin,' she whispered.

'Too many of them in any case,' he murmured. 'Play along with me.' The Duke raised his voice again. 'How much?' he enquired, much as if he was discussing the purchase of a snuff box.

He turned Sarah so that she was in the crook of his arm. It gave her a feeling of safety that she knew was entirely illusionary, but which somehow helped to stiffen her spine.

Lockhart stared at the horizon, meditatively chewing his wad of tobacco. 'Two.'

'Thousand?'

'Aye. Each.'

'Oh, come now. You do not expect me to pay

two thousand apiece for *servants*, do you? Five for the four of us.'

'Six. In notes. I'll not risk bonds.'

'Very well. It will take a while. I must send to my agent, who will have to arrange it with my bank, then have it transported. Where are we, exactly?'

'Never you mind. Jed, open the hatch. *His Grace* can write his letter in the saloon. You and Dan get them all down there. Keep 'em up the far end, out of trouble.'

'Aye-aye, Cap'n.' The man heaved up the hatch one-handed and jerked the pistol. 'Down you go, nice and slow, hands where I can see 'em.'

It would be best to establish herself as a feeble creature, Sarah thought, stifling false sobs as she stumbled along after the Duke, mind spinning with the shock and the mystery that seemed almost as bizarre as their kidnap: what on earth was *any* member of the aristocracy, let alone a duke, doing on board a shabby little coaster?

He stopped outside his cabin. 'My writing desk is in there.'

The man, Jed, grunted. 'The rest of you down to the saloon. Dan, you keep an eye out, look sharp.'

Sarah huddled obediently at the far end of the

bleak space with Millie and the manservant, taking the opportunity to give Millie's hand a reassuring squeeze. Then the Duke emerged carrying a portable writing slope which he set on one of the plank tables and opened out.

'I will need a candle for the seal,' he said, unscrewing the lid of the inkwell and lifting out a pen and a sheet of paper.

'You'll not seal nothing 'til the cap'n sees it. You get on and write.'

The Duke dipped the pen and began to cover the page with flowing black writing. 'Where shall I tell them to bring the money?' he asked, pen poised.

'Tell them to give it to my messenger.' Lockhart appeared and leaned against the bulkhead.

'No.' The Duke laid down his pen. 'My men bring the money. You bring us. And there is an exchange. Under no circumstances will my agent pay a ransom without the security of seeing that I am alive.'

'We could send him fingers until he does,' Lockhart mused. 'Or one of the lady's pretty little ears.'

Sarah gave a little shriek and buried her face in her hands, hoping she sounded convincingly helpless. In truth she felt sick, but so angry, so very angry. On the other side of the table she heard Millie mutter something that sounded exceptionally vulgar.

'Which would be no proof of life,' the Duke pointed out with a calm that made the owner of the ears in question want to kick him. 'You know this coast, you must know of a place where you can effect an exchange with no fear of being ambushed.'

'How do you know that I know it?' Lockhart straightened up, frowning.

'You are sailing along it, are you not? I assume you are a smuggler.'

'You keep your assuming to yourself. All right. Tell your man Horsey Gap. He's in London?'

'Yes. At the address on my card.'

'Aye. Well, it will get to him tonight and—'

'That's fast.'

'I've got the ways and means, never you fret, *Your Grace.* For a duke's neck I reckon he can get money at the snap of his fingers. Tell him he'd better be at the Gap by midnight, three days' time.' Sarah saw his smile and did not need to pretend to shudder. 'If he ain't there then we can start cutting off the bits that ain't fatal. Tell him that.'

The Duke wrote, signed, took out a small sand

sifter and shook it over the page, then handed it to Lockhart. 'Give me a candle for the wax. Without my seal Fawcett will not act.'

The captain flicked the letter back to the Duke, then put one of the lanterns on the table. Sarah watched the blue wax drip onto the folded paper like so many drops of aristocratic blood. The Duke pressed the signet on his left hand into it.

One of the sailors came in and dumped a double handful of items on the empty table. Sarah saw her clasp knife and a case that looked as though it contained pistols, along with two canvas rolls that flapped open to show razors. 'Naught else that looked dangerous, Cap'n. They must have sent their heavy baggage by road.'

'Right. Into your cabins.' Lockhart jerked the pistol at the Duke. 'You and your lady together, the lass and your lad in the other. I don't want you men plotting together.'

They were bundled into the cabins. Sarah had just a second to reach out a hand to Millie. 'Are you all right? Don't provoke them.'

'Provoke? Oh, no, miss. More like, cut off their todg—' The door slammed shut on Millie's threats.

'Would you care for the bunk or the stool, Miss Parrish?' The Duke might have been offering her a seat in an elegant drawing room and not the dingy little cabin that was littered with the contents of two men's luggage. The searchers had been thorough and not at all concerned with replacing what they had ransacked.

'I suggest one each end of the bunk,' she said as she kicked off her shoes and curled up at the head of the lower bunk. 'That stool is going to become very uncomfortable, very quickly.'

He inclined his head and sat, leaned his back against the support for the upper bed, and turned so that he could look at her. 'They are not going to kill us, Miss Parrish. Nor harm you. There is no need to panic.'

'No, there is not.' Sarah met his steady gaze, wondering why she had ever thought his eyes blue. In this mood they were decidedly black. 'Not until they have their hands on the money, that is.' She was not going to pretend she could not perceive the danger, but she was determined not to let him see how frightened she was. She crossed her arms and tucked her hands in tight against her sides. No one else was going to give her a hug and, in any case, she rather suspected that her fingers were trembling.

The Duke studied her for so long that she felt

her colour rising. 'You have steady nerves for a lady, Miss Parrish.'

For a lady, indeed! Patronising creature.

'Would you prefer me to be hysterical? Panic is not going to help us, is it?' she enquired tartly.

'No.' The faintest flicker of a smile touched the corner of his mouth. It seemed to her to be grim, rather than humorous. 'My agent, Fawcett, was a captain in the Rifle Brigade,' he said, his voice pitched low. 'He is intelligent, inventive and, I am happy to say, exceedingly ruthless. He will know exactly where the danger lies. You may put your faith in him, as I do.'

'Your Grace—'

'Nicholas. We are married, remember?' He appeared to find that mildly amusing, although it was hard to tell. No, definitely not a man of much humour.

'And I am Sarah.' She believed his abrupt re-assurances, she realised. Fulsome protests that everything would be all right would have left her even more anxious, because that would mean he had poor judgment. But she was not alone and she had responsibilities. 'Your man—is he to be trusted? Millie is very young, for all that she appears confident.'

'Jamie Pendell is young too, but he's a decent

lad. He won't do anything to make her uncomfortable and he will look after her as best he can.'

'Thank you.' Sarah found that she could let her hands lie on her lap and that they were quite steady now. The gold band of her mother's wedding ring on her right hand no longer seemed to shiver in the faint light from the porthole. *Wedding ring. Of course.* She tugged it off and moved it to her left hand.

'A good thought, Sarah. What are you doing on this ship?'

'I am—I was—travelling to take up a post as a lady's companion. Mrs Gladman, a widow, lives near Great Yarmouth. And you, Nicholas?' She used the name deliberately, getting used to the feel of it on her tongue. 'Why is a duke travelling incognito and in discomfort?'

He isn't used to being questioned, she thought as those dark brows drew together.

'I have no wish to pry into your business, but it will seem strange if I am ignorant of your affairs.'

The Duke inclined his head, acknowledging her point. 'I am interested in steamships. It appears to me that there is the potential for advantageous investment in them as passenger vessels. Various proposals have been made to me and I wished to see for myself what competition there might be from the existing coastal craft that have cabins.'

'If you want to attract a better class of passenger, then there are some quite easy improvements to be made to the accommodation, even in sailing vessels,' Sarah said, interested despite everything. 'And with steamships, built from scratch, it would not take a very great investment to create clean and comfortable cabins, superior food, some better arrangements for, er, washing.'

'I was coming to that conclusion myself. I do not choose to have my interest in the matter widely known, however. You will oblige me by not mentioning it once this is over.'

If we get out of this alive.

Sarah gave herself a brisk mental shake. Letting her imagination run riot through all the possible dreadful outcomes was a self-fulfilling prophesy. She would be no help at all if she was in a state of panic.

'I promise I will not mention it,' she assured him. Dukes invested in canals, she knew. And many noblemen were promoting schemes to lay rails for steam engines to run on. But both those endeavours needed expensive Acts of Parliament and the purchase of thousands of acres of land.

Steamships needed none of that. How interested Papa would have been.

Thinking about that helped quell the horrible sick sensation inside her that seemed to be getting worse, not better. Shock, she told herself with a glance at the man sitting at the other end of the bunk. He seemed calm enough, though. Was it courage? Or a lack of imagination? She could only hope it was the former: his quick thinking up on deck was reassuring.

Silence fell, except for the sound of the waves slapping against the side of the ship, the creaks and groans that made the *Gannet* seem like a living thing, the murmur of voices from the next cabin, and the occasional shouted order from on deck. It almost felt normal, safe…

'Why are they doing this?' she asked suddenly. 'Discovering that you are a duke stopped me wondering about it, but *they* did not know that is who you are until you told them, and they were ready to kill you along with the rest of us, which means they had no thought of ransoming you. So why should they decide to murder six people? No, seven, because I am sure that horrible man Lockhart killed poor Captain Barlow. If they wanted to steal the ship, then why not simply sail it away from the docks?'

Chapter Three

It was disconcerting to have his thoughts echoed by a woman. This one, Nick was beginning to realise, was completely outside his experience as far as holding a conversation was concerned. Young ladies of rank were not raised to offer their opinions and, as far as married ladies were concerned, their exchanges with a duke covered social matters—they left politics, current affairs and anything that concerned science or finance to their husbands. And this was not even a well-bred debutante, this was a paid companion, and they were expected to be self-effacing, tactful and, so far as gentlemen were concerned, invisible.

But he would be closeted with Sarah Parrish for days and he could hardly ignore her. 'I have been puzzling over what is behind this,' Nick admitted. He got up and began to pace slowly up and down the cabin, suppressing a wince as his leg muscles protested.

Four paces one way, turn, four back, turn. It helped him to think and to quell the suicidal urge to kick down the flimsy cabin door and punch the first of the pirates he encountered.

'I am quite certain they did not know who I was and you are quite correct: stealing the ship away would have been simplicity itself. Which means that there is something on board that they want and to sail early, or to remove it at the dockside, would have aroused suspicions.'

Sarah swung her feet down and sat forward, elbows on knees, chin on her clasped hands. It was hardly a ladylike posture. 'I agree, the authorities are much more on their guard against the water pads and ark ruffians than they used to be.' He must have looked askance at the cant that she used, because she added, 'The water pads operate on the docks, the ark ruffians actually get on board ships to steal cargo, so Papa told me.'

'What if those two men who were killed were not merchants, as they seemed, but guards for something?' Nick said, digesting that. He looked at Sarah, puzzled by her calm, although the absence of hysterics, or swooning, was very welcome, if surprising. 'What if something valuable is being shipped and they wanted to steal it well clear of London? They picked up extra hands in the Blackwater.'

'If I was doing this, then I would want the men I most trusted with me to take away the prize, whatever it is, once it is landed,' Sarah said, clearly working it out as she went along. 'That means they need extra crewmen to sail the ship back to port, looking quite innocent.' She seemed to ponder a moment, then she added, 'Or, if I was them, I'd change the name of the vessel and put a new set of sails on her. She's got very patched red ones now. A set of white ones would change the appearance of her quite significantly.'

'It seems I am imprisoned with an expert mariner,' Nick remarked.

The colour rose in Miss Parrish's cheeks as though she suspected him of disapproving of her. He did, he realised. Well-bred young ladies did not display an acquaintance with dockside crime or the workings of ships. They did not sit in a locked room with a strange man with murderers outside the door and behave calmly and rationally.

'You are related to the late Richard Parrish of the shipping company, are you not?'

'He was my father. I have no wish to discuss him,' she said flatly.

Nick told himself that a gentleman dealt courteously to all females and he must keep a rein on his tongue, even if trapped with one like this. He ignored the snub, and set aside his question. 'So what can it be that is so valuable they will kill for it?' he wondered aloud, not expecting an answer. After all, she had arrived at the ship at the same time he had and could have no idea. Still, talking it through would help keep her calm.

'Perhaps it is in the large crate that was lowered down to this deck before we sailed,' she mused.

'What crate, Miss Parrish?'

'Sarah,' she reminded him. 'You must still have been in your cabin. It was this size.' She held out her hands to sketch a large cube. 'It hardly fitted through the hatch. It was covered tightly in canvas, but stitches tore along one seam as they lowered it and I could see it was a well-made wooden box. Heavy too, from the way it landed.'

'Not labelled, I suppose? *Gold ingots, this way up*, for example.'

'No.' She narrowed her eyes at his sarcasm, but did not retaliate. 'However, there was a brand on the wood.' Her brow furrowed with the effort of recollection and she closed her eyes.

'What did it say?'

'*Shh.* You are distracting me.'

People did not *'shh'* a duke. Nick bit back the put-down that leapt to his lips and waited.

'An *R* and a *B* and… Another *B*? No, the letters *R B* and *R*, that was it. The *and* was written as an ampersand.' She sketched the shape in the air with one finger. 'And there was another mark—I remember thinking it looked like a crown. Not very helpful, I am afraid,' she added, opening her eyes.

'You are mistaken. That is very helpful indeed.' Nick crouched down to open the portable writing desk that had been tossed carelessly on to the floor after them when they had been locked into the cabin. The compartment for papers held the post that had arrived for him the day before he had left for the dock and he had tucked it in to look at more thoroughly on the journey. The bill he was searching for was at the bottom, smudged with the dirty fingers of the sailor who had checked the box for weapons. He unfolded it and handed it to Sarah Parrish.

'The repair of a gold watch chain… Refixing a sapphire in a loose setting in a tie pin… A diamond-and-pearl cluster brooch.' Her eyebrows rose, presumably at the sight of the total. She frowned, then looked at the engraved head of the bill. 'Rundell, Bridge & Rundell. Goldsmiths and Jewellers to Their Majesties,' she read slowly. 'And there is the royal coat of arms. Oh, my goodness. Those are the initials I saw. You think it must be a consignment of valuables? Whatever can it be?'

'Nothing for Their Majesties, at least,' Nick said. He took back the bill, folded it and tucked it away again. There was no point in letting their captors know they might have guessed what was afoot by leaving it lying around. 'But something of significant value is being sent. Not jewellery, not in a crate of that size. Something like a set of very opulent silverware perhaps—epergnes, platters. Or a new set of municipal regalia. It would explain the two guards. We do not even know the direction it was supposed to be going in.'

'But on this shabby little ship?'

'It would attract less interest,' Nick said as he took his place at the end of the bunk again. 'A bulky crate on an insignificant coastal trader?

That would pass unnoticed, unlike land transport with armed outriders. Someone within the firm has obviously informed a criminal gang of what was intended to be a secret.'

'I do not know why it should be the case,' Sarah said, 'but knowing why this is happening makes it somehow easier.'

'Easier?' Had this female ice water in her veins that she felt no fear, or was she so foolish that she did not realise the situation they were in? He had spoken with confidence about their rescue and release, but anyone with the slightest imagination could see that this could go very, very far wrong. Lethally so.

'I mean, understandable,' she explained. 'We know who our enemy is and now we know what their motives are, what they stand to gain.' She regarded him, head cocked to one side, and Nick found himself stiffening against the post at his back. People did not look at him like that, as though assessing him, judging him. 'I imagine that whatever is in that case is very valuable, but now they have gained something worth even more in *you*, don't you think?'

'I imagine so. It would be a dinner service fit for the Regent to cost six thousand pounds.' The gain of whatever was in that crate *and* the ransom money would be significant, he realised. Once that sank in, the temptation might be for Lockhart and his crew to hold on to them, to attempt to raise more money. But Fawcett was good, he reminded himself. Very good. The word *ruthless* might have been coined to describe him.

'Do you think they intend to feed us?' Sarah said, breaking into his less than comfortable thoughts about how their captors might choose to capitalise on the asset they represented. 'I brought no food on board and we have no water, either, and none of us has had any breakfast.'

'They might consider that keeping us hungry will render us more docile, but they cannot keep us without water for long, not if they expect to have live hostages at the end of it.'

He walked to the door and banged on it; then, when there was no response, kept up the tattoo until, eventually, a voice on the other side demanded to know what the devil he was about.

'We require water and food for ourselves and our servants.'

'All in good time.' There were the faint sounds of bare feet moving away.

Perhaps ten minutes later there was a thump on the other side of the door. 'Stand back!'

Nick moved to the bunk. He had no desire to provoke retaliation, not with two women to be considered. Not yet.

The door opened to reveal two sailors, one with a pistol. The other put a jug down. 'That'll last you today.' Then he dropped a knotted cloth on the deck. 'Breakfast and dinner. Just like your fancy Frenchie cook would make, *Your Grace.*'

Nick waited until the door was closed again, then carried jug and bundle over to the bunk and set the food on the stool. 'I somehow doubt this contains lobster patties, a fricassee of veal and some lemon tartlets, but we can hope.'

'So long as it is not those herrings again.' Sarah untied the knot and revealed half a loaf, a hunk of cheese and a brown knobbly object. She prodded it cautiously with the tip of one finger. 'What is that?'

'Some kind of Continental sausage, I think.' Nick managed to break it in half and took a cautious bite. 'Better than it looks.'

'They haven't given us anything to drink from.'

Nick rummaged in his valise and produced a silver travelling cup that seemed to have escaped the searchers' notice in its leather case.

Sarah set about dividing the food into two portions. 'I think we should make it last for breakfast, luncheon and dinner,' she said earnestly. 'That will give us something to look forward to, as it were.'

She ate a third of her share and drank a beaker of water, grimacing at the taste. 'I am sure they have never scrubbed out the casks.' Then she took a handkerchief from her valise, poured a small amount of water onto it, and wiped her face and hands. 'I think the sacrifice of a splash of water is worthwhile, don't you? I am sure we will feel better for a little cleanliness.'

Nick thought that he would feel a lot better for the deep bathtub at his London house, Sicilian lemon soap and the long-handled back brush, followed by a close shave and clean linen, but he kept the thought to himself while he chewed his way through his breakfast, resolutely banishing fantasies of kidneys and bacon, kedgeree, beefsteaks and ale.

Sarah Parrish gathered up the remains of the food tidily and set it and the water jug to one side, then went to put the tumbled luggage in order.

'All my things are in the other cabin. Do you think we could prevail on our captors to bring my valise in here and take your valet's to him?'

'I can try,' Nick said. 'I'll give them a while.

They have brought us food; they may be thinking we have been indulged enough for the present.'

She made a pleasing picture as she knelt on the deck, folding and tidying, her skirts swirled around her. A domestic scene painted by a Dutch master, perhaps, although with her dark hair, her slender height and those sherry-brown eyes she bore little resemblance to a plump Dutch *huisvrouw*. Sarah would pass as a society lady easily enough, he thought idly. If someone were to dress her well, style that heavy mass of hair in the latest fashion...

Sarah turned, still on her knees, and caught his gaze. Her colour rose, her eyebrows lifted and an indefinable coldness crept over her expression.

Damn. 'My apologies. I did not intend to stare you out of countenance. I was pondering the best approach to persuade them to exchange some of the bags.'

'Of course.' But she finished her tidying with rather more haste and got to her feet, took a step towards the bunk, then changed direction and went to the porthole. 'Do you think you could open this? I tried earlier, but it is too stiff for me. More light and air would be welcome and we might get a better idea of where we are, if we can see out properly.'

Sarah sidestepped neatly to allow Nicholas access to the porthole, then retreated to her end of the bunk. She felt hot and prickly under her skin and was not sure why. He had not been leering at her, or ogling, just studying her steadily, as though he had not seen a female like her before.

He probably hasn't, she told herself. *I do not expect he really notices servants, and that is what I must seem to him. But he is a gentleman. Or, at least, he has behaved like one so far,* she corrected herself.

His language, when she caught the muttered swear word, was not particularly gentlemanly. 'Is it giving you trouble?' she enquired.

'Merely a broken fingernail. I wonder if they have taken my manicure set?'

'So that you may trim your nails?'

'So I can scrape this hinge and catch and see if I can free it,' he said with as much of a snap as she had yet heard in his voice.

Sarah searched through his newly ordered possessions and found it, with all its little implements intact. 'Here you are.'

It took him ten minutes and, by the sound of

it, another broken nail, but the porthole swung open at last, bringing with it a gust of salt-laden air and the rush of the waves against the side of the ship.

Constraint forgotten, Sarah pressed close to peer out. 'We've moved further out to sea, but we are still heading northward. I was worried that he might be taking us across the Channel to drop off the cargo. I do not recognise the coast, though.'

'Nothing that I would call a landmark, only low cliffs and sand. I do not know this part of the world. I assume this is still Suffolk.'

'I think so. Of course, he may have turned and beaten south during the night, then turned again and it is Essex, but I don't think so. Horsey is in Norfolk, I believe, so he will have to pass Great Yarmouth. Perhaps he feels safer here on this quiet bit of coast.'

'Interesting that Lockhart does not sail on, unload the cargo he is intent on stealing and then go to Horsey Gap with us.' Nicholas appeared to be thinking out loud, so Sarah kept quiet and let him ponder. 'I can only assume that he is ultimately heading further north but knows Horsey is a safe place to make the exchange. I wonder—'

He broke off at the sound of raised voices from the cabin next door, a thud, a shout and, unmistakable, Millie's voice raised in a screech that would have been envied by the fierce Billingsgate fishwives.

There was the pounding of running feet and their cabin door was thrown open. Lockhart looked in, a pistol in one hand, then he slammed the door and they heard his voice raised outside.

'He didn't lock it,' Nicholas said, then, 'Stop, you little fool!'

Sarah ducked past him, wrenched the door open and found herself in the passageway in the middle of what looked like the entire crew. She used her elbows, kicked an ankle and wriggled through to the door.

The young manservant, Pendell, was flat on his face on the deck with a thin trickle of blood running from beneath his shoulder. One of the sailors was slumped against the bulkhead, rubbing his jaw, and Millie stood in the middle of the cabin, the stool gripped by the leg in her small, determined fist.

'Silence!' Everyone stopped shouting. 'Put that down, you hellcat,' Lockhart said.

'He tried to grab me.' Millie brandished the stool towards the groaning sailor. 'Said he fancied a bit. James here, he pushed him away and your man knifed him, so I hit him.'

'If you have killed my man,' said a silky-smooth voice from behind Sarah, 'then you have thrown away one thousand pounds. And if my wife's maid is damaged, I'm not prepared to pay you the agreed price for her, either.'

Chapter Four

Sarah, shaking with anger, spun around to face Nicholas. 'You—' The warning glint in his eyes stopped the words on her tongue. He was playing Lockhart at his own game, she realised. Cold, hard calculations about money would have an effect where pleas about humane behaviour would fall on deaf ears.

'He may be bleeding to death while you argue,' she said and pushed her way back through the knot of men in the doorway and into the cabin. 'Millie, can you find me some clean linen?' She wanted to hug the white-faced girl, but perhaps giving her something practical to do would help.

'Make room, damn you.' Nicholas was beside her, shouldering past the sailors. 'The valise in my cabin, girl. There are neck cloths in the bottom.'

He straightened up and confronted Lockhart,

apparently unconcerned about the weapon in the man's hand. 'Lockhart, get your men out so we can work on him. Leave both cabins open so we have access to our baggage. Put a man at either end of this passageway with a pistol apiece and draw chalk lines on the floor that we may not cross—whatever it takes to make you feel secure. I have no patience for this.'

The captain snarled some orders, the dazed sailor was dragged away and the cabin emptied.

Nicholas looked out of the door, a rapid survey up and down the passageway. 'They have left the other cabin open and, yes, he has stationed a man at either end.' As he spoke there was a loud splash and a yell and he stepped over Pendell's body to look out of the porthole. 'He's thrown that sailor overboard, the devil.'

'Almost lost him some money, didn't he?' Millie said, her voice flat. 'I've come across rum coves like him before. Ruthless. He won't give anyone a second chance.' She knelt beside Sarah and helped her roll the young valet on to his back. He was without his coat or waistcoat, which was helpful, and they managed to pull his shirt off over his head without rousing him. 'Got him through the shoulder and he banged his head on the way down. I don't reckon it's too bad if we can stop the bleeding.'

'You have seen a great number of knife wounds, have you?' the Duke enquired, turning from the window.

It was meant to be sarcastic, Sarah knew, but Millie merely nodded. 'Aye, a fair few. This isn't deep.'

She had also suffered many unwelcome encounters with men as she was growing up near Covent Garden, Sarah was certain, but that did not mean it was any easier for her to deal with this time. 'Well done for fighting the man off,' she said as she wound another length of muslin around to keep a folded neck cloth tightly in place. 'Pendell would be better off on the lower bunk. I think the bleeding has stopped, and he is starting to stir.'

They removed his shoes and stockings, Millie pulled off his breeches without turning a hair and, with the Duke lifting his shoulders and Millie and Sarah supporting his legs, they managed to get the young man on to the bed. He opened one eye, groaned and tried to sit up.

'Stay flat,' the Duke said.

'Millie—'

'I'm all right, James. Here, help me sit him up,' Millie ordered.

Sarah bit her lip to control the smile at the Duke's expression. To give him his due, he did support his valet while Millie slid a rolled-up coat behind him and then passed him water in a cracked beaker.

'You have been given something to drink out of,' she remarked.

'That sailor was holding it when he came in. Had gin in it, I reckon,' Millie said. 'He'd drunk it all, though,' she added regretfully.

The laugh did escape Sarah that time and she received a wintry stare for it from those blue, blue eyes.

He really is a very good-looking man, if only he was not so intolerably top-lofty. Does he ever smile? I wonder. Or would that be beneath his dignity?

'Now they have opened both cabins to us I shall remain in here,' he announced. 'Pendell requires some attention.'

'They won't believe that you're a real duke if you do that,' Millie observed. She was tucking in the thin blanket around the wounded man's legs.

'Here, who took my breeches off?' Pendell demanded, recovering enough to discover he was clad in only his drawers.

'I did,' Millie said. 'Nothing special to see, is there?'

He subsided, blushing, and Nicholas turned to Sarah, eyebrows raised. 'I believe I may indeed be superfluous.'

'Very likely,' she agreed, causing him to narrow his eyes at her. 'If you can decide which of your bags James needs, I will take mine through to the other cabin. Millie, is there anything else that you require? Did they give you food?'

'Yes, ma'am. Your Grace, I should say.' The maid dimpled a wicked smile at her. 'I can take care of James here.'

'I am not at all easy in my mind about what that young woman means by *take care*,' Nicholas said when they regained what Sarah was startled to find herself thinking of as "their" cabin.

'Nothing you need worry about. She likes to tease and I have no doubt they will enjoy a flirtation when he is feeling more himself, if they haven't begun one already, but I doubt very much that his morals will be corrupted.'

'How did you come to employ such a girl?' He had finished arranging his baggage and resumed his seat on the end of the bunk.

'You mean someone as cheerful, honest and hardworking as Millie Greene? It was just my good fortune, I suppose.'

'I mean someone who appears to have grown up in a back slum, judging by what I have heard of her language and her prowess with a blunt instrument.'

'I fear, Your Grace, that we may fall out if you persist in insulting my maid. She was born into a harsh world, through no fault of her own, and has bettered herself through hard work. I was brought up in a very comfortable gentry home and find myself classed as a servant by such as you, and therefore beneath your notice. Again, through no fault of my own. You occupy the highest position in the land beneath the royal family—and that through no *effort* of your own.'

She swung her feet up on to the bunk and wrapped her arms around her knees. 'I think for the comfort of us all, just now, it would be as well to pay as little attention to rank as may be and concentrate on the character of those who hold us prisoner.'

Nick bit back the stinging set-down that was on the tip of his tongue, as much for the realisation that he could not possibly top the one he had just received as any restraint about speaking harshly to a lady. Insolent chit! But he had to admit that Sarah had intelligence and wit and also, grudgingly, that he probably deserved her rebuke.

He inclined his head in acknowledgment, too irritated to reply, although which of them he was most annoyed with would be hard to say. It was difficult to recall the last time anyone had actually reproved him: it was not something that happened to dukes, but now he had to swallow the realisation that this woman considered him to be a complete coxcomb.

Annoyance improved her looks, he thought. The colour was up in her cheeks and her eyes sparkled. Pursing her mouth—probably to contain further cutting observations on his character—made the full lower lip pout. He stood up abruptly to lean one shoulder against the bulkhead and stare out of the window. Becoming aroused by his fellow captive was thoroughly inconvenient.

When he glanced back at her she had closed her eyes and it occurred to him that she must be exhausted. However intelligent and strong-willed Sarah Parrish might be, a night at sea followed by witnessing a double murder, being threatened with ravishment at the hands of a piratical crew and then finding herself forced into intimacy with a strange man was enough to exhaust anyone.

'If you wish to sleep, and it would make you more comfortable, I can retire to the upper bunk,' he offered.

'Thank you.' Sarah opened her eyes and smiled at him and something caught in his throat, strangling whatever cool response he was prepared to make to her reply, whatever it was. 'But I could not sleep now. I was simply trying to think if there is anything to be done to make Pendell more comfortable and I have just remembered that I have some bascilicum powder which will be useful when we redress his wound.' She lapsed into thoughtful silence again.

It seemed to Nick that she was a very restful companion when she was not putting him firmly in what she considered to be his place. His experience of women, although extensive, had not included any who did expect his attention, or require it, or who hung on his every word. Sarah Parrish, who was not his servant and who, quite clearly, felt absolutely no desire to cast lures in his direction, was rather soothing.

'I have a travelling chess set if you would care to play?'

'You would have to teach me, I fear.' She sat up straighter. 'Do you have cards? I can play piquet.'

'I appear to have fallen in with what one might term a beau trap,' Nicholas remarked after half a dozen hands had been played.

'And what might one of those be?' Sarah made a note of her gains. They were playing for imaginary shilling points and she was feeling rather smug.

'A card sharp who lies in wait for innocent country gentlemen.'

'I am no such thing and you are not an innocent countryman, either. I know precisely why I am ahead at the moment—you thought I would be a poor player and were not concentrating on your game. Now, admit it!'

Nicholas held up a hand in a gesture of surrender. 'You have the right of it. Be assured I am concentrating now.'

'No, do not deal another hand. I must go and see how Millie and Pendell are and then, I think, it is time for luncheon. If you are to put your mind to my defeat later, then I shall need all the sustenance I can find,' she said with a laugh and tossed down her hand.

The afternoon passed slowly after their meagre ration of food was eaten. Pendell protested that he was as fine as five pence and only needed a night's rest to be back on his feet—Millie rolled her eyes at this—but he did appear to be recovering well, so there was nothing to be done there.

'The benefits of youth,' Nick remarked when he and Sarah resumed their card game.

'And you so ancient,' she said abstractedly, her attention seemingly fixed on her hand. 'Oh, you have dealt me the most impossible cards!'

'I am twenty-nine, Miss Parrish,' he retorted, then saw her pursed lips and realised he had been drawn into a defensive answer and that it amused her. 'And how old are you, might I ask?'

'Four and twenty. It is a good thing that our captors have not thought that through. If I was betrothed to another man and wished to marry you instead, then I am quite old enough to have broken my engagement and married where I choose—and there goes the justification for our dashing elopement.'

'Your fortune is tied up until you are thirty

or marry with the consent of your trustees,' Nick said.

'Is my fortune so very large? Oh, dear, perhaps that is your motive for carrying me off. I am quite cast down. The disillusion! I have fallen for the wiles of a fortune hunter.'

A snort of laughter escaped Nick. Then he looked again at the cards and swallowed an oath.

'My trick, I think,' Sarah said.

'You were deliberately distracting me.'

'It worked, didn't it?' She looked up at him through her lashes. 'And you laughed.'

'It did and I can assure you that my motives in eloping with you were anything but mercenary.'

That earned him a dubious look, but he focused on the cards in his hand and they played on.

It was disconcerting to realise that, beneath the general tension of their situation and his determination to get them all out with whole skins and to see Lockhart and his crew in the hands of the law, there was a growing awareness of Sarah Parrish and the need to protect her. Not as a young woman for whom any gentleman was bound by chivalry to shield, but as someone for whom he had a liking. It was an unsettling sensation.

He had sisters, but they were married and independent of his care. Women, in Nicholas's experience, were divided into a series of groups, none of which involved actual liking. There had been Grandmama, a remote, aloof figure from his childhood, and his mother. He had been informed that, of course, he loved them and that they loved him. Looking back, he could not detect any real evidence of this. His memory was of soft hands, rustling silks, sweet perfumes and a sensation of being on display during the hour before Mama had gone to change for dinner every evening.

Then there were the servants. Nanny, but she was a distant, blurred memory now, pensioned off when he was deemed, at the age of seven, to require a tutor. The others had treated the youthful Lord Nicholas with rigid, distant respect and he, in turn, understood that a gentleman treats his staff with dignity and consideration.

His father had instructed him in what his relationships should be with the women who entered his adolescent life, as he had done with his brother, Frederick, before him. Firstly, there were married ladies and their daughters, who must be treated with carefully formalised respect—and a degree of wary self-preservation, because the second son of a duke was a very significant catch on the Marriage Mart.

And then there were the members of the muslin company. For a man in his position there was no need to risk association with the lower, or even the middle, ranks of that flock of birds of paradise. Only the highest fliers, the loveliest, most sophisticated companions would do for him.

'One at a time, my boy,' his father had counselled. 'Gets too complicated else. Treat them well, pay them off when they start to cling or they begin to bore you. Be generous.'

By the time Nicholas turned twenty-one he had learned to move through the upper ranks of society with ease and to negotiate his relationships with equal confidence. Some of his many friends had sisters, with whom they were on good terms, and some had wives with whom they appeared to share a depth of understanding and friendship that surprised Nicholas with his memories of his own parents. But he had never observed a lady with whom he could imagine sharing confidences, or jokes or deeper thoughts. Even when he had fallen in love, blindly and disastrously, he could not recall this strange companionable feeling.

Sarah Parrish was not awed by his rank, cowed by his aloofness or intimidated by his set-downs. She had surprised laughter from him and aroused admiration for her courage and her common sense. He would, naturally, have done his utmost to protect any woman in distress, but he doubted he would have experienced this nagging worry that his utmost might not be good enough.

'If your employer cuts up rough at your belated arrival on her doorstep I will, naturally, ensure that the situation is made clear to her,' he said abruptly.

'I am not certain that being told that I have been captured by pirates and have spent days and nights in the company of a gentleman, however elevated his rank, is going to reassure a respectable widow.'

'In that case I will request my sister, the Countess of Wellingfield, to provide you with impeccable references.'

'That is very kind of you,' Sarah said warmly. 'Oh! My trick, I believe.'

It also appeared, he thought before fixing his attention back on the game, that it had not occurred to Miss Parrish that flirting or casting out lures might be a way out of her predicament when they finally escaped from captivity.

Yes, *refreshing* was definitely the word for his temporary bride.

Sarah had thought the day's experiences would banish all hopes of sleep, but when it grew dark and the lanterns were lit and they had eaten the third portion of their rations, she found it hard to keep her eyes open.

Pendell was resting comfortably with no sign of fever and Millie said firmly that she was quite comfortable where she was and that it was safest for Miss Parrish to stay with the Duke and maintain the appearance of their marriage. She returned to her own cabin, feeling somewhat awkward at the prospect.

It was not that she feared the Duke would take advantage. He had not so much as touched her, let alone made any warm remark, but she did not look forward to the prospect of sleeping in her gown, nor of trying to change into her nightgown.

But when she did enter the cabin she found that one of the old sheets from the upper bunk had been hung over the side so that her own bed was screened, and that Nicholas was already under the blankets in the top bunk, his back turned to her.

With a smile she closed the door, took off her gown, splashed the remains of the water jug on to as much skin as she dared bare, and then got behind the screening blanket to take off the rest of her clothes and pull on her nightgown.

There was something very comforting about the all-enveloping softness of good, plain flannel, she decided as she made herself as comfortable as possible on the thin, lumpy mattress.

'Goodnight,' she whispered, not expecting a reply.

'Goodnight.'

The motion of the boat moving slowly through the water was soothing and so, surprisingly, was the sound of deep, regular breathing from above her. Sarah slipped into sleep.

When she woke only flickering candlelight held the dark at bay. She was terrified and strong hands were gripping her. She opened her mouth to scream and a palm was slapped across it.

'Be quiet,' ordered a voice that was somehow familiar.

Chapter Five

'Stop struggling,' said the deep voice. 'You are quite safe. You were having a nightmare.'

Sarah batted at the arms that held her, made contact with a very solid, bare chest and realised by the flickering lantern-light that she was in her bunk on the *Yarmouth Gannet*, and that the man holding her was the Duke, clad in breeches and not much else.

She had seen a marionette once, its strings cut by a naughty small boy, and thought vaguely that this must be what she looked like as she lay against Nicholas.

'What is it?' he asked, his breath warm across her ear.

'Marionette…'

'You were having nightmares about a puppet?'

'No… I do not know. I am confused. I'm sorry.' She became aware that the hand that was supporting her was making small, comforting circles against her back.

I should sit up...

But it seemed that her strings truly were severed, because she simply did not have the strength.

'You were calling for your father,' Nicholas said. *"'Papa, don't trust...'"*

'Oh, yes. I remember now.' Her strength seemed to be returning with the memory and Sarah sat up away from him. She immediately regretted it. Not only was the support and comfort of that strong arm removed but she now had an unimpeded view of considerably more of the Duke than was comfortable. Smooth skin over discernible muscles, a dusting of dark hair, nipples.

Nicholas stood up, probably, she thought with an inward cringe, blasted by the heat from her cheeks. He picked up his shirt and pulled it over his head. 'Do you want to talk about it?' He sounded perfectly matter-of-fact, but even so, it took her a shocked second to realise he was talking about her dream, not her reaction to finding a half-naked man on her bed. 'It might help clear it from your mind,' he added, which Sarah had no trouble interpreting as, *And you will therefore not disturb my sleep again.*

'I think I was trying to warn Papa about Josiah Wilton, his business manager. I was uneasy, although I was not certain why. Papa had been ill, you see. An inflammation of the lungs caught after he had fallen getting into a rowing boat taking him out to one of the ships. Wilton had to manage all of the business for several months. I offered to help because I understood enough to keep the books straight, but he was very evasive.

'By the time Papa was well enough to get himself to the office he found that Wilton had gone, taking our best ship with him, that the others had vanished, somewhere abroad, and the safe had been cleared out.'

'And shipping companies run on credit a great deal, do they not?' Nicholas asked. 'So when the news got around, confidence collapsed, people called in their loans and your father was bankrupted.'

'Yes,' she agreed. Nicholas had the tact not to mention what happened next.

'You cannot force someone to listen to what they do not want to hear,' he said. 'You had no evidence to show your father to explain your worries about the man and I suppose the absence of the ships was easy enough to explain.'

'That was the trouble. All manner of things

cause shipping delays and my father's instructions to the captains was to change plans if they learned of a profitable cargo. Wilton could not have done it if Papa had not been so ill, and he could not have got away with it for many more weeks, but the damage was done.'

'Where is Wilton now?'

She shrugged. 'Operating out of a Continental port, I would imagine, with a new name and a small fleet of renamed vessels. I try not to think about him.'

'Very wise,' he said drily. 'Imagining revenge when there is no way you can inflict it does damage, I always feel.'

'You have been in such a situation?' Sarah asked. She sat up against the bulkhead, hugging her knees. Nicholas sat at the other end of the bunk.

'Fortunately not.' His sudden smile was wolfish. 'I have always been in a position to exact my vengeance.'

Sarah shivered.

'And now you are cold. Try and sleep again.' Without waiting for her reply he climbed up to the top bunk and, a moment later, there was a soft *flump* as his shirt landed on the stool.

Sarah snuggled down as much as she could

under one sheet and a threadbare blanket and tried not to remember how he had looked in the faint light. *So male,* a treacherous little inner voice said. Which was ridiculous, the sensible Sarah told herself, because of course he was male. What else would he be? He was an adult man.

In his prime, whispered the inner voice.

Well, he isn't quite thirty yet, she agreed and then pulled herself together. *And he is healthy and privileged and well able to keep himself in prime condition.*

Mmm, murmured the voice appreciatively.

Stop it, Sarah thought, cross with herself. *He is arrogant, top-lofty, and however warm his chest might be, the rest of him is as cosy as an iceberg. I will not think about him any further.*

Sarah woke the next morning wrapped around her pillow and all too aware that she had been dreaming about Nicholas. The dreams of a respectable maiden lady ought not to have been very explicit, given her ignorance of sensual matters, but Sarah, having an enquiring mind, had a reasonable idea of what went on between a man and a woman in bed and was sincerely regretting that now.

She could only hope that any self-consciousness she showed this morning would be put down to the disturbance in the night and not to the fact that thinking about the Duke was making her toes curl and creating a very uncomfortable sensation in places she did not wish to think about. Focusing on the many disagreeable attributes of Nicholas Terrell, Duke of Severton, would surely send those night-time fantasies back into the mists where they belonged.

The sound of his voice from the passageway—clear, authoritative, demanding—was a help. 'I fail to see why the provision of hot water for washing should be such a burden. I assume that even if none of *you* ever wash, the galley does produce such a thing. If you wish to have the four of us in a reasonable state and recognisable to my agent it would be in your interests to maintain us in civilised conditions. And as for these buckets—'

She stuck her head under the pillow and drifted back to sleep, her mind safely diverted from thoughts of dangerously attractive dukes.

Nick informed Millie that hot water was on its way and that if she took the buckets to the end of the passageway nearest the hatch someone would toss them over the side on a rope's end and tow them through the sea until they were clean.

'I suggest you take hot water through to the other cabin for yourself and my wife. I will assist Pendell here.'

'Your Grace—' His valet struggled up against the pillow. 'It isn't right.'

'It certainly is not right for this innocent young maid to wash you,' Nicholas said, straight-faced, and got a very sideways look from Millie, on her way out. 'And it certainly isn't right for the pair of us to smell any more offensive than can be avoided, given the state of this ship.'

That left Pendell with very little to do other than to submit to being washed, shaved, and helped into a clean shirt and breeches. 'Thank you, sir. There's something quite lowering about being told what to do by a female when one is in one's nightshirt.'

Nick was hard put to keep a straight face and it occurred to him that, despite being kidnapped and held to ransom, he had found more to entertain himself over the last two days than he normally did in a month.

Pendell turned bright red as his ears appeared to catch up with his mouth. 'I mean… One is at such a disadvantage without one's breeches.'

'Quite,' Nick agreed. It would be unkind to tease the lad, who was certainly in no position to retaliate.

He tipped the dirty water out of the porthole and poured himself some fresh, then stripped off. The luxury of a scoop of hot water and soap under these circumstances was as satisfying as the deep hot bath he had been fantasising about.

Through the wooden bulkhead he could hear Millie's voice and, under it, the softer tones of Sarah answering. There was a ripple of laughter which meant, he supposed, that she had recovered from last night's bad dreams. Had he done the right thing in encouraging her to talk? He couldn't imagine ever telling anyone about the things that disturbed his own sleep, but talking had seemed to help her.

It had done little to help him sleep, he had to admit, he thought, frowning at his reflection in the small mirror propped up on the top bunk as he drew the razor across his chin. Not the tale itself—a common enough story of a crooked employee defrauding and ruining his trusting employer—but the proximity of Sarah Parrish, warm, frightened and clinging.

The clinging had not lasted long, nor had the fright. The woman had backbone and she had recovered a great deal of her poise the moment she was fully awake. But the memory of that softness pressed against him, the feathering of her breath across his naked chest, the scent of sleepy woman, had been powerfully arousing and had kept him awake for a good hour after her breathing had settled.

It was not as though she was a great beauty, he told himself now, working around the tricky area under his left ear. He was used to ladies more lovely, more sophisticated and infinitely more experienced flirting—and more—with him. It was not as though Sarah was attempting to attract him, either. Which was, he admitted ruefully, attractive in itself when one was used to being a target and knowing that was so very often because of his title and not any personal attributes he might possess.

There was a sudden knock on the door which almost had him slicing off the tip of his nose with the razor. His nerves must be more on edge than he thought.

'Come in!'

It was Millie brandishing a dripping wet bucket. 'There you go, sir,' she said cheerfully, dumping it in the corner behind the curtain.

'*Your Grace,*' Pendell said. 'I keep telling you, Millie.'

'I think that *sir* will do under the circumstances,' Nick said, wiping the last of the soap from his face. 'But not in front of any of the crew. I want to keep reminding them that I am a duke and therefore valuable. Do you understand, girl?'

'Yes, sir. Your Grace,' she added with a wicked twinkle at the valet. 'My lady says—' She broke off at the sound of Sarah's voice in the passageway.

Nick opened the door and stepped out, braced for trouble, to find her facing Captain Lockhart.

'I cannot see what possible difference it can make to you if we eat in the saloon and not in our cabins,' she was saying. 'It is even further from the hatch and it would be easier to keep an eye on us all, would it not?'

Nick reached Sarah's side in two strides, his hand closing around her upper arm so that he could thrust her behind him if Lockhart made the slightest move.

'Stubble it,' Lockhart said, narrowing his eyes

at Nick. 'I'm not going to tangle with your lady. You want to eat down there? You go ahead. You can say grace nicely before you eat and pray your man is on his way with the money. He's got about forty hours, by my reckoning.'

'He'll be there,' Nick said easily, releasing Sarah and offering her his arm instead. 'Come, my dear. Breakfast awaits us.' He took one step towards Lockhart and the man grinned and stepped back to allow them to make their way to the bleak saloon. Behind him he heard Pendell muttering to Millie that he could manage perfectly well and he did not need supporting.

'It'll be a pleasure to take your money, Your Grace,' Lockhart said as they passed him. 'A right pleasure.'

Pendell and Millie would have taken a separate table, but Nick waved them towards the larger one. 'We need a conference.' He broke off as a sullen crewman dumped food on the table, followed by the cabin boy with mugs and a jug of the dubious coffee.

'That lad has a black eye and a cut lip,' Sarah said, when they found themselves alone again. 'This is no place for a child.'

'Could be up a chimney with a fire lit below to hurry him up or learning to pick pockets,' Millie countered. 'Sorry, ma'am, but it's a tough life for young 'uns.'

'Perhaps we could—'

'No, we couldn't,' Nick said firmly. 'Pendell, how is your shoulder? The truth mind. Heroics are not of any help whatsoever.' He kept his tone conversational and his voice low, but not suspiciously so.

'It's sore and I can't move it much,' his valet admitted. 'But it isn't bleeding and I can use that hand.' He reached for a mug and picked it up. 'I don't think I could hit anyone with it, though, sir.'

'I very much hope you will not be required to. Can you run, do you think?'

The freckled face scrunched up as he thought. 'Some, sir. But I'll be better tomorrow.'

'Will we need to run?' Sarah enquired. Her voice was steady, but he could read the anxiety in her eyes.

'We may have to. I do not know this coast, but I believe Horsey is in Norfolk. Therefore the coast will be low with crumbling cliffs or marshes or sand dunes, possibly all three. I assume the gap is a way through to the beach, doubtless used by fishermen and smugglers. Underfoot it may be sand or shingle or mud—heavy going whichever it is. Wear your sturdiest shoes or boots, and if you think they may slip off, tie them in place.'

They all nodded, clearly paying close attention.

'And may I recommend no tight lacing, no skirts that you cannot move freely in?'

To his relief Sarah nodded briskly. He had not been too certain how she would react to mention of her stays, but she clearly valued common sense above modesty.

'And our possessions?' she asked. 'I imagine taking our baggage would only impede us.'

'That is a good point. However, I believe we should take them with us from the ship: it will reinforce the impression that we are not prepared to react swiftly. But if you can conceal any valuables about your persons, then, if we have to, we can drop the bags and run.'

'Very well. You expect trouble, I assume?' Sarah asked as though she was soliciting his opinion on whether it would rain in the morning.

'I think it inevitable.' Nick had come to the conclusion that attempting to hide the seriousness of the situation was both impossible—Sarah was too intelligent—and dangerous: they all had to be alert. 'But I have every confidence in Fawcett. I will tell you more as we eat.'

The food was no improvement on their last rations and, if anything, the bread was harder and the coffee worse. 'I am convinced the cook boils up the leftovers from the day before and just adds more water,' Sarah commented, grimacing over her first sip.

'It is quite dreadful,' Nick agreed. 'Now: Fawcett. He was an officer in the Rifles who sold out after Waterloo. I have known him since we were boys and when he left the army he became my confidential agent.'

'But he has so little time,' Sarah began.

'Fawcett is cunning and quick-thinking. It will be a dangerous mistake for anyone to make to assume he is some desk-bound clerk who spends his time studying rent books. He has a number of connections from his army days, all of them Riflemen. The first thing he would have done was to dispatch them up to Horsey Gap to scout out the land and to get into position well before Lockhart's men arrive.'

'There will be others besides the crew, you think?'

'It will be an ambush, I am certain. Lockhart is going to want the money and, I have no doubt, to dispose of us once he has it. He will not want witnesses.'

Sarah shivered. 'You do not sugar-coat the pill, do you?'

'If I thought any of you were likely to be paralysed by fear, then yes, I would. But you have courage, all of you. It is better that we are fully prepared.' He looked at the three faces staring back at him. The maid, Millie, was a tough little thing. She would know how to duck and run—and she'd know where to plant her knee if a sailor made a grab for her too. Pendell was young, fit, and a mixture of excitement and willpower would carry him through, even with his wound.

And Sarah Parrish? She was a gentlewoman unused to violence. She might have come down in the world, she might be from a merchant background, but the brutality and danger she was facing now would be utterly alien to her. She must be his chief concern once they were on the beach, he told himself, wondering just why he felt so apprehensive, given his trust in Fawcett and his irregular little army.

Nicholas squared his shoulders and reached for the cheese. It must simply be the enforced inactivity that was wearing on his nerves.

Chapter Six

The night passed without any dreams bad enough to awaken her screaming. Sarah blinked into the subdued morning light as Nicholas climbed down from his bunk and let himself quietly out of the door. A few minutes later Millie came in to join her, a jug of steaming water in her hand.

'Are you all right, Millie?' Sarah sat up and pushed her hair back out of her face. As usual her long plait had come apart in the night. She supposed she really ought to wear a nightcap, but the thought of being seen in one by the Duke made her wince.

'Right as rain, miss. Ma'am, I should say. And James is a lot perkier this morning—his freckles aren't showing like they were, so he's got some colour back.' She moved about for a minute or so, finding things and setting out Sarah's soap and a towel. 'What about you, ma'am? Shut up again all night with a man like that...'

'A man like what?' Sarah swung her legs out of bed and wriggled her toes.

'A lord. A duke, I should say. He's used to getting what he wants, you can tell that. And taking what he wants if it doesn't come willing, like.'

'As the Duke is behaving like a perfect gentleman *and* as I am confident in saying that he does not want me, I am perfectly comfortable here with him,' Sarah said tartly.

'Yes, ma'am.' Millie muttered a curse as the ship gave a sudden lurch, sending water splashing from the jug. 'I'll be glad to get back on solid earth, I will. If we'd been intended to float about on the sea we'd have been given fins.'

'It is not going to be an easy landing.' Sarah stood up and began to wash. 'Remember we must sort out which things we need to carry on us and find the best clothes and shoes to wear. I'm sure we will be able to collect our bags when it is all over, but just in case they get dropped in the sea it would be as well to remove anything that cannot be replaced.'

'I want to hang on to mine for as long as possible so I can get one of those—' She caught Sarah's eye and found another word. 'One of those *swine* right in his wedding tackle.'

'You will just have to resist the temptation,' Sarah said firmly. 'We cannot risk one of the men having to rescue us because we have become involved in a fight. They will have enough on their hands.'

They had only two bags each, so sorting and repacking was hardly a difficult task, but Sarah tried to make it last as long as possible. Now that the midnight rendezvous was approaching it was the only way she could think of to keep her mind off what lay ahead.

Millie was wearing a plain round gown and Sarah put on one very similar, with plenty of room in the skirt. They both wore small stays, tightened just enough to remain in place, a chemise and a single, equally wide petticoat. Millie's shoes were sensible solid leather ones and Sarah wore half-boots that she thought would be flexible enough to run in.

Her few items of jewellery went in a pouch hung around her neck under her clothes and everything else was put back in the valises. She had nothing with her that was worth encumbering herself with.

'I've just realised, our heavy luggage will have

arrived with Mrs Gladman by now and she will have no idea what has become of us.'

Millie shrugged. 'At least she'll know you meant to come. Will we go to her afterwards?'

'If she will still have me. It is the only employment I have, after all.' Before, she had been looking forward to a change of scene and a new start. Now the prospect of being a companion in a quiet Norfolk village had lost its charm.

Although it ought to be considerably safer than this.

When they made their way to the saloon the men were already there and Pendell got up to call to the cook that they were ready for breakfast.

'He is moving more easily,' Sarah remarked, low-voiced, to Nicholas, who had stood as she came in and now folded himself back down into the rough bench, managing to look elegant as he did so, despite a creased coat and a handkerchief in place of a neck cloth.

'He is a mere youth,' he said with his rare smile. 'He heals easily.'

'You sound as though you are middle-aged,' she said in a rallying tone.

'He has seven years on me.'

He was hardly so insecure as to be fishing

for compliments, but Sarah wondered if being a very handsome and well-built man brought the same nagging consciousness of time passing as an accredited beauty must feel.

Feeling herself merely passably well-looking, Sarah had never sought anxiously for the first grey hair, or sign of sagging under the chin.

Wait until you are thirty, my girl, she told herself. *You will be aware of every little line then.*

But by then she would be on the shelf, a confirmed spinster, and no one would care, provided she was clean, tidy and decent.

That was not as liberating a thought as it ought to be, she decided, eyeing the plank-like bread with even less appetite than usual.

The day crawled by. The ship was definitely heading north, they realised, watching what they could see of the sky through the portholes. North and then, finally, as the light was fading, Sarah thought their heading had changed towards the west.

'We are past Yarmouth now,' she said out loud to herself, trying to recall the exact point when the coast of Norfolk began to sweep around to eventually reach the Wash. There was a full moon rising. Would that make their escape easier or more dangerous?

Sarah stood at the porthole trying to steady her breathing. It seemed to be coming shorter and shorter as the daylight dwindled. Now that it was dark the fear she had been fighting from the moment she had seen murder done was threatening to bubble to the surface. She gripped the salt-encrusted rim of the open porthole with fingers that had begun to tremble.

'Not long now,' Nicholas said right behind her.

A gasp escaped her and she spun around. 'I didn't know you were there.'

'I'm sorry. I did not intend to startle you. Come here.' He gathered her against him, as he had done after her nightmare, and held her firmly until her breathing steadied.

It was quite an impersonal hold, for all that his arm was right around her and her forehead was pressed against his shoulder. Sarah wanted to melt against him, feel both his arms tighten. She would be safe then, safe from everything except the awful awareness that she wanted this man.

Desire was not something she had even felt before, except for the occasional twinge of admiration for a fine pair of shoulders, a rangy athletic frame or a handsome profile. The streets of London provided an ever-changing array of men who might be designed to set female hearts aflutter—but that was all it ever had been, a passing, rather pleasant tremor.

Now this cool, hard-headed aristocrat, who could have only one use for the daughter of a disgraced merchant, was causing not so much a flutter as an earthquake in her well-regulated and sensible heart and the problem was that what she wanted was quite shocking, because she was not in the slightest bit in love with the man.

She wanted Nicholas to kiss her. No, she realised, ruthlessly honest now as she breathed in the scent of his skin, she wanted him to lay her down on that bunk and make love to her.

He didn't move, didn't speak.

Of course not. He doesn't want me; he is simply calming me down, he thinks.

She felt anything but calm.

Sarah found the self-control from somewhere to place her hands firmly on Nicholas's chest and push. 'Thank you. That was... I was having the most foolish attack of nerves.'

'Not foolish at all,' he said easily as he moved away from her and propped one shoulder against the upright of the bunk. 'You are far too intelligent not to see how tricky this could be and far too resolute to give way to nerves when it comes to the point.'

Of course, it was far better that Nicholas thought her a sensible female he could rely upon and not some swooning, fluttering little creature. It must be nice, just sometimes, to be a fragile blossom and to be swept off one's feet and out of danger by a masterful male. On the other hand, that was a demeaning situation and, day to day, one simply had to be able to rely upon oneself in every situation.

The motion of the ship changed and they met each other's eyes in the dim lantern-light. 'They have taken in sail,' Sarah said.

There was the sound of increased movement on the deck above, orders being given and the little ship slowed further. With the rattle of the anchor chain the motion changed.

'We have stopped and she is swinging around. There, a lighthouse.'

To the south, as the shore came into sight, there was the glow of a light and, closer, two more small, low ones.

'That may be the Winterton Light,' Sarah said, racking her brains to think back to the days when she had loved to play with the charts in her father's office, tracing the shoals and the headlands, the lights and the harbours. 'I am not certain, though. There are no lights on the shore,' she added dubiously as she gave way to Nicholas at the porthole.

'I doubt there will be until they are certain we are the ship they are expecting. Imagine showing lights and having the coastguard land a cutter. Ah, there, now—see?' He made room for her to squash in front of him, his cheek against hers as they strained to make out the moon-shadowed beach. 'Against the pale of the sand there are figures behind the light. Two, no three.'

There was a bang on the door. 'Time to go,' Nicholas said, stepping back and picking up two of the bags. 'We need to be as free as possible, so we should carry two valises each and, the moment you need to run, drop them or throw them clear. I've already told Pendell: co-operate. As for you, do not appear to be too independent.'

'Cling and stumble?'

'Yes,' Nicholas said. 'And if I shout, *Drop!* then fall flat on the ground.'

'I understand. We will not let you down, Millie and I.'

Nicholas opened the door, then looked back at her. 'I know.' He stepped back into the cabin, caught her against him and kissed her once, fast and hard. 'For luck.'

Sarah had no trouble appearing flustered as she emerged from the cabin. The problem was in clinging when every instinct was telling her to run, fast, in the opposite direction before she did something irretrievably foolish, like wrap her arms around Nicholas's neck and kiss him back.

Millie was making a fuss over Pendell, carrying three bags herself and supporting him while scolding all the while. 'I told you not to lift that bag with your bad arm—and now you have torn the wound again.' And sure enough, the valet had his arm back in the sling and he had his lower lip caught hard between his teeth as though he was in pain.

We are all going to be fit for leading roles at Drury Lane if we get out of this, Sarah thought as they were hustled down the passageway and up to the deck.

Sailors took the bags from them and dropped them over the side into one of the two rowing boats beneath, then prodded Nicholas towards the side.

'You first,' Lockhart said. He held a long-barrelled pistol at his side.

Sarah clung to Nicholas's arm and let herself be dragged away as Millie was sent down next, giving faint shrieks of alarm, then Pendell, who made clumsy, slow work of the descent.

Sarah had never had to climb down a rope ladder before and was grateful for her sensible footwear and the ease of her skirts as she swung and bumped her way to the boat.

Lockhart followed and sat facing them, the pistol on his knee, as they crowded into the middle between the rowers. Behind them more of the crew dropped into the second boat and they rowed hard for the shore through the surf until the prows grounded and men jumped out to pull them up further.

Someone threw their bags at their feet and they snatched them clear before the next wave reached them.

'Up.' Lockhart gestured towards a wide gap in the sand dunes that rose ahead of them, furred with what she supposed must be some kind of rough grass, although it was hard to tell with the moonlight turning everything into shades of black and white. 'You, boy, take the lantern and go in front.'

The cabin boy scampered forward, picked up

the light and started towards the gap which, she guessed, was over fifty feet wide.

'Now you. Women first. Single file.'

Sarah let Millie take the lead, then lagged behind, frequently half turning, as though to reassure herself that the Duke, her husband, was behind her. Pendell stumbled in her wake.

The gap widened out and, for a moment, Sarah was not certain what was before them. There was the glint of the moonlight reflected on water, dark clumps of what looked like bushes and areas of open ground. Marsh, she guessed, seeing one long, narrow ribbon of water. Marsh that was half drained and would be criss-crossed with treacherous ditches, pools of water, tussocky ground.

In front the boy walked on, dragging his feet. He seemed as reluctant as any of them and Sarah wondered if he had been put there as an expendable target if Lockhart feared an ambush.

Then, perhaps two hundred yards ahead, she saw another light. From the height it looked as though it was hanging in a tree. As they got closer she saw the moving shadows of horses, shifting uneasily in the shafts of a carriage, and realised that a lantern had been placed on the roof.

'Stop!' Lockhart called and the boy halted,

so did Millie and Sarah. Pendell came up close behind her.

Crew members passed them on either side and she saw two had pistols in their hands. The moonlight glinted off the cutlasses the other pair held. They stopped a little way ahead and formed a rough circle.

'Bring the money! Boy, get on!'

A shadow detached itself from the carriage and resolved into two men carrying a large oblong box swinging between them from rope handles. In their free hands they held pistols. The box seemed heavy and they moved slowly, weapons trained on the sailors, as the hostages followed the cabin boy towards them.

The men with the box reached the four sailors and stood holding their burden just short of them, then slowly lowered it and stood, pistols steady as they each drew another from their belts.

If they were good shots, then they could take all four, Sarah thought. But Lockhart and at least another four men were behind them and goodness knows how many of his contacts on land had concealed themselves in the marsh.

Millie and the boy had reached the four sailors now. A few more steps and Sarah had too, then Pendell was at her side and Nicholas close behind him.

'Walk up to the box,' Nicholas said, his voice without any expression, and suddenly Sarah's feeling of fear became dread, so severe that she could almost taste it, bitter on her tongue. This was the moment of greatest danger.

She made her feet move, sensed the other three close beside her, and then they were facing the two men guarding the ransom, so close that she could see the stubble shadowing their chins.

'Come past us, Your Grace,' one of them said loudly. 'Be careful of your footing. The ditches on either side of the track are steep ten strides back and the way is slippery.'

'Stop right there,' Lockhart shouted behind them. 'That's far enough.'

'Now,' the man facing her said, as he caught the cabin boy by the arm and swung him around, sending the lantern flying. The boy disappeared with a splash. 'Jump!' the man ordered as he and his companion dropped to their knees on either side of the box.

Millie didn't hesitate and Sarah was just a second behind. They caught up their skirts and leapt over the chest. Behind her she heard Pendell swear under his breath, then he was behind her. The crack of gunfire had her half turning and she saw Nicholas, long legs eating up the ground between them as more guns spat from the marsh, then he was on them.

'...nine, ten. Down with you,' and he pushed her, then Millie, off the path and into the water-filled ditch, Pendell sliding behind them.

Sarah stifled a scream as figures rose out of the water, half-seen monsters, dripping and stinking. 'Is that all of you?' a surprisingly cultured voice asked.

'Yes. Except Nicholas,' she added, looking back as her arm was taken and she was half led, half dragged through the ditch away from the beach.

'He's gone back. You won't catch Nick Terrell running from a fight,' the man said and laughed.

The volume of gunfire increased. 'How many of you are there?' Sarah gasped as they halted to gather up Millie, who had tripped and was spitting water and expressing herself freely on the subject of its taste.

'Twelve out there. Thirteen now, now Terrell's joined in. Unlucky thirteen for someone,' her guide said and this time the laugh was a wicked chuckle. 'Here we are.'

They were hauled and pushed up the bank,

their clothes a mess, and found themselves bundled into the carriage.

'You'll be safe here,' the man said. 'Two men on the top and the coachman and groom are armed. And here come the rest,' he added at the dull sound of hooves on the sandy ground. 'All ready to pick up the lads when it's all over. Ha! Almost forgot this little one.' He pushed something into the coach and slammed the door. 'Keep away from this side until the shooting stops.'

Sarah peered down in what little light penetrated the interior. 'You! What are you doing here?'

Chapter Seven

Nick dropped to one knee and waited until he saw Harris start to move the little group back along the ditch, then, finding he could breathe easy again, ducked low and scrambled along the path back to where Fawcett and one of the Riflemen were using the box as a firing platform. Crouching hurt his leg like the devil, but standing up was asking to get his head blown off. On either side of them in the marsh, rifles barked.

'They're falling back on the beach,' Fawcett said. 'How many now, Jack?'

'Five firing.' There was a scream, abruptly cut off. 'I misspoke. Four now.'

In the moonlight they could make out running figures in the gap, dark against the paler sand of the beach.

'They are getting away,' Nick said.

A voice shouted from their left, followed by

an answering call from the right. Fawcett stood up. 'We can follow now. The marsh is clear.'

'Give me a gun.' Nick took the pistol Fawcett thrust at him and led the way at a run down the track towards the gap, gritting his teeth against the pain in his leg as he jolted over the rough ground.

They reached the beach to find two sprawled bodies and saw the second rowing boat clear the surf and follow its companion back towards the *Gannet*.

The Riflemen at Nicholas's side dropped into firing positions and loosed a volley of shots. There was a scream from the boat, but it kept going.

'Tidy up the rubbish, lads,' someone said. 'Rendezvous back at the carriage.'

Figures melted into the darkness as two men lifted the bodies, some of them groaning and feebly trying to hit back, and carried them back through the gap. Nick and his two companions followed them, ploughing through the heavy sand.

'Thank you. I knew I could rely on you.'

'My pleasure. The lads couldn't have been happier.' They reached the wooden box and Fawcett tipped it on its side, sending a rattle of large stones to tumble down the bank and into the water. 'It felt good to plan an operation again, carry it out. We've been here since before dawn, they came at five this evening—too cocky by half, they deserved all they got.' After a few more steps he said, 'You all right, Nick? It must have been hell, having your lady involved.' The last sentence wasn't quite a question.

'I met the lady concerned on board. In order to keep her safe I told them she was my wife and that we were eloping,' Nick said as they drew closer to the carriage. Figures emerged from the marsh towards them, several carrying bodies slung over their shoulders.

'Well, she's a game one, whoever she is. No panicking, no shrieking, just leapt that box and took to her heels. What do you intend for her now?'

'To restore her to where she ought to be,' Nick said repressively. 'What the devil are we going to do with these bodies?' There was a chorus of pitiful groans. 'We've a few live ones too, by the sound of it.'

'The Preventives have a look-out just south of here, at Winterton. They'll know how to get hold of the local Justices and how to deal with this.' Nick felt his friend's attention on him. 'There's no need for you to drag along. Take the carriage and however many of the men that you need.'

'Lord Sutton's place is just to the west of here, if I've the map straight in my head,' Nick said. 'I'd thought of finding a respectable inn in Great Yarmouth, but a private house would be more discreet.'

Fawcett grunted agreement. 'There's a road book and maps in the carriage. If I don't hear from you at the inn at Winterton, then I'll assume that's where you are.'

Nick limped his way to the carriage, too tired to try and hide the halt in his step. The driver had a groom up beside him and two men, rifles slung, were holding on behind. The lantern was still burning. 'Lord Sutton's house,' he told the driver. 'It's near East Ruston. There's a map in the carriage, I'm told.'

'If you'll pass it up, Your Grace, we'll sort out the way. North up to Waxham and Palling to start, then across and a bit to the west, I'm thinking.'

Nick swung open the carriage door, found the route book and two folded maps in the door pocket, passed them up, then swung inside and collapsed, thankfully, onto the seat beside Sarah. The interior stank of marsh water, but in the gloom he could see all three of his charges sitting up and apparently fully conscious. No—four.

'Who the devil is that?'

The small form wedged between Millie and Pendell ducked and seemed to try and burrow through the back of the seat.

'This is Charlie,' Sarah said. 'Someone threw him into the carriage along with us.'

'Well, he can get flung straight back out again. The bodies and the prisoners are being taken to Winterton.'

'He is the ship's boy.'

'And that is where he belongs, with the rest of the crew.'

'Nicholas, he is ten years old. He cannot be held responsible for any of this. He was terrified. You must have seen that.'

'I am not dragging some misbegotten ship's rat along with us,' Nick said flatly.

'In that case you may leave us here. I am not having this child taken off to prison with that murdering gang.'

'It is past one in the morning, you are soaking wet, we are miles from any decent habitation—' He broke off as Sarah reached for the door handle. 'Of all the confounded sentimental, idiotic…' Nick dropped the glass in the window beside him and leant out. 'Drive on! If we all catch lice, I will not be surprised,' he added as he sat down.

'Very likely,' Sarah said tartly. 'There appear to be some rugs under these seats and we would all be better for being wrapped up in them. Where are we going, Your Grace?'

He almost snapped back at her to call him Nicholas and then remembered that there was no need now to pretend that she was his wife and that when they found themselves under Sutton's roof it was essential that the deception was not revealed, or her reputation would be in tatters. Bad enough that she had been kidnapped and held prisoner, but at least she'd had her maid with her and Nicholas would present the story in such a manner that it would seem Sarah had been safely locked away in her cabin the entire time.

'To the country residence of a friend of mine, Viscount Sutton. It is north of here, about fifteen miles, I would guess. It will take us at least two hours on these roads and in the dark.'

'That is a long way. Four of us are soaking wet and one is carrying a wound,' Sarah said dispassionately, setting his teeth on edge. 'Would it not be more prudent to stop at the first decent inn we come to?'

'If you want to be the talk of the county, yes. Gossip will spread about the fight on the beach and the captives taken. Add that to a party of wet travellers arriving in the early hours and every hope of discretion is gone. Is anyone seriously cold? And, Pendell, how is your shoulder?'

'Aches, but it isn't bleeding, Your Grace, and I'm warm enough now we've found the blankets.'

'And I'll do,' Millie said. 'The nipperkin has stopped shivering and he's warming up, aren't you, lad?'

There was a muffled squeak from the space between the maid and the valet.

'And you, Miss Parrish?' Nick reached out and took one of her hands. It was damp, but not cold. 'Best to move that wedding ring.'

'I am sure I will survive for two hours, Your Grace, if you deem it necessary. Is Lord Sutton in residence?' Sarah slid her hand out of his and tucked it under the blanket. Under its cover he could see that she tugged off the ring and replaced it on her right hand.

'He said he was spending the summer in Norfolk and invited me to join his house party. I had left it that I might well do so if my investigations on board ship left me at a suitable point. I was undecided at that stage whether to sail up as far as the Yorkshire coast.'

'So, not only are we going to arrive in the small hours, unannounced, but he will have a house full of guests.'

'We are hardly descending on a small villa. I imagine they can make up twenty beds without difficulty.'

Sarah subsided into silence. Pendell, probably more out of tact than any desire to sleep, closed his eyes. Millie fussed a little over the boy and Nick began to massage his thigh, discreetly attempting to knead away the penetrating ache. This was going to be a long two hours.

The absence of movement woke Sarah and she blinked into darkness, wondering why the pillow her temple was resting against was quite so hard and unyielding. Then she remembered where she was and found that she had slid sideways so that her head was against the point of Nick's shoulder. She sat up, disturbing the disgusting skirts that had half dried around her legs.

Opposite her Millie straightened and yawned

and gave a gentle shake to the boy, who was curled up with his head on her lap.

Pendell knuckled his eyes. 'Are we here, Your Grace?'

'We are.' Nicholas opened the carriage door and climbed out. 'And, thank heavens, they have an alert footman on duty in the hall.'

As he spoke Sarah saw the dim light that had been visible through the transom above the front door intensify, then the door itself opened and a man appeared, holding up a lantern.

Nicholas got down and went towards him and she saw with a pang that his limp was worse. The footman was bowing now and ran back into the house and, by the time that they were all out of the carriage and the bags were handed down, three more footmen had joined the first. All had the appearance of men who had just dragged on their livery and the two grooms who came running from the rear of the house were actually still in their nightshirts, with breeches underneath.

Sarah was ushered into the hallway in time to hear Nicholas say, 'On no account disturb Lord Sutton. But if rooms can be found for myself and for Miss Parrish—my man and the boy can sleep on beds in my dressing room and Miss Parrish's maid in hers—and if hot water for baths can be obtained, that would be very welcome. As you can see, most of the party has been tumbled into a drainage ditch.'

At this point they were joined by a personage who could only be the butler, closely followed by a stout woman with a mob cap firmly pulled down over a head full of curl papers.

'Your Grace! Some accident has befallen you? I shall have the doctor sent for immediately.'

'Thank you, Ramage. None of us is injured, at least, not to the extent that requires immediate attention. But as you can see, hot baths—'

'At once! Mrs Watson, the Octagonal Bedchamber for the lady. Your usual chamber, the Chinese Room, Your Grace, with a bed for your man. And the boy?'

'Stays with Pendell,' Nicholas said firmly, one hand on Charlie's shoulder.

Footmen snatched up their battered valises, leaking sand on the marble floor. Sarah and Millie followed the housekeeper up the stairs to be delivered into the hands of a chambermaid with apologies that the water might be a few minutes, given that the kitchen range had been banked down for the night.

Sarah fought back the urge to simply throw

herself on the wide bed with its froth of gauze draperies and blue silken coverlet and set herself to respond civilly—and coherently—to the housekeeper's anxious queries without mentioning kidnapping, murder or gun fights. Nicholas would explain it all to their unwitting host in the morning and she had no intention of saying anything that might reveal whatever he chose to leave unsaid.

She insisted that Millie sit down too, and left the maid to unpack their valises, shake out their nightgowns, and bustle about making up a truckle bed in the dressing room and putting a pair of tin baths in front of the hastily kindled fire. The room became warmer and she closed her eyes for a moment.

There was a vague memory of someone helping her out of her filthy gown, of the bliss of hot water and the scent of rose soap and the comforting embrace of warm towels, then she was sinking into the depths of a feather bed. The voices around her dropped to a murmur and then were silent as the light behind her closed lids became darkness.

'What the devil is going on?'

Nick belted the sash of the heavy silk robe that

one of the footmen had produced for him. 'We woke you—I apologise, my dear Reece. I hope you are not going to throw us out on our ear.'

'Terrell!' Andrew Reece, Viscount Sutton, also in his night robe, strode across the room and clasped Nick's hand. 'I could hardly believe my ears when Ramage said the Duke of Severton had arrived on the doorstep accompanied by a sodden lady, her maid, a valet and a scruffy urchin. Carriage land in a river?'

'I will tell you the tale in daylight,' Nick said. 'At this hour it is too Gothic to be believed. But to cut a long story short we were kidnapped by pirates, held to ransom and escaped after a gun fight in the marshes.'

Reece grinned and shook his head. 'Of course you were, dear boy. Only you would arrive on my doorstep at this hour with such a tale. And who is the lady?'

'A fellow passenger,' Nick said, his tone indifferent. It was beginning to occur to him that extracting Sarah from this with her reputation intact was going to require some careful manoeuvring. 'Fortunately a level-headed and sensible woman and her maid is a creature of spirit. It would have been a thousand times more dangerous if they had not been so courageous.'

'I'll not keep you from your bed,' Reece said, turning back to the door. 'We can talk of this tomorrow when you finally emerge from it. I draw the line at believing in the pirates, you know. Will you be able to remain here now that your voyage has been curtailed? As you know, I have a party staying.'

'I am not sure it will be possible,' Nick admitted. 'I may well have to go down to Winterton to deal with the local magistrates and the survivors of our escape.'

His friend halted, one hand on the door. 'I should perhaps tell you that your sister-in-law is here. Prunella invited her when we thought you would not be joining us.'

'Marietta?' An idiotic question. He only had one sister-in-law, the widow of his older brother, Frederick, Marquess of Farne.

'Er...yes. She and Prue are old friends, as you know.'

'Of course.' Nick found a smile that he hoped would be reassuring. The last thing that Reece needed was discord between two of his guests. He wondered, not for the first time, if Lady Sutton had any idea of the events leading up to the betrothal of Marietta and Frederick.

'I doubt I'll trouble you beyond breakfast. Beside anything else, I must take Miss Parrish to her destination near Great Yarmouth. If she has recovered sufficiently I will combine that with discovering what the situation is at Winterton.'

'Of course. A pity, but I must hope you can make a prolonged stay later in the year. Off to your bed now.'

Once his friend was safely out of the way, Nick tapped on the dressing room door and looked inside.

Pendell, clean and looking about fifteen in his nightshirt, was sitting up in one bed, glaring at Charlie, who was curled up defensively in the other. He had the air of a boy who had been subjected to quantities of unfamiliar, and unwelcome, soap and water and his hair was now tow-coloured rather than dark brown.

'A problem?'

'Charlie was used to sleeping squashed into the sail locker where nobody could get at him,' Pendell said. 'I have explained to him that my tastes do not run to undersized brats, but he appears reluctant to accept my word for it.'

'So might you in his shoes,' Nick said. 'Charlie, have you any notion what I mean if I give you my word of honour?'

'You're a gent, so you think you'll go to hell if you break your word?' Charlie ventured after a moment's thought.

'Yes, that is more or less right. Well, I give you my word that nobody will misuse you in any way while you are under my protection. Will that do?'

'Aye. I suppose so.'

'Your Grace,' Pendell prompted.

'*Sir* will do, Charlie.'

'Aye-aye, sir.' There was no lightening of the boy's expression, but his tense body visibly relaxed.

'Goodnight, sir,' Pendell said, turning over and lying with his back to the other bed. 'Keep the lamp lit if you want, Charlie. Just turn it down.'

Nick closed the door on them and limped back to his bed, snuffing candles as he went. He blew out the one by his pillow and lay down, willing the cramps in his thigh to subside. He had a sneaking suspicion that the realisation that Marietta was in the house was making him more aware of the old injury than usual and cursed himself for allowing it to affect him.

He had been a fool to fall for a beautiful face. In fact, he should be grateful for the damage to his right thighbone, he thought, punching the pillow in an effort to get comfortable. It had saved him from worse than a broken heart.

Chapter Eight

Nick had expected to sleep instantly, but his treacherous memory insisted on presenting him with image after image of that time seven years ago.

After a whirlwind romance in London where he had won the hand of one of the diamonds of the Season he was on his way home to Severton Hall to give his father, the Duke, and his older brother, Frederick, the Marquess of Farne, the good news in person. Then he planned to continue on his way to ask the formal permission of Miss Langley's father, who lived about ten miles further on. The families had known each other for ever, it seemed to him, which was why the sight of Marietta at her come-out ball, transformed from a gawky girl into a radiant young beauty, had struck him like a lightning bolt.

That day he had sent his curricle on ahead to

enjoy a nostalgic ride over the familiar countryside that crisp morning with the snow lying over the hills.

No one had known that one of the supports of that little bridge in the Home Wood was rotten, so there was no warning notice. It gave way, throwing him into the stream where his mount landed on his legs, breaking his thigh and trapping him in the frigid water for several minutes until the animal thrashed its way free. He owed his life to the fact that his horse had been bred at Severton and that, when it arrived riderless at the stables, the grooms could follow its tracks in the snow.

Pneumonia and the agonising process of setting such a major break took him almost to death's door and, for a long while, the doctors were gravely warning that his leg would have to be amputated. He was delirious, too ill to tell his family of Marietta's acceptance of his proposal.

His love, hearing of the accident, travelled to Gloucestershire and her family and called to see the invalid. With tears in her big brown eyes she had told him that she could not marry a cripple. She was very sorry, but she was simply repulsed by the idea, fight it as she might. It broke her heart, but it would not be fair to marry him and she begged him not to tell anyone of her weakness. It was, she pointed out, a good thing that he had told nobody of his proposal because he would be spared any embarrassment now.

As a gentleman Nick could only accept what she said. He was hurt and angry, shaken at the realisation of how mistaken he had been in her to argue. As for his anxious family, he was too ill, in too much pain, to contemplate telling them of his broken heart. He knew he was helpless to change Marietta's mind, even if he had wanted to, but there was one thing he could control: he was damned if he was going to let them take off his leg.

By the time his family considered that he was well enough to cope with any excitement they were delighted to be able to tell him that dear Miss Langley, who had been such a comfort to his mama throughout the ordeal, was to marry his brother, Frederick.

It was, Nick discovered, the perfect antidote to a broken heart to discover that the lady one had loved was very happy to forget you, if the prospect of one day becoming a duchess was before her. He told her so, quite frankly, when he next found her alone.

Marietta wept, of course, and accused him of being selfish, with all the defensive anger of someone who knew perfectly well that they were in the wrong. Nick had too much pride to allow anyone to see what he was feeling. It was a small comfort to know he could not dance with the bride at her wedding.

Then, four months later, both Frederick and their mother, the Duchess, succumbed to a virulent influenza that swept through the county. Marietta was left a childless widow and, even though she was a marchioness, she knew that the man she had spurned was now the heir to the dukedom.

She had tried weeping on his shoulder but Nick had pointed out to her, with grim satisfaction, that she was wasting her time. 'It is not permitted to marry your late husband's brother, you know. You may spare yourself the effort.'

They behaved with perfect, brittle courtesy to each other from the day of the funeral onwards and, wherever possible, avoided each other's company. Marietta liked to drop tiny barbs implying that he still longed for her. Nick refused to show he had heard them but he was aware that, along with the injury to his leg, something inside him was broken. Trust perhaps, or a belief in romantic love. Whatever it was, he suspected that the damage was as permanent as the halt in his gait.

And lying awake, unable to sleep because Marietta was under the same roof, was weak-willed. He had once found her wide-eyed assumption of innocence and her air of needing a man to help her deal with every problem from a spider in the corner of the room to the fact that it had rained on a picnic, feminine and charming. That had not lasted beyond the discovery of her betrayal, but he had never, somehow, compared her to any other woman. Now he found himself lying sleepless and contrasting her with Sarah.

Miss Parrish was not as pretty, not as delicate, but she had grit and intelligence and the kind of good humour that carried her through difficulties with grace. She was loyal too, he thought, thinking of how she treated Millie and the fierceness with which she defended her decision to bring Charlie with them.

He must take care not to expose Sarah to Marietta's sharp tongue, but unless his sister-in-law had taken to early rising, there was not much danger of that. They'd be out of the house before Her Ladyship emerged from her boudoir.

He could deliver Sarah and her maid to her new employer and be on his way to deal with the captives at Winterton.

Sarah had fallen asleep resolving to be up bright and early the next morning, to be ready to leave as soon as possible so as not to inconvenience her hosts any more than she could help. But Lord Sutton had thoughtfully instructed his staff not to disturb the unexpected guests and it was nine o'clock before she blinked awake to find a yawning Millie drawing back the curtains.

'Sorry, miss. I didn't mean to wake you yet. I thought I'd ring for some hot water and have things all in order first.'

'I think we had best ring immediately. I would not like to be late down for breakfast.'

The maids had done their best with the crumpled contents of their valises, but Sarah was aware that she hardly looked the part of a guest at a viscount's table and wondered, as she was directed to the breakfast room by a footman, whether she should not have joined Millie below stairs.

The sunny little room had only two occupants when she reached it and, judging by the pristine state of the table, they were the first down.

A short brunette jumped up and held out her hand to Sarah. 'You must be Miss Parrish! Welcome. Do take a seat. John, tea for Miss Parrish. Or coffee perhaps? I am Amanda Reece.'

'Lady Sutton.' Sarah shook the proffered hand and sat down. 'Thank you for your hospitality. I do hope our arrival did not disturb you. Thank you, tea, if you please.' She smiled at the footman and turned back to find the other occupant of the table regarding her with undisguised curiosity.

'Do allow me to introduce Lady Farne.' Lady Sutton said it with a slight emphasis, as though expecting her to recognise the name. Sarah must have looked blank because she added, 'The Marchioness of Farne. Severton's sister-in-law, you know.'

'Good morning. Forgive me, I am afraid I know nothing of the Duke's family. I was not aware that he had a brother.'

'No longer,' Lady Farne said with a brave smile. 'My poor Frederick was taken from me six years ago. He was the heir, you know.'

'Oh. I see. How sad. Thank you,' she added to the footman who was indicating the buffet to her. 'Just some toast and an egg.'

Her hostess put down her cup and rose, begging them to excuse her.

'You know so little of us?' Lady Farne enquired, eyebrows raised, as the door closed behind Lady Sutton, who was followed by the footman carrying the empty teapot.

'I know nothing. How should I? The Duke and I met only by chance as passengers on a ship and then found ourselves held to ransom when the crew, a set of complete villains, discovered his identity.'

'Ah. I had assumed that you and he were... But of course not.'

'Of course not what, exactly, Lady Farne?' Sarah enquired politely, feeling her hackles rise.

'A very good friend?' There was no mistaking the edge to the Marchioness's smile now. 'But dear Nicholas always chooses the prettiest of the highflyers for his *chère amies*. And always blondes.' Her hand fluttered to her own ringlets.

They were alone in the room. Sarah took a bite of toast, chewed it while she counted to ten and then decided that she might as well say exactly what was on the tip of her tongue. 'Lady Farne, you may wish, for reasons I cannot comprehend, to insult me, but I can assure you, you are wide of the mark. I am not any man's mistress, and if you do not understand your brother-in-law well enough to know that he would never offer insult to a lady by presuming on her distress, then you have learned less in the years that you have known him than I observed in an hour. Might I trouble you to pass the salt?'

The other woman sent the silver salt cellar sliding down the polished table with an irritable shove. 'Just who are you?'

'The daughter of a ship owner, on my way to take up a post as a lady's companion. So you see, Lady Farne, you have absolutely nothing to fear from me.'

'*Fear?* Why—? Oh, Nicholas, good morning!'

Nicholas came in and sat opposite Sarah, his shoulder to Lady Farne. 'Marietta. Miss Parrish. I hope you are rested?'

'Yes, thank you. I feel quite recovered.' Which was more than could be said for the Duke, she thought, studying him while Lady Farne was distracted by the arrival of the footman with more tea.

He looked as though he had barely snatched an hour's rest, with dark shadows under his eyes and taut lines bracketing his mouth. His leg must be causing him a great deal of pain, she thought, wishing there was something she could suggest that would help. All that running over rough ground and through sand must have been a terrible strain on it.

What had happened to cause it? He was clearly a fit, strong man with the broad shoulders and flat stomach of someone who exercised regularly. There was no obvious distortion in his legs, either, she mused, so it had not been a childhood illness like rickets. A break or a gunshot wound were the most likely causes, she concluded. Someone had once told her that a broken femur was a very difficult bone to set because it was so large and because, in a fit person, the muscle surrounding it was so strong.

'…don't you think, Miss Parrish?'

'I beg your pardon.' She blinked at Nicholas, who was clearly expecting an answer. 'I am afraid I was not listening.'

Lady Farne made a faint sound that Sarah suspected was a snigger. She kept a polite smile fixed on her lips.

'I was suggesting that we set out as soon as possible so that you may put your new employer's mind at rest. I will take you and then continue to Winterton to consult with the local magistrates about their prisoners.'

'Thank you, Your Grace. That is very obliging of you. We can be ready whenever you wish to set out.'

Lady Farne began to twit Nicholas in a light, mocking tone. 'I declare you are becoming positively eccentric, my dear Nicholas, with your obsession for these new-fangled steamships. So noisy and with all that awful smoke! Why, people will begin to think you are descending to *trade.*'

Sarah caught the sharp glance in her direction and was struck by a sudden realisation.

She is bitterly unhappy. And perhaps she loves him—or believes that she does. Poor creature, she thought compassionately. *Here is the one man she cannot marry.*

She had once distracted herself during an interminable sermon by reading the *Table of Kindred and Affinity* in her prayer book. It had a list of thirty categories of person one might not marry, according to church law. She had later seen an article in a newspaper saying that in civil law a man might marry his dead brother's wife, if he could find a clergyman willing to perform the ceremony, but that the marriage might be declared void at any time if it was challenged, thus making any children illegitimate.

No duke would risk such a situation, she was

certain, and doubtless Lady Farne was well aware of that. All it would take would be for the next heir after the children of that marriage to contest the match and they would eliminate the offspring from the succession at a stroke.

Nicholas finished helping himself to mustard to accompany the sirloin steak on his plate. He smiled thinly. 'If the Duke of Bridgewater could achieve fame—and retain his position—as the Canal Duke, I have no qualms about being labelled the Steamship Duke. We are talking about investment, Marietta. I am not considering stoking boilers or running the offices.'

He spoke patiently, even with a touch of humour, but Sarah detected constraint. Was he aware of his sister-in-law's feelings for him? He certainly did not even glance in her direction.

Sarah finished her own breakfast and rose, gesturing him back to his seat as he made to stand. 'I will go and make certain we are ready to leave as soon as you wish, Your Grace. Good day, Lady Farne.'

Millie had returned from her own breakfast and was checking through the rooms to make certain nothing had been forgotten. 'Is everything all right, miss? Only you look a bit—'

'No, nothing at all is wrong. I shall just be very

glad to arrive at Mrs Gladman's house so we may begin to establish ourselves again. I have had quite enough adventures to last me for the rest of the year.'

'Me too, miss,' Millie said, giving one of the luggage straps a final tug. 'I thought I'd miss London, you know. But after all this I quite fancy a nice quiet village for a bit.'

'I couldn't agree more,' Sarah said firmly. But she couldn't completely convince herself. It had been frightening, uncomfortable and downright dangerous, and unemotional dukes were not at all the right travelling companions for impoverished females who had a respectable living to earn, yet… She was going to miss Nicholas, she had to be honest with herself.

She and Millie kept in the background in the hallway where Nicholas was talking to Lord Sutton.

'Thank you for your hospitality, Reece. I'll not be returning this time—too much to do following up this band of rogues.'

'Oh, quite. Come again in the autumn. We'll have some sport, you can be certain!'

Pendell and Charlie, who was startlingly clean and combed, were already in the carriage, occupying the seat with their backs to the horses.

'You are looking very smart, Charlie.'

'It's the boot boy's outgrown Sunday best,' Pendell confided when Charlie wriggled uncomfortably and tugged at his collar.

The Duke did not appear to be in the mood for conversation. He gave the driver Mrs Gladman's address and, as soon as he was seated, closed his eyes. Sarah was certain he was not actually asleep, but she hushed Millie's chatter with a finger to her lips and they all sat in silence.

Mrs Gladman lived in Acle and Sarah's spirits lifted at the sight of her little house, a neat two stories with a roof thatched with reed and a garden bursting with flowers at the front.

Pendell jumped down, carried their bags to the front door and knocked for her while Nicholas got out and handed her and Millie down. 'It will probably be as well if I do not intrude,' he said.

'Of course. Thank you very much for everything, Your Grace. You saved our lives and—'

Nicholas made an abrupt gesture as though to dismiss her thanks. 'The door is opening. Good day to you, Miss Parrish. Good fortune.'

She waved to Charlie, thanked Pendell and then set off up the garden path with Millie behind her.

The maid who answered the door to Pendell's knock gaped open-mouthed when Sarah told her who she was.

'Is Mrs Gladman at home? I assume you are going to let us in?'

'Yes, miss. Of course, miss. If you'll just wait here, miss.' She stood back to allow them into a narrow hall encumbered with a large trunk and two smaller ones. 'I'll tell Madam you are here, miss.'

'At least our luggage has arrived,' Sarah observed. 'You'd have thought they'd have had it carried up by now.'

'Perhaps there isn't a manservant,' Millie suggested. 'That maid didn't look as though she could lift a—'

'Well! So here you are at last, Miss Parrish.' Mrs Gladman advanced down the hall, reminding Sarah of nothing more than an irritated Bantam chicken, all bosom, red hair and indignant clucking.

'Yes, I am so sorry, but we had the most unfortunate experience—'

'Unfortunate! I should certainly say so indeed! William, my coachman, heard all about it on the third occasion—third!—that he went into Yarmouth to fetch you. That ship you perversely decided to travel on captured by pirates or some such thing! Battles on the beach! Some cock and bull story about ransomed dukes—'

'There was a duke, ma'am.' Sarah managed to get a word in edgeways. 'The Duke of Severton. The crew held him to ransom and he persuaded them to ransom us as well, otherwise we would have been thrown over the side.'

'A duke? On a coastal trading ship? What lies are you telling me, girl?'

'I do not lie,' Sarah replied sharply. 'It is the truth. We fortunately came off safe and—'

'And where have you been, might I enquire? The news is that the villains were captured last night. You do not appear to have spent the night in the sand dunes.'

'We spent it at the home of Lord and Lady Sutton, friends of the Duke.'

'Hah! More taradiddles. If there was a duke, which I very much doubt, then he is not going to take young women of your type off to meet his fine friends. You have spent the night—and all that time on the ship—with some man. And I tell you, my girl, that you can take your bag and baggage and remove yourself from this house.'

Chapter Nine

'I should have known better than to listen to recommendations from Agatha Walgrave; she was always a flighty piece, even when we were at school together,' Mrs Gladman announced.

'But—' Sarah managed.

'I have a position to maintain in this community, Miss Parrish. I am chairwoman of the parish League of Purity, a patron of the local School for Indigent Infants, a member of the Parish Wives' Committee...'

'And a thoroughly un-Christian woman, by the sound of it,' Sarah broke in, letting her temper fly. 'You assume the worst on the basis of gossip, you call me a liar on no evidence whatsoever other than your own prurient imagination—'

'Get out of this house! Never have I been spoken to like that in my life!'

Sarah felt a tug on her sleeve and the draft as the front door opened.

'Come out, Miss Sarah,' Millie said. 'She's not in her right mind, that one.'

'You insolent drab!' Mrs Gladman surged forward and Sarah took an involuntary step back, then another, until she and Millie found themselves on the path.

'Don't you call me names, you cross-grained old trot,' Millie shouted.

'Dorothy! Dorothy! Throw their bags out of the hall and then run for the constable!'

'Is something amiss?' a cool, deep voice enquired.

'Oh. Your Grace. This… This is Mrs Gladman and she is saying the most awful things about me. Mrs Gladman, this is the Duke of Severton.'

'Libertine,' the widow pronounced, fists on hips, the light of battle in her eyes.

'Is this the person for whom you were intending to work, Miss Parrish?' Nicholas was ignoring the spluttering little woman with admirable calm.

'Yes.'

'Then may I take leave to tell you that, in my opinion, she is hardly a fit employer for a gently reared lady such as yourself? Her imagination appears to be salacious, she is reckless enough to put herself at risk of a suit for defamation by a peer of the realm and she is—'

One of the small trunks landed on the path with a thud and Sarah saw the maid struggling with the other.

'Oh, our things. Do be *careful*, you clumsy girl.'

Nicholas turned and called something and Pendell and the groom came up the path. 'Kindly remove this lady's trunks from the hallway. Is that everything, Miss Parrish? Do you wish to check to make sure nothing has been taken?'

'Taken? Never in my life have I been so insulted—'

'That strikes me as unlikely, madam, if this is your normal manner. Is that everything, Miss Parrish? In that case, let us remove ourselves.'

He took her arm and guided her, shaking, to the front gate, which Millie slammed vigorously behind them.

'In you get, Miss Parrish, Millie. Drive on.' Nicholas swung himself in as the carriage moved off.

'Cor, what an old catamaran,' Charlie said,

peering out of the window. 'She's giving that mop squeezer a right bear garden jaw.'

Sarah blinked back tears that she told herself were anger, and craned to look. Mrs Gladman was indeed haranguing the unfortunate maid, both of them still in the middle of the front garden. They were beginning to attract an audience of interested villagers.

'Poor girl.' She looked at Nicholas and had to take a moment to get her voice under control. 'Thank you, sir. I do not know what we would have done if you had not returned. What brought you back?'

'I was uneasy about the reception you might receive, although that seemed extreme.'

'She'd heard gossip,' Millie said. 'The old cat. Miss Sarah's well out of it, I'm thinking.'

'I have to agree. I had intended waiting until you had been inside long enough to explain the situation and then, I confess, I intended to send Pendell around to the back door to discover from Millie what the situation was.' He produced a large and spotless handkerchief and handed it to Sarah without comment, his expression austere.

She mopped her eyes, blew her nose with more energy than elegance and decided that if Nicholas had expressed any sympathy she would probably have given way to her tears completely. This cool, practical help was just what she needed.

'Thank you. I suppose… Perhaps if you could set us down at a respectable inn in Great Yarmouth, we could take the stage into Norwich, or perhaps go up-river by boat.'

'Why do you wish to go to Norwich, Sarah?'

'It is the nearest large town. I could find lodgings and enquire for work at a domestic agency. I really do not know what else I can do.'

'But I do. I shall send you to my eldest sister, Lady Julia Marten, the Countess of Wellingfield. As I suggested some days ago, she will provide you with an excellent character and give you shelter until you can find a new employer. Or she may even have an acquaintance in need of a companion.'

'That would be wonderful, thank you so much. But why should she help me?'

'Because I ask her,' Nicholas said. 'I hope you will forgive me if we first go to Winterton so that I may deal with the magistrates. We can then return to Sutton Lodge; I will write to Julia and arrange for a post-chaise tomorrow.'

'I do not think I can afford a post-chaise,' Sarah ventured. 'The stage will be perfectly adequate.'

'I wish the servants to see you arriving in style. We are establishing your reputation, Sarah.'

There did not seem to be anything to be said. 'Thank you, Your Grace.'

The carriage rattled on over roads that became rougher and sandier the nearer they got to the coast. 'Is it far?' Sarah asked once she was sure she had her voice and emotions back under control again.

'About ten miles. It should take less than two hours unless the roads become much worse,' Nicholas said without glancing up from the road book he was studying.

Millie was playing cat's cradle with Charlie and Pendell was staring out of the window at the flat landscape around them.

'Is your shoulder better?' she asked the valet. 'I hope you did not strain it carrying the trunk just now.'

He smiled at her, a quick grin. 'It has almost healed, thank you, Miss Parrish. His Grace says it is because I'm so young, but I put it down to virtuous living.'

Millie snorted and dropped one corner of the complex cradle she was weaving with Charlie.

Sarah glanced at Nicholas and could have sworn she saw the ghost of a smile on his lips, just for a second. She looked away and found she was staring at his long legs, encased in tight buckskins, and rapidly shifted on the seat to stare out at the dull, flat expanses of pasture, enlivened only by hedges and flocks of sheep.

Should she accept Nicholas's offer of help, made without even consulting his sister? It was asking a lot of the Countess to give refuge to a complete stranger, one under a cloud, and then to be asked to vouch for her, putting her own reputation on the line. On the other hand, the alternative of finding cheap lodgings in a strange city and then trying to obtain respectable employment without any references or a reasonable explanation of what she was doing in Norfolk seemed insurmountably difficult.

Was it principal or a lack of common sense that was giving her qualms about accepting the Duke's offer? Sarah was still undecided by the time they reached the tower of Winterton church, then a straggle of cottages of flint and red brick.

The coachman slowed and finally stopped in front of a small ale house, flagged down by a tall man in frieze coat, breeches and much-scuffed boots.

Nicholas dropped the glass in the window as

the man called up to the driver. 'George! Is the Duke with you?'

'Aye.'

The man came up to the window and doffed the battered hat he was wearing. 'Good day to you, Your Grace. They are waiting at Warren House for you. Take me up and I'll guide you.'

The coach body dipped as the man scrambled on to the box seat behind the driver, then they moved off out of the village.

'Where are we going?' Sarah asked.

'The home of one of the magistrates, I imagine. That is one of Fawcett's brigade of irregulars, left to look out for us. One of my gamekeepers, in fact.'

'You have a private army, by the sound of it,' Sarah said, half joking.

Nicholas shook his head. 'Not mine—they follow their old captain. I can only hope it never occurs to them to turn to crime.'

Warren House proved to be only half a mile from the village. A rambling brick property of little architectural distinction, it seemed to hunker down in the sandy heathland as if turning its back on the sea. Around it was a spinney of beech trees, their shapes stunted and swept at strange angles by the prevailing salt-laden winds.

There were more men, this time with rifles slung over their shoulders, lounging around the forecourt, but they came alertly to attention as the carriage drew up and one went to bang on the front door.

The Duke got out and handed down Sarah. Pendell helped Millie and then turned back for Charlie. 'Come on, out you come.'

'No.' It was a barely audible mutter.

'Why not?'

'Don't want to go to prison.'

'You will not.' Nicholas moved to the open carriage door. 'You are not in trouble with the law, Charlie, nor are you in any danger from the crew, who are all locked up. I need you to tell the Justices what you know, that is all.'

'You swear?'

Sarah expected an abrupt order and for the boy to be hauled out of the coach, perhaps with a boxed ear for his disobedience.

'Upon my word of honour, Charlie,' Nicholas said patiently.

'Aye-aye, Ca— I mean, sir.' The boy scrambled down and stood by Pendell, his bottom lip stuck out and his shoulders back.

Trying to look tough, Sarah thought with an

inward smile and the front door opened and they followed Nicholas inside.

There were three local magistrates gathered in the drawing room, along with a senior officer of the Land Guard, another man in battered uniform who proved to be a retired naval captain working with the coastguard on the local smuggling problem and a doctor to report on the state of the wounded.

'They'll all live,' he was saying as Nick ushered in his party and found them seats to one side.

'Until they meet the hangman,' one of the Justices said with a bark of a laugh.

Nick felt Charlie, wedged between him and Pendell, twitch and laid a hand on the boy's shoulder, uncertain whether he was reassuring or restraining him.

'Your Grace.' A tall, white-haired gentleman stood up. 'I am Sir Henry Pettigrew. My colleagues, Claude Bunyan, Alfred Gordon. Captain Rogers, Lieutenant Grady.' There was a flurry of bowing before everyone was seated.

'Miss Parrish, her maid, Millie Greene, my valet, James Pendell, and Charlie here who was taken in London and forced to work on the ship.'

'Indeed?' Sir George fixed Charlie with a hard stare. 'And how did that happen?'

'Cap'n Lockhart was with me ma,' Charlie said. 'An' then she died and 'e said I was to come wiv 'im or go to be a chimney sweeper boy.'

'How old are you?'

'Dunno, sir. Ten?'

'All the time we were on the ship he was bullied and knocked about,' Sarah said. 'He was forced to do as he was told: he is quite innocent in all of this.'

'I see. Then if we are all agreed, we will leave the boy in your custody, Your Grace. I assume you will deliver him to the workhouse.'

'I shall find him employment,' Nick said and felt a responsive quiver in the thin shoulder under his palm.

Sarah turned to look at him. 'Oh, thank you,' she mouthed and smiled.

Nick felt a warm glow at her approval and told himself not to be ridiculous. He had only done the humane, charitable thing and he should not expect, nor welcome, thanks for it.

They were led out to the stable yard where the bodies had been laid out in an empty loose box. Sarah insisted on coming too, much to the clear disapproval of the Justices.

Two of the dead men they recognised as crew and Charlie confirmed it, his voice cracking as he said, 'That's Dan, an' that's Jed. Dunno who the others are.'

Fawcett, who had been waiting in the yard, stepped forward. 'Those were amongst the ones we observed taking up position in the marsh for the ambush,' he said and the Justices scribbled notes.

Then they went to inspect the prisoners. Charlie said that one of them was Long Tom, a crew member, and Nick agreed that he recognised the man. 'Good boy,' he murmured to the lad, who squared his shoulders and gave him a shaky smile.

Lockhart and the rest of the crew had escaped back to the *Yarmouth Gannet*, it seemed.

When they regrouped in the house Lieutenant Grady reported that the men who were not crew members were from local smuggling families. 'Ready for hire for any underhand business, they are. It proves that this Captain Lockhart has contacts on this coast, but that's no surprise, I fear.'

'So where have they gone now? Have you any idea of Lockhart's home port?' Nick asked. There was a general shaking of heads. 'Then I propose we get Long Tom in here and question him.'

The sailor was silent and surly when he was brought before the magistrates until Sir George said, 'Is this one of the men who murdered the two passengers, Your Grace? No? Then, fellow, I presume you would prefer not to hang?'

'What, you'll let me go? Nah, I won't fall for that.'

'Transportation instead of hanging. A few years labour and an opportunity to make a new life afterwards.'

'You can do that?' The man was suspicious, but underneath the hardened expression Nicholas detected eagerness.

'We can, provided the information you give us is accurate and helpful.'

'The captain came from Yorkshire. Near to Whitby. But we're working out of Blakeney these days—better for London.'

'What is in the crate that was loaded in London?' Sarah asked suddenly, making most of the men turn and look at her. 'It was marked with the Rundell, Bridge & Rundell stamp.'

Long Tom shrugged. 'Dunno. Captain Barlow never said. Right tight-lipped about it, he was. Got in a huddle with those two what went over the side—we could tell they weren't passengers.

Guards more like. But he wouldn't tell Lockhart anything about it.'

'And then Captain Barlow had his *accident*?'

'Lockhart was bosun, so he said he was taking over. Some of them weren't so keen—he'd only just joined the ship, but there was more of us than them. Only a couple by then.'

'What do you mean?' Nick asked sharply.

'There was the original crew, along with Captain Barlow, and then some of them went missing, like, and we came on board. Lockhart had got the papers that looked all right and tight, so Barlow believed we were from his ship owner.' The gap-toothed grin was not a pleasant sight.

'So who employed Lockhart?' Nick asked. He couldn't believe this degree of planning, involving contacts within the Crown jeweller and forged papers was all the work of Lockhart.

Long Tom shut his mouth and looked shifty. 'Daren't say.'

'Then you hang,' Sir George said.

'Damn it! You'll keep me safe? He'll kill me himself if he knows I've blabbed.'

'There is no reason anyone should know and you'll be locked up, don't you worry.'

'All right, then. But I only know it's a cove called Axminster. Never saw him, but Lockhart said he's a cunning one and he's got half a dozen ships. He's a coming man who's not too worried about ways and means, if you get my drift. A ruthless one. Lockhart was scared of him, I could see that, and it takes a lot to rattle Caleb Lockhart. Didn't sound too frightening, if you ask me—they call him the Glass-Eyed Man. Jed had seen him, said he looked like a clerk.'

The name seemed faintly familiar to Nick, but he was intent on getting every last scrap of information from Long Tom. 'What else do you know about him?'

'That's it, sir. I swear it.'

They led him away and Nick suggested to Sir George that he write immediately to Rundell, Bridge & Rundell to warn them of what had happened.

'I will certainly do that. Thank you for your assistance, Your Grace. To what address should I send to acquaint you with the progress we are making in the case? I imagine you will wish to know.'

'I wish to do rather more than be informed, Sir George. I intend to run these pirates to earth. Fawcett, you take half a dozen of your best men and another carriage. I must secure a post-chaise for Miss Parrish and I have a letter to write, then we will be on our way.'

'To Blakeney, Your Grace?'

'Yes. That seems to be the only firm piece of information we have. That and the name Axminster.'

He turned to find Sarah in whispered conversation with Millie. When she turned back he saw she was pale and tense. She must be exhausted.

'I hope that was not too distressing for you. Now, I will write a letter for you to take to my sister and drive you into Aylsham where there are a number of decent inns and we should be able to find you a post-chaise.'

'No,' she said, and he realised that she was not upset or tired, but excited. 'I am coming with you.'

Chapter Ten

'I am coming with you,' Sarah repeated. 'Don't you realise who Axminster is?'

'No, I do not,' Nicholas said.

'Wilton—my father's business manager. Don't you see? Wilton and Axminster, the two great carpet-making towns.'

'Coincidence,' he said.

'Really? Two crooked ship owners with those names? The Glass-Eyed Man? Wilton wears thick-lensed spectacles and he looks as meek and precise as any office clerk.'

'That is one coincidence too many,' Nicholas said thoughtfully. 'But you are most certainly not coming with me.'

'Why not?' Sarah demanded. 'I am the only person who can identify him. And besides, I want to see him brought down, brought to justice. The man ruined us, as near as killed my father.'

'Yes, I can understand how you feel. But it would be scandalous, you travelling with a party of men and only a maid as chaperone, and besides, it would be dangerous.'

'Might I remind you that I have been travelling with a party of men, as you put it, for days now? If your sister is able to salvage my reputation now, then why not in a week's time? We are hardly likely to be flaunting ourselves at society functions, are we? And as for danger,' she said quickly, seeing he was on the point of speaking, 'just what do you envisage as being more dangerous than the situations I have been in this last week?'

'Miss Parrish—Sarah—please be reasonable about this—'

She almost smiled. This was not a man who was used to people contradicting him, refusing to obey his orders or disagreeing in any particular. 'If you put me in a post-chaise I will instruct the postilions to go to Blakeney as soon as you are out of sight. And do not think that paying them a large sum to ignore me will work, because I will tell them that you are abducting me for evil purposes.'

For a long moment he stared at her and she stared right back into those dark eyes until she felt she was swaying towards him, mesmerised, her heart thudding, although why, when she was not frightened, she could not tell.

And then Nicholas laughed, a genuine burst of laughter that had everyone else in the room turning to stare at them. 'You will be the death of me, Sarah Parrish. Why couldn't I have found myself on a ship with a meek little spinster.'

'I *am* a meek little spinster,' she retorted, then realised how ridiculous it was to say that when she was standing in the middle of a room full of respectable gentlemen brazenly defying a duke. 'Well, a spinster anyway.'

Nicholas sank onto the nearest chair, put his head in his hands and laughed until his shoulders shook. He looked up and wiped tears from his eyes with the back of his hand. 'Come, then. I am undoubtedly all about in the head to even contemplate it, but I have no faith whatsoever in you not arriving at Blakeney—probably in the middle of a gun battle—having begged rides in farm carts right across Norfolk.'

'You are *amused*?'

'I am probably hysterical at the turn my well-ordered existence is taking,' Nicholas retorted, getting to his feet. He bowed towards the group of magistrates and officers who were studiously pretending to ignore them. 'Excuse me, gentle-men. An ill-timed jest, I fear. I will keep in touch with news as it arises.'

Nicholas swept her down the steps. 'Now where the devil have Pendell and Millie got to?'

'And Charlie.' Sarah looked around her, anx-ious. What if he had run off, frightened by the magistrates and the nearness of members of Lockhart's gang? 'I will look this way.'

Without waiting for Nicholas's agreement she gathered up her skirts and ran along the right-hand front of the house, through a gateway in the flanking wall, found herself in a garden and stopped, enchanted.

High walls sheltered the plot from the sea winds and it was full of roses, with grass paths dividing the symmetrical beds and mounds of lavender and Russian sage spilling out in wanton abandon. Her nostrils full of the heady perfume, Sarah followed the sound of trickling water and found a stone basin in the centre with a fountain running over mossy rocks. Charlie was perched on the rim, gazing about him with his mouth half open.

'Are you all right?' she asked, sitting down be-side him. 'We thought we had lost you.'

He blinked up at her. 'Wot is this, miss?'

'It's a garden, Charlie. Haven't you ever seen one before?'

'No, miss. Nuffin grows in the docklands. Is it 'eaven?'

'Heaven? No, although in some countries they think gardens are like heaven come to earth.'

'Who looks after it, miss?'

'Gardeners, Charlie. They start as apprentices and learn the skills. They grow fruit and vegetables as well as flowers. Look, there's one now.'

A middle-aged man in a leather jerkin, breeches and gaiters came out from one of the paths and touched a finger to his hat brim. 'Good day to you, miss.'

'Good day. My young friend and I were admiring this lovely garden.'

'Thank you, miss. Like flowers, do you, lad? What kind do you like best?' He spoke kindly and Sarah guessed he might have children of his own.

'Don't know any names,' Charlie admitted. 'I like those.' He pointed at a deep crimson rose.

'Now that's a rose. She's a beauty, isn't she? Here you are, lad, have one for your buttonhole.' He broke off a half-open bud and handed it to Charlie. 'And one for the lady, of course. You need to make sure you take off the thorns first so she doesn't prick her fingers. See?'

Ten minutes later Sarah finally managed to drag Charlie out of the garden, stunned into speechlessness. Millie was looking out of the coach window and Pendell and Nicholas stood on the gravel, both with hands on hips, the perfect models of exasperated menfolk waiting for a woman.

'Where did you find him?' Nicholas demanded. He picked Charlie up bodily and dumped him into the vehicle, then gave Sarah a hand to mount the step.

'There is an enchanting walled garden. Charlie has never seen one before and we were talking to the gardener.' She looked at the boy, who was peering down at the rose attached to his jacket and touching it tentatively with one finger. 'Here, Charlie, look at the one he gave me. It is more open and you can see inside.' She raised an eyebrow at Nicholas. 'You don't happen to have a vacancy in your gardening staff for a boy, have you?'

'I expect one could be found.' Nicholas regarded the absorbed child. 'Charlie.'

'Cap'n? I mean...sir?'

'Would you like to work in a garden?'

'Me? Wot, like that one?'

'Bigger,' Nicholas said, with a glance out of the window. 'Much, much bigger.'

'Oh, yes, sir. Please, sir.'

'We'll see if you still think the same once all this is over. If you do, I'll take you to see my head gardener, see what you make of each other.'

That rendered the boy utterly silent. All he could do was nod.

'That was kind,' Sarah said when Charlie's attention was back on a minute study of the rose.

Nicholas shrugged. 'He may change his mind or he may not suit, but he deserves a chance.'

They took luncheon at the King's Arms in North Walsham where the landlord had the charming conceit of filling half-barrels with a mass of cottage garden plants. Pendell had to march Charlie inside past them and, as soon as he had finished wolfing down his pie, eating as though he might be back on crusts and slops at any moment, he escaped outside to stare at them. Sarah followed him and through the open window of the private parlour Nick could hear her identifying them.

'That's a marigold and those are larkspur and

that is a dandelion, but that's a weed. What is a weed? Well...'

He leant back in his chair, closed his eyes and let the voices wash over him.

Pendell cleared his throat and Nick came to himself with a jerk. 'Good Lord, I was dropping off to sleep there.'

'I don't think so, sir. You were humming.'

'Humming? Don't be ridiculous. I do not hum, Pendell.'

'You were, sir,' his valet persisted. '"Early One Morning," it was. You know, the one about the maiden singing and the sun rising and her picking roses for her lover. I expect that's what put you in mind of it.'

Nick got to his feet and tugged his coat into order. 'Ridiculous. I do not hum folksongs in public houses. You were dreaming.'

'Yes, of course, Your Grace. I'm sorry, Your Grace.'

'Here, take this and go and pay the reckoning.'

Outside he found Sarah and Charlie were still exploring the flower tubs. 'And this one is Sweet Cecily and that's a daisy.'

'Cor... I knew a Daisy once. And a Cecily, only they called her Ceccy. Why are flowers called girl's names?'

'I think it is the other way around,' Sarah said.

'I disagree,' Nick drawled. 'It is because ladies are beautiful and so flowers are named after them.'

'Daisy weren't beautiful,' Charlie objected. 'Her teef stuck out and she had a squint.'

Nick met Sarah's amused glance. 'All ladies are beautiful, Charlie. It is important for a man to remember that.'

'Well, Millie's pretty,' Charlie agreed. 'And Miss Sarah's beautiful. But Daisy weren't, honest she weren't.'

'His Grace is teasing you, Charlie,' Sarah said composedly. 'The girls are named for the flowers. And beauty is not important, although it is not polite to comment on people's appearance.'

'So 'is Grace is wrong?'

'His Grace is a duke, Charlie, and they are a law unto themselves and may be as rude as they like. You and I, we must mind our manners.'

Behind him Nick heard a choking sound and turned to find Pendell pink about the ears and attempting to stifle his sniggers with his hand.

'You heard Miss Parrish, Pendell: you must mind your manners.'

'Yes, sir.' Pendell emerged from behind his

hand, biting his lip, but otherwise managing to keep an admirably straight face.

'Right. Time we were going. The others should have finished by now.' They should be on their way and he should be thinking about bringing Lockhart and his crew to justice, not lounging around in inns humming—*humming, for heaven's sake!*—and talking inanities with a cabin boy and a paid companion.

In the stable yard he found Fawcett and his six men waiting and both teams harnessed.

'Where to tonight, sir?' Fawcett had the road map in his hand. 'It's another twenty-five miles or so to Blakeney.'

Nick studied the map. 'I don't want to arrive in two carriages without scouting the area first. Holt is just inland and looks large enough to have a decent inn or two.' He opened the route book. 'Yes, the King's Head and the Feathers. We'll split up, go to one each and then ask about Blakeney—is it a good port to take a coastal vessel to London? Can they recommend a skipper? Anyone to avoid? You know the sort of thing, Matt.'

'That's a good idea. I'll send some of the lads out to the ale houses, ask the same questions.'

'Then tomorrow we'll go to Blakeney early,

before sunrise. Leave the coaches a way out and walk in. I'll leave Pendell with the women and the boy.'

'What about the local Justices, sir?'

'I think we'll leave them out of this until we have a clearer picture. This is smuggling country and it isn't always clear where loyalties lie. This Axminster fellow may have established himself as a local gentleman, for all we know.'

'Right, sir. We'll follow you twenty minutes or so back: no point in advertising that we're all together.'

Nick strolled back to his carriage, whistling under his breath, caught himself doing so and stopped mid-verse. What the devil was the matter with him? Anyone would think he had been drinking heavily when all that had passed his lips had been a pint of ale with the meal.

It was not until the carriage was moving off that he finally realised what was happening. He was enjoying himself. This adventure—there was no point in pretending it was anything else—was a total novelty and couldn't be further from his normal routine. And that routine had begun to pall, he had to admit. The business of the dukedom was considerable and, however many excellent staff one employed, there was a great deal to keep on top of. His social life was, of course, lavish and, he realised, utterly predictable.

His friends and acquaintances would think he had taken leave of his senses if he told them that he was relishing the discomfort and the danger, to say nothing of the company of one urchin, one pert Cockney maid and one young woman who appeared to think it her mission in life to depress the pretentions of top-lofty aristocrats.

There were dangers, of course. He made himself think seriously about the situation. This was not some storybook adventure. He had people depending on him for their lives if this went wrong, and Sarah Parrish was relying on him to keep her reputation intact, which should be achievable with his sister's help.

But there was more than reputation at stake here, he acknowledged frankly, shifting on the seat and wedging his shoulders against the angle of coach back and window so he could stretch his legs out more easily.

Sarah, he could see clearly now he had shifted his position, had curled up in the other corner and was looking past him out of the window.

He found her attractive and he must not let that show, must not alarm her or make her feel uncomfortable. She had insisted on accompanying him, true, but that was, surely, because of her own innocence. Presumably she was confident that he would behave like a gentleman and, of course, he would. But it might be rather more difficult not to let the effort show...

Goodness knows why he was finding her presence disturbing. She was attractive enough, but his world was full of far more lovely women. She used no wiles to beguile, she did not flirt, she was given to saying just what she thought in flattening detail and she looked absolutely nothing like Marietta, whom he had always assumed was the perfect example of the kind of looks that most attracted him.

Surely it was not because she made him laugh, or because she used her brain in ways that no young lady was encouraged to do? And she had courage and that was attractive. But she was patently respectable and he was not going to offer her a *carte blanche* as his mistress: ruining innocents was not something he would contemplate for a moment. It would be sensible to be careful what he said.

'What is it?' the innocent in question demanded, jerking Nick out of his abstraction. 'You have been staring at me for quite ten minutes.'

'I apologise.' The truth was clearly inadmissible, but insult would always distract. 'I was lost in contemplation of that quite awful bonnet.'

'Oh, yes, isn't it dowdy?' she agreed earnestly, giving the ribbons an irritable tug. 'My last employer bought it for me as a present and I cannot afford to simply discard it. I wondered about new ribbons, or a spray of artificial flowers, but I do not think that would answer.'

'I will buy you a new one. Holt, surely, has a milliner.'

And there, within a minute, goes my resolution to be careful.

'I cannot accept gifts of clothing from a gentleman,' Sarah said stiffly.

'And my reputation will never survive being seen with a female in that bonnet,' Nick said, finding his balance again.

'Very well, thank you. But as a loan only.'

'And what am I supposed to do with a lightly used bonnet?'

'Give it to your housekeeper to present to a deserving housemaid.'

Nick made a gesture of defeat. If he bought her a pretty enough hat, then she would keep it, he was sure. He had never yet found a woman who would not. He met Sarah's speculative gaze and wondered if here was the exception.

'Who are we?' she asked suddenly.

'Theologically, philosophically or biologically?' Nick asked.

'No, *actually*,' Sarah said. 'We can't arrive in a little market town announcing that you are the Duke of Severton. Not without creating a stir anyway. And no one will believe you are Mr Smith—I certainly didn't. And who am I supposed to be?'

Nick pondered the question which was, he acknowledged, something he should have considered. 'I have it. I am Lord Wendover and you are my sister Sarah. George, the third Baron Wendover, was at university with me; he has a sister Sarah and is very much wedded to his country estate in Buckinghamshire. If anyone should look in the *Peerage* I am the right age, and the chances of anyone we might encounter in Norfolk ever having met George are remote in the extreme.'

Sarah nodded. 'That would be perfect, although you do not *look* like a George.' She appeared to find this worrying and frowned at him while her lips shaped the name. 'Charlie, we will be pretending that the Duke is actually Lord

Wendover. Can you remember that? You must call him *my lord*.'

Charlie nodded. 'Who am I?'

'That's a very good point, Charlie. How would it be if you are the new gardener's boy? You had best stay with the coachman and groom tonight.'

The boy went very still and Nick recalled his fear at being left alone with his valet that first night. He seemed to trust Pendell now, so he said, 'On second thoughts, you *are* the new gardener's boy, but you are also Pendell's young brother, so you stay with him. Is that better? His name is James.'

'Jimmy,' Charlie said with a cheeky grin, caught sight of Nick's expression and added, 'My lord.'

Nick, who had been suppressing a smile, and had clearly produced a scowl, merely nodded and tried to avoid catching Sarah's eye. She appeared to find his new name amusing.

Chapter Eleven

Travelling dukes either had elaborate arrangements made by their staff in advance or simply
arrived somewhere and the best possible accommodation was supplied by their gratified hosts.
Mere barons appearing unannounced and demanding good bedchambers, a private parlour
and stabling with accommodation for coachman
and groom were met with rather less enthusiasm
on market day.

'Think how much worse it would have been
if you had been plain Mr Smith,' Sarah pointed
out when he had eventually negotiated a parlour and two acceptable bedchambers, one for
him with two truckle beds in it for Pendell and
Charlie, and one for Sarah with a bed for Millie.

It seemed to Nick that she was on edge and
hiding it behind a facade of amusement. He wondered what was wrong, until he realised that if

she was expecting this to end with an encounter with Wilton, the man who had caused her father's death, then she would be feeling considerable anxiety, if not distress.

The waiter brought tea and a tray of cakes and biscuits to the parlour and Millie and Pendell made as if to leave, Charlie between them. 'Not so fast!' Nick called the man back. 'Three more cups and plates, if you please. We need a council of war,' he told the others. 'Come and sit down.'

'The innkeeper is going to think it very strange, Your—my lord.'

Nick shrugged. 'He may think what he likes and will keep quiet about it if he wants my money.' He waited until Sarah poured tea, Pendell moved the plate of cakes out of Charlie's reach and they were paying attention, then told them what he had agreed with Fawcett.

'Tomorrow morning, before dawn, you and I and Charlie will join Fawcett and his men and we will see what we can find at Blakeney. Charlie, you will stick to Pendell like glue, do you understand? Whatever happens, whatever you see, you stay with him and he will look after you.'

'*Mmm.*' Charlie nodded, his mouth full of fruit cake.

'And what do you propose for myself and Millie?' Sarah asked.

Nick took out his pocketbook, removed two banknotes and passed them to her. 'Buy a new bonnet for yourself and some more clothes for Charlie.'

'But—'

'You cannot possibly accompany us,' Nick said firmly.

Sarah opened her mouth to protest, but one look at Nicholas told her it was impossible. He had that look, the one of ineffable superiority that men wore when laying down the law to mere females. Dukes, she was realising, were able to produce it at the drop of a hat—it was probably in the blood. She would protest and he would counter with calm arguments which boiled down to one—that women were poor, feeble creatures who would get in the way, need saving from themselves and would probably have the vapours or hysterics, or possibly both at once, if confronted by danger.

He is rather splendid, looking down his nose like that with just the one lock of hair falling on his forehead and his mouth—that mouth—set in a firm line. Rather like a marble bust of a Roman senator, only not in cold stone...

'No, of course not. Whatever was I thinking of?' She smiled, putting every ounce of rueful apology she could into it.

'It seems a pleasant town. I imagine you will find plenty to amuse you for a day,' Nicholas added.

'I am sure I will. No doubt there is a haberdashery shop. I shall buy a shuttle and thread and commence some tatting. Or perhaps there is a bookshop and I can find a distracting novel,' Sarah added sweetly. 'And to cap all the excitement, a new bonnet, of course.'

That earned her a sideways look, more for her tone than for her proposed programme, she thought. Just so long as Nicholas believed her to be sulking rather than contemplating active disobedience, she would be safe.

'What are you planning, Miss Sarah?' Millie asked as they went up to their bedchamber that night.

'Why, to go shopping, of course.'

'And then?' Millie perched on the end of her bed and made no effort to begin undressing.

'Hire a gig and go to Blakeney. I want to make

enquiries about this mysterious Mr Axminster and I am the only person who can recognise him if he really is Josiah Wilton. We must take care to dress in clothing that Lockhart and his crew have not seen. A new bonnet for both of us, I think, and brighter colours than we wore on the ship. I want to look like a respectable lady of the middling sort out for a drive with her maid.'

'And if we speak to anyone, why are we in Blakeney?'

'Let me think.' She needed an excuse that would sound respectable and not arouse curiosity. 'I know. I wish to leave London and I am looking for a pleasant area to move to.'

Millie nodded and stood up. 'Right you are, Miss Sarah. I won't be a minute.'

When she came back she had something wrapped in the edge of her shawl. 'I thought we might need this, Miss Sarah. Can you use one?'

This was a small but effective-looking pistol. 'Um. Point it and pull the trigger? Is it loaded?'

'I think so, and it is safe until you pull back the hammer, I do know that,' Millie said, putting the sinister thing down cautiously on the dresser. 'I saw there were a pair in the door pocket of the carriage when we were driving this afternoon.'

'What if it is needed?' Sarah bit her lip as she bent over it, not touching.

'That Mr Fawcett and all his men had enough guns for a small war and they are all going together.'

'That is true,' Sarah agreed. 'Yes, we will take it.'

She was tired enough to sleep almost as soon as Millie snuffed out the candle, but exhaustion did not stop her dreaming.

It was a vivid dream, and it made total sense at the time. Nicholas was mounted on a magnificent black stallion and held a golden pistol in one hand. Only a duke could use such a fine weapon, he told her, and she must not have one at all. She should have a kitchen knife because she was a woman and only a paid companion. It was important that she remember her place, he told her, looking down his nose at her as she stood humbly next to his horse.

Sarah woke with a sensation of embarrassment, as though she had just received a resounding snub. She lay in the half-light feeling miserable and blinked into full consciousness, the leaden weight of misery in her stomach. Any moment now she would remember just what had happened the day before to cause this sick sensation.

Nothing came back to her and she sat up, racking her memory until, at last, the dream returned in all its strangeness. Nicholas had never said anything specifically to put her in her place—not that she admitted that she had one—so was this her own common sense warning her that she must not forget just who he was and how infinitely remote he was from her usual existence?

I do not need reminding of that, she thought crossly.

Don't you? an uncomfortable little inner voice asked. *Aren't you becoming just a little too friendly, just a trifle familiar with him?*

I am pretending to be his sister, she argued back.

'What time is it, Miss Sarah?' Millie sat up, stretched and yawned. 'Early by the light.' She hopped out of bed and opened the curtains a crack to look down on the street. 'There they go—both carriages and two riding horses, as well. Oh, he's a handsome man, isn't he, miss?'

'Who? Pendell?' Sarah asked, knowing perfectly well who Millie was talking about.

'Oh, miss! He's all right if you like skinny lads with freckles. His Grace, of course.'

'Yes, I suppose he would generally be considered handsome,' Sarah said with careful indifference.

'Do you think he might…you know.'

'No, I do *not* know, unless you are suggesting that the Duke might make me an improper proposal.'

'Improper, miss?'

'He is hardly likely to make me an honourable one, now is he, Millie?'

'He might. You're a lady and you are pretty.'

'Thank you for that, Millie. But I can assure you that his family and friends would consider me genteel at best. I work for my living, just like you do, which means that I am not the sort of woman to receive anything but a *carte blanche* from an aristocrat.'

Millie tossed her plaits over her shoulder. 'Pity. I fancied being lady's maid to a duchess, I did.' Sarah smiled at her and, clearly emboldened, Millie added, 'So you didn't come with him just to give him a nudge?'

'No! Goodness, Millie—I came because I want to see the man who cheated my father brought to justice.'

The fact that she enjoyed being with Nicholas, even when he was at his chilliest and most duke-like, was beside the point. Any woman might be excused for allowing a foolish daydream to creep into their heads but sensible ones also had nightmares where they were reminded firmly of their place.

They dressed in fresh clothes from their trunks, then shopped after breakfast for Charlie's new shirts and stockings, a modest but flattering bonnet for Sarah and a jaunty flat straw for Millie.

There was plenty left over from Nicholas's banknotes to hire a gig, but the groom waved it away, saying he would put it on Lord Wendover's account.

'I think that will be useful,' Sarah said, putting the money away again carefully in her reticule. 'We have money to spend in any shops or stalls we find at Blakeney which will give us an excuse to ask questions.'

Millie climbed up to sit beside her as Sarah took the reins. 'I didn't know you could drive, miss.'

'It is a long time since I have, but I'm sure it isn't something one forgets.' The smart bay cob behind the shafts set off at a brisk trot out of the yard. 'And it is only about six miles, they say,' she added, mentally crossing her fingers that she was right.

It proved a pleasant drive with considerably more up and down than she had expected after the flatness of the south of the county. There were scattered farms, plenty of woodland and charming valleys, but no cottages until they arrived at the tiny village of Wiveton with its church that looked large enough for somewhere three times the size.

A pair of elderly men outside the inn directed them on the right lane for Blakeney and the cob set off willingly again, although the rise and fall of the road had removed some of his initial exuberance, much to Sarah's relief. Her arms were beginning to ache intolerably and so was the small of her back, and it was with considerable relief that she drew to a halt by a church with a view of the sea in the distance, like a darker blue line drawn below the sky on the horizon.

'Those are wide salt marshes beyond the cottages,' she said, looking down the slope before them. 'I suppose there must be a channel into the port.'

They proceeded slowly down the narrow street past little cottages built of flints and red brick. Tall gateposts hinted at larger houses to the side and, as they reached the bottom and could see vessels tied up against a dock that seemed to run at right angles to the street, there were more substantial, double-fronted houses.

'It looks small but prosperous,' Sarah commented.

'Busy too,' Millie said as they reached the harbour. There were groups of men standing talking with the air of business deals being completed, ships were being unloaded and, as they watched, half a dozen boats came in with nets piled on the decks. There was no sign of Nicholas or Fawcett and his men and they had passed no empty carriages.

They drove the length of the dockside. With the crowd and bustle they had to move slowly until they reached a low, whitewashed inn at the point where the road curled uphill again, away from the water.

Sarah drove in and when a groom came forward asked him to look after their horse for an hour while they took a stroll along the harbour.

'We're being watched,' Millie said as they lifted down the baskets they had borrowed in Holt.

Sarah turned casually and saw two loungers studying them. 'Just idle fellows,' she said, seeing the impertinent stare one was giving Millie. 'Ignore them.'

They strolled along, studying the ships. 'I can't see anything that looks like the one we were on,' Millie said.

'There are more in the open water where the creek turns towards the sea.' Sarah shaded her eyes. 'Yes. See that one with the very white sails? There's something about it—I think it's the *Gannet* with a new set of canvas. There's a general store next to the ship's chandler's: let's try in there.'

She pushed open the door of A. & G. Pegg, General Merchants and Receiving Office, causing a bell to tinkle wildly and all the occupants to turn and stare.

'Good day,' Sarah said to three women with laden marketing baskets, a small boy clutching a list, an old man with a parcel and the two women behind the counters. It was one of those shops that seemed to sell a little of everything, from mousetraps to lamp oil to buttons and cheese.

'How may I help you, ma'am?' enquired the nearest shopkeeper, reaching out a hand for the list the boy held at the same time. The old man dumped his parcel on the other counter and demanded to know how much for the carrier to take it to Norwich and the three women returned to their conversation.

'Do you have any ribbons?' Sarah asked at random.

'Aye, ma'am. Here you are.' The shopkeeper pulled out a deep drawer and laid the whole thing on the counter. 'Now, Tommy Bishop, let's see what you've got here. Boot laces, tapioca, dried peas, linen thread...' She began to walk about the store collecting things up as she went.

Sarah began to sort through the ribbons and lifted two spools up to the light. The old man went out muttering about the wicked cost of the carrier and the gossiping women followed him.

The other assistant came around the counter to Sarah. 'That's all we have. You'll need to go into Holt for more.'

Sarah smiled at her. 'This pink one is just what I need. Can I have a yard of that, please?' She waited while the woman measured and cut. 'This is a very well-equipped store and the village is busier than I was expecting.' She took off her gloves to open the stiff catch of the coin purse in her reticule and caught sight of the ring she wore on her right hand. It gave her an idea and she put her gloves on again hastily. 'Are there any small houses to rent around here, do you know? I have been thinking of moving out of London—it is a year since my husband died.' She paused while the women made sympathetic tutting noises, then added, 'A chance acquaintance said it was a pleasant area.'

'Someone from around here, ma'am? Who would that be, I wonder?'

'A Mr Ax… Oh, what was it? One of those introductions at a social gathering… Oh, yes, Axminster. That was it. It reminded me of carpets.'

A subtle change came over the atmosphere in the stuffy little shop. The boy, half his purchases packed away, paused, a packet of dried peas in his hand, and stared at her. The women looked at each other, then one said, 'Mr Axminster at Green Lodge, was that, ma'am?'

'Oh, I have no idea if that is his address,' Sarah said casually, still rummaging amongst the ribbons in the hope that it hid her sudden excitement. 'I'll have two yards of that narrow green one as well, please. I was just making conversation with him, you know how it is? Saying I wished I could get out of London before the summer became any hotter and he said this coast was good for blowing away the cobwebs and I said I enjoyed making watercolour sketches and he said there were some fine skies to paint.'

She handed the reel of ribbon to the assistant. 'And that was it, really. Only it made me restless, thinking of getting away.'

The ribbons were carefully wrapped, she paid for them and then, finally, they were able to leave.

'That's wonderful,' she said to Millie as soon as the door closed behind them and the faint tinkle of the bell died away. 'I never expected it to be so easy.'

They turned to continue along the waterfront, then stepped aside quickly as two burly men barged along towards them, gesticulating as they shouted aggressively at each other. People moved aside and Sarah and Millie stepped quickly into the mouth of a narrow alleyway beside them.

A hand seized Sarah's arm, a palm was slapped over her mouth and she was dragged, kicking and struggling, back up the alleyway.

Chapter Twelve

Sarah tried to bite the hand over her mouth, dug back with her elbow and was still dragged inexorably into a small, dark yard out of sight of the quayside. She glimpsed Millie kicking and wriggling, then she was behind the bulk of a carriage. She tried again to make contact with her elbow, felt it hit home.

Behind her a man said, *'Ough,'* and let her go.

'Nicholas? *Nicholas?'* She spun around, her back to the carriage, and confronted him. 'What the devil do you think you are doing?'

'What am *I* doing?' He had lost his hat, wore a Belcher handkerchief tied around his neck and a shabby frieze coat and he looked as furious as she felt. 'I told you to stay in Holt. You lied to me—'

'I did no such thing. We shopped, as you can see by this bonnet which you have probably ruined. Then we hired a gig and came here. I do not see why I should do what you tell me.' Behind her, on the other side of the carriage, she could hear Millie expressing herself forcefully and Pendell replying, equally heated.

'Because you should have more sense,' Nicholas said. She could almost hear his teeth gritting in the effort not to shout. 'Because we are dealing with very dangerous men and this is not a game, not some exciting tale in a trashy novel.'

'I know they are dangerous. I was there when they murdered those men—remember? I do not want to encounter them again. I will most happily leave them to you and your little army. But if Axminster is Wilton, then he drove my father to his death, he stole and cheated and he ruined my life. I will not stand back from any chance to bring him to justice.' She took a step forward and prodded her index finger emphatically into his breastbone. 'I will *not.*'

Nicholas caught her hand as she began to jab him again. Did she stumble towards him or did he pull her? Sarah was not certain, only that they were so close that she could feel his breath on her face. His hand moved from her wrist, up her arm. Her hand flattened on his chest and slid to his shoulder and then they were kissing, open-mouthed, urgent, angry.

His arm tightened around her shoulders, her hand fisted in his hair, and still they clung until, panting, they fell apart.

As though at a distance she could hear masculine voices, calm now, placating, and Millie laughing. Here, in the space between the carriage and the wall was another world, filled with the sound of their breathing, of her heartbeat pounding in her ears, of unspoken words.

After what seemed like an age Nicholas said, 'I apologise.'

'What for?' Sarah realised that under a tumult of confused feelings she was still angry. At herself because she wanted to kiss him again? At Nicholas for making her want that? 'We kissed each other. Or are you apologising for man-handling me, frightening the life out of me and dragging me off the street?'

The effort it took to answer her was written plainly on his face. 'Two of our men saw you at the inn. We had to get you off the street before any of the crew from the *Gannet* encountered you. Lockhart came ashore an hour ago with two sailors who are waiting in a rowing boat you'd have passed in a few more yards. Our men, making a row, distracted attention so we could get you clear without anyone noticing.'

'They would not recognise us. They have never seen us in clothes of these colours; they are not expecting us.' There was a small scar that she had not noticed before, just below the curve of his lower lip; his eyes had gone the deep inky-blue she had seen when he was angered—or aroused, she realised now.

Nicholas's lips moved and she guessed that he was counting. 'I apologised for kissing you,' he said finally. 'I refuse to apologise for attempting to keep you safe.'

'We kissed each other,' Sarah said. 'Angrily,' she added, puzzled.

There was the faintest twitch of his lips, so faint that if she had not been studying his mouth with painful intensity she would not have seen it. 'I thought at one point you were going to bite. Are you always so fierce?'

'I have no idea. I have never kissed anyone before,' she admitted, looking up to meet his gaze. 'Except you kissing me in the cabin that time. And that was hardly...'

'I see,' Nicholas said. 'In that case perhaps I should tell you it is not normally so angry.'

'No. I never expected it to be. I suppose people kissing each other are usually rather more in accord.'

'That is the case in my experience,' Nicholas agreed gravely. Now he was unmistakably smiling.

It was difficult to know what to say next. Difficult to speak, her mouth was so dry. A sophisticated woman of the world would no doubt extract herself from this situation with a witty quip or a provocative toss of her head. Both wit and provocation appeared to have completely deserted her, as had even the faintest idea of what she wanted to do next.

'I have discovered where this Mr Axminster lives,' she blurted out. 'Green Lodge. It is local, but I do not know where that is—I did not like to draw attention to my interest in the shop.'

If Nicholas was taken aback by her abrupt change of subject he did not show it. Perhaps he, too, was relieved to be saved from any further intimacies. 'We can find out when we return to Holt,' he said, moving out from behind the shelter of the carriage into the yard. 'Enquiries here might not be wise.'

'I can see that.' Both carriages had been brought into the space which seemed to be at the rear of a tavern, judging by the stack of barrels in one corner. 'It is the *Gannet* out in the deep-water moorings, isn't it? With a new set of white sails.'

'Yes. The local Revenue officer has sent out a fishing boat with some of his men on board to shadow her if they leave harbour, but we do not want to intervene until we hear from London. Ideally we should let them out on a long leash and see if we can capture the entire gang, but Rundell, Bridge & Rundell may have different ideas, and so might the owner of whatever they have stolen.'

'But we can still find Wilton and have him arrested,' Sarah said. Half a dozen men stood around, two of them watching the entrance to the yard, another lounging against the entrance, smoking a pipe. Millie was talking to Pendell, her good humour quite restored, it seemed. He was holding the pistol they had taken and was shaking his head in reproach: it appeared to amuse her.

'No.' Nicholas said it flatly.

Sarah spun around to face him, her expression incredulous. '*What?* It is easy, surely? We wait until Lockhart and his men are back on board the *Gannet*, then go to the local magistrate. I tell him who their Mr Axminster really is and he is arrested. If we don't make a great fuss about it Lockhart will not know.'

'I cannot trust the local magistrates,' Nick said. 'Smuggling is rife along this coast and some, at least, of the Justices will be involved: it is always the way.'

He could see the disappointment, the instinctive urge to argue and protest, clear on her face and could hardly blame her for it: in her position he would want to be after Wilton with a shotgun. He braced himself for an outburst because there would be no kissing another quarrel away, much as he might like to.

'I see. Yes, that could ruin everything; he might even escape,' Sarah said slowly. She was pale and her hands were clenched, but she had herself under control. 'But you will not just forget him, will you? When we take Lockhart and recover the stolen crate, you will return and deal with him?'

'I promise. Give me your hands.'

She put her tight fists into his and he raised them to his lips, kissed each on the knuckles that stretched the thin black kid over the bone.

'Nicholas—what are you doing?'

'Endeavouring to stop you splitting the seams

of your gloves, otherwise I will have to buy you some new ones and, frankly, what with clothing that brat Charlie and buying you new bonnets, I will be out of funds within days.'

'You—' She glared at him, then gave a choked laugh. 'You are impossible.'

'I fear so,' he said, releasing her and walking further into the yard. He was certainly confused, presumably by that kiss, which was ridiculous. It meant nothing, merely the release of tension and anger on both their parts. He shouldn't be kissing virginal paid companions, of course, but there was no harm done: Sarah was thoroughly sensible.

He watched her making her way to Millie, skirting around the yard so as to keep out of sight of the entrance onto the quayside. Yes, thoroughly sensible, he reassured himself. Sarah would know he was not attempting to seduce her and she was not going to behave as though he had compromised her.

Which he had, of course. It was an uncomfortable thought, but if Miss Parrish had been the daughter of one of the *ton*, or of a respectable ship owner, come to that, he should be offering marriage.

But she is not: she is one step up from a servant, just like a governess.

His duty was to ensure that her reputation did not suffer and he could do that easily enough with his sister Julia's help.

Even so, he thought, watching her, calm and determined now, he would make it his personal mission to bring Wilton to justice. The memory of those small, fierce fists enclosed in his own hands would be a long time fading.

As will the taste of that kiss, he thought ruefully.

He found he was running the tip of his tongue around his lips. He was losing rather too much sleep on account of Sarah Parrish.

One of Fawcett's men, signalling from the entrance to the yard, put a stop to inconveniently sensual musings. Nick strode across and looked cautiously around the corner. The man at the entrance was knocking the used tobacco out of his clay pipe against the wall in the rhythm that signalled that someone was on the move. He held up one finger, then a second and jerked his head in an unmistakable *Come on* gesture.

Nick walked to the entrance and looked out. There was Lockhart, seated in the stern of the rowing boat, and two sailors on the oars pulling hard down the creek.

Someone was pressing against him, craning to look around. Someone soft who smelt faintly of jasmine.

'Get back,' he muttered. 'Wait… Our man who followed Lockhart into the inn has come out and he's signalling. The person Lockhart was meeting is coming this way.'

He did not have to wait for the lookout to signal who it was. Behind him Sarah stiffened. 'That's him,' she whispered. 'That's Wilton.'

He could have been any moderately prosperous local landowner or merchant. His suit of clothes was well-made but not of the latest fashion, his linen was crisp and white, his low-crowned hat of best beaver was at a jaunty angle and there was a flash of bright blue from his waistcoat as he half turned to bow acknowledgment to a greeting. A pair of gleaming round-lensed spectacles was perched on the end of his nose.

Medium height, comfortably portly around the midriff, with a cheerfully nondescript face, Josiah Axminster, *née* Wilton, looked anything but a thoroughgoing villain. He also appeared completely comfortable strolling along. This was no cautious criminal skulking in the shadows for fear of discovery, Nick thought.

'You sound like a kettle that is about to boil over,' he remarked without looking around.

Sarah made a sound that was almost a laugh. 'He makes me so angry.'

'I can understand why.' Nick turned and put his arm around her, shielding her from the view of passers-by on the quayside. 'He will not escape justice, I promise you.'

It felt strange to hold her like this, to feel so protective of the independent, brave young woman. For a moment she leaned in, rested her head against his shoulder and murmured something.

'What did you say?'

There was a sigh. And she pushed away from him. 'I said that sometimes I get so very tired of this grieving and hating.' Then she straightened up and, once again, was the aggravating Miss Parrish. 'What do you intend to do next?'

'Go back to Holt and see if there are letters from Winterton, or from Rundell, Bridge & Rundell, wait for a report from the Revenue men here on what Lockhart does next and make our plans from there.'

'Are they going to sink the *Gannet* with cannons?' That was Charlie.

'I thought I told you to stay in the carriage in case anyone recognised you.'

'I did. Sir,' he added as an afterthought. 'But they've gone now, ain't they?'

'Haven't they,' Nick corrected automatically. 'Yes, they have and no, we are not going to sink the *Gannet*, you bloodthirsty brat. She belongs to someone—Lockhart stole her.'

The council of war after dinner, held in Nick's private parlour at the Feathers, consisted of himself and Fawcett, Pendell, Millie, Sarah and Charlie, because, as Millie said, it was the only way to keep an eye on a boy she described as a limb of Satan. Nick had the sneaking suspicion that she approved of Charlie.

The cloudy June day had turned to rain, a damp, persistent drizzle, and Nick had ordered a fire to be lit. It gave their meeting a cosy, homely air, out of keeping with the subject under discussion.

Millie curled up on the hearthrug with Charlie leaning against her, playing the cat's cradle she had taught him. Pendell sat opposite her, ostensibly to wield the poker and keep the fire going but, Nick suspected, to look at her. He sat down in one of the armchairs, close enough to nudge his valet in the ribs with his toe if his attention started to stray too much. Fawcett pulled up a chair next to him and Sarah, who had, he noticed, slipped off her shoes, curled up opposite him on the battered sofa and seemed intent on watching the flames.

She looked sad, or perhaps merely thoughtful, and he wondered if all of this was bringing back too many painful memories to cope with. There was not a lot he could do about that, he decided. Nothing except bring Wilton to justice.

'There is post,' he told them, holding up two letters. He cracked the seals and everyone seemed to sit up straighter to listen.

'This is from Rundell, Bridge & Rundell.' He studied the first. 'Apparently they have spoken to the owner of that crate who has authorised them to tell me of the contents and their destination. It is a complete and lavish silver gilt dining set sent as a wedding present to the Duke of Findlater's eldest daughter, who has returned with her husband, the Earl of Tranley, to their home in Yorkshire after their honeymoon trip. They were aware that word that it was ready for shipment had got out and therefore decided to send it by sea. Apparently whoever is leaking information was able to discover what they had believed to be a well-kept secret.'

'What do they want done, sir?' Fawcett asked.

'The Duke wants it retrieved, regardless of publicity, and the culprits prosecuted to the utmost severity the law allows. Reading between the lines the directors of the company feel he is ordering the medieval dungeons in Findlater Castle put in order and the rack and thumbscrews oiled and that they themselves will be the first to try them if the silver is not recovered urgently.'

'This makes it easier,' Fawcett commented. 'At least we know what we are looking for now.'

'And the other letter?' Sarah asked. She wriggled into a more comfortable position against the plump cushions. Nick discovered that he was uncomfortably aware of her.

He cleared his throat and opened the letter. 'Not much. Long Tom has given more information about where they might be heading—a little fishing village called Saltfleet, just south of Grimsby.'

'I do not understand why they haven't delivered the crate to Wilton,' Sarah said, frowning at the fire.

'My guess would be that it is not destined for a buyer in this country,' Nick said. 'It would be too risky, given the prominence of the owners and the distinctiveness of the work.'

'I agree.' Fawcett, who had been brooding in the shadows, leaned forward. 'They intend to ship it abroad, possibly through Edinburgh. Increasing the distance from London can only make them more secure.'

'Then why come here at all?' Sarah queried.

'Because either Wilton is their agent for the sale and wanted to be certain it was safely in their hands, or he is their leader,' Nick said. 'We will wait until we hear what Lockhart does—if he sails north, then we follow by road. Wilton will stay snug hereabouts, I have no doubt. We can leave a couple of men behind to keep an eye on him.'

Fawcett stood up and announced that, if His Grace no longer required him, he would make his way back to the King's Head. Charlie had fallen asleep under the settle and Pendell hauled him out and carried him off, Millie following.

Nick stood and stretched, then sat down at the other end of the sofa to watch Sarah, who seemed to be on the point of dropping off to sleep.

'This is like being back on the ship, with one of us at each end of the bunk,' she said. 'Only more comfortable.'

The mention of the ship started a chain of thoughts in Nick's head. 'What exactly did Wilton steal from your father?' he asked.

Sarah blinked at him, but she answered readily enough. 'Six sailing vessels, their cargoes, and fifteen thousand pounds in cash and bonds.'

'And Wilton was an employee, not a partner?' She nodded. 'Then I think you will have no need to seek employment after this is all over and Wilton is arrested. You can demonstrate ownership of that money, the ships and the value of their cargo. I am no lawyer, but I suspect you will also have a claim for damages on anything that remains of Wilton's assets after that.'

Sarah sat up straight, wide-awake now. 'You mean I will be *rich*?'

Chapter Thirteen

'Not *rich*,' Nicholas said. 'But very comfortably off. If the ships are sold for a good price and the money is invested carefully, then you will have a very respectable competence—enough for a house, servants, a carriage of your own.'

'That *is* rich,' Sarah said. Of course to a duke, someone laden with lands and investments and family heirlooms of great value, it was probably less than his annual bill for candles for all his establishments. 'It might be a respectable competence to you, but as far as I am concerned, it is wealth. Everything was tied up in the business, so we lived quite simply when Papa was alive. Very respectable and comfortable, of course, and Papa had promised that I would have a comeout when I was eighteen, but this…this would be entirely different.'

'We will have to act quickly, once he is arrested,' Nicholas said, frowning as he thought it through. 'Have accountants move in to establish exactly where all his assets are, have lawyers ready to organise the seizure of the ships and his accounts, and to present the case in court.'

We?

'That will take a great deal of money,' she began.

Nicholas waved away the rest of what she had been about to say. 'I retain both accountants and lawyers: it will all be taken care of.'

'I cannot accept that!' Sarah swung her feet to the floor and began to pace across the small room. 'I would pay you back, of course, but even so—'

'Wilton is responsible for murder, mayhem and, although it is trivial in comparison, putting me to a great deal of discomfort and trouble. It is on my own account that I will pursue him. I have every expectation that what you can claim will pay all the legal bills without impinging upon your rightful inheritance.'

Sarah's steps had brought her to the door. Now she turned around and leaned against it. She felt slightly dizzy as though she was being buffeted by a strong wind. 'You have no need to look after my interests in this. You have saved my life—'

'I did nothing that any other gentleman would not have done in the same situation.'

'You have taken care of me. And do not tell me that any other gentleman would have done the same. You took me to your friend's home, you waited to make certain I was received by Mrs Gladman. You have transported, fed and accommodated me.'

'Only because you would have followed on my heels like a small dragon, breathing fire and vengeance on Wilton if I had not,' Nicholas pointed out. 'You would probably have arrived at a critical juncture and ruined everything. Really, you gave me no option—as you very well know.'

'That is true,' Sarah admitted ruefully. 'But before—you had no need to inflict me on your friends.'

'Of course not. I could simply have left you and Millie by the side of the road in the middle of that blasted fen at some ungodly hour of the morning, miles from anywhere. I am sure I would have slept very soundly in Sutton's best spare bedchamber after that.'

'You did not have to wait outside Mrs Gladman's house.'

Nicholas got to his feet in one abrupt movement and strode across the floor until they were virtually touching. 'No, I did not. But, confound it, I was worried about you. I... You are the most complete nuisance; you are argumentative, disobedient, unladylike, stubborn, but I care about you.'

'Indeed? After that catalogue of my failings I must say I cannot imagine why,' she retorted. It was hard to keep her voice from shaking, she was so mortified, but she was not going to admit to any of those faults. Not one. Of course he cared—it was his duty to care for those he saw as his dependents.

'Why?' Nicholas turned on his heel, strode back to the sofa, turned and glared at her. 'You want honesty? I care because, despite giving me a permanent headache, you are courageous, intelligent, you make me laugh at the most inappropriate moments and I like looking at you.'

'You like *looking* at me?' Sarah could not have been more dumbfounded if he had informed her that she had grown another head. 'I am not pretty. Not in the slightest.'

'I know that perfectly well,' the infuriating man said crossly.

Sarah snatched up the nearest object—fortunately a cushion from the settle—and hurled it at Nicholas's head.

He caught it.

Of course he caught it, she raged as she flung open the door and virtually ran to her bedchamber. *He's perfect. He's a duke.*

'Miss?' Millie eyed her cautiously from the far side of the bed where she was laying out Sarah's nightgown.

'Men!'

'Oh. Yes. He's a bossy one, but I suppose that's dukes for you.' Millie plumped up the pillows vigorously. 'Has he kissed you again, Miss Sarah?' she added casually.

'No, he has not— What do you mean, again?'

'I could see your feet under that carriage, Miss Sarah. I don't think anyone else noticed.'

'That was not a kiss,' Sarah said, kicking irritably at the bed leg and stubbing her toe. 'Ouch. That was anger, plain and simple. We both lost our tempers, and I don't know how, but we ended up kissing each other.' She sat on the end of the bed and looked at her maid, who was busy doing something in the chest of drawers and seemed to be fighting a smile.

'That would do it,' Millie said sagely.

How much experience with men Millie had

had Sarah wasn't certain and had no intention of asking, but she certainly had more than Sarah and there wasn't anyone else to ask.

'What do you mean?'

'He was anxious about you, that was plain. And there you were safe and sound and acting like he was a fool to have worried himself, so he lost his temper and so did you. And all those feelings you've been pretending weren't there come bubbling up and if one of you touched the other…' Her voice trailed off and she looked at Sarah, head cocked to one side.

'I poked him in the chest,' she admitted and gestured with her forefinger.

'There you are, then.'

'But I don't *like* him,' Sarah protested.

Millie dumped the little pile of underwear she had lifted from the drawer back into it and put her hands on her hips. 'Oh, Miss Sarah, what a taradiddle.'

'He is arrogant.'

'He's a duke.'

'And autocratic.'

Duke, Millie mouthed.

'And—' And that was all, really. He had been kind and thoughtful and brave and decisive. He was intelligent. He had looked after Charlie.

'He has no sense of humour,' she added, doubtful that was true. It was just that he kept it quietly to himself.

Millie looked unconvinced too. 'But you want him.' When Sarah just stared at her the maid shrugged. 'Nothing more natural. He's a good-looking man and he's got...you know.'

'No, I do not know,' Sarah said flatly, suspecting that she understood precisely what Millie meant.

'He's a real man, that's what he is. And he looks at you like he sees full well you're a woman and he knows what to do about it.' Millie shrugged. 'Makes your toes curl, I'll be bound.'

It wasn't her toes that were curling, it was her insides that felt tight and hot and her emotions were somewhere between eager and terrified. And her skin felt sensitive when she was near him, like it had after she had spilt near-boiling water over her hand once and for days she had flinched at even a breath of air over it. And as for the parts of her that a lady did not discuss at all—well, the less she thought about those the better, which was easier said than done.

'Yes,' Sarah admitted. 'He is...disturbing. But, Millie, even if he was only a baron, I am still a paid companion. An unemployed, unpaid companion. Aristocrats either ignore the fact that women like me exist or they have dishonourable uses for us.'

Millie nodded, her smile gone. 'I suppose so. Never come across the likes of even a baron before, so what would I know? But I see what you mean, miss—you can't expect a duke to make it permanent, and then where will you be?'

'I am hardly beautiful enough to have a career as a courtesan,' Sarah said with a painful attempt at humour.

'No, miss,' Millie agreed, flatteningly.

But, *I like looking at you.* What had Nicholas meant by that, when he agreed, all too readily, that she wasn't pretty?

Charlie thinks I'm pretty, she thought ruefully.

'I am not going to become his mistress and I do not for a minute believe he would ask me,' she said firmly. 'Now, enough of that. Has Charlie gone to bed?'

'He's got a mattress on the floor next to James in his room. He's happy enough now he knows he isn't going to be beaten every time we're cross about something.'

'In that case I think we should both try and get some sleep. Goodness knows what we will find ourselves doing in the morning.'

Sarah could tell by her breathing that Millie dropped off to sleep almost as soon as her head touched the pillow. She looked across as the figure curled up like a hedgehog under the blankets, gave her own pillows a thump, blew out the candle and curled up too.

Sarah was tired, it had been a long day; it should be easy to slip into the darkness. But it wasn't. Her body was restless, her mind was filled with images that refused to be ignored.

Finally she sat bolt upright and stared into the darkness. 'All right, I give in. Let me go to sleep and I promise I will dream about you,' she whispered.

It worked. She lay down, turned over, closed her eyes and made herself relax. Toes, feet, knees, those disturbing bits in the middle. Her shoulder became heavy, her thoughts blurred…

Nicholas stood up as Sarah came into the parlour the next morning, Millie at her heels. Breakfast had just been set out, the bacon was sending curls of appetising steam into the air, the coffee pot was competing with its own tantalising odours and his bed had been comfortable.

He should, in fact, have been feeling up to whatever the day threw at him.

Sarah met his gaze, went a charming shade of peony pink and sat down with a muttered, 'Good morning.'

'Good morning.' He was blushing too, he realised as he sat down, although he doubted it was anything but an embarrassing adolescent scarlet. It had taken him hours to fall asleep in defiance of his body which was informing him in no uncertain terms about exactly what it wanted. He had finally managed to drop into a restless doze filled with fevered and exceedingly explicit images of himself and Sarah and a large bed covered—for some reason best known to his unconscious mind—in sheepskins.

In his dreams he had kissed her and caressed her and sated himself with her in ways that no gentleman should even allow to cross his mind in connection with an innocent young lady. And now she sat there, the curve of her cheek still pink. For a hideous, stomach-swooping moment he thought he had said something, blurted something out or leered or—

Nicholas got his rioting imagination back under control with an effort that was almost physical. 'Bacon? Or may I pass you the eggs?'

The look in Sarah's eyes as she glanced up

might have been appropriate if he had said what was truly on his mind.

Last night I dreamt about how soft the skin on the inside of your thighs would be under my hand. I imagined kissing your nipples until you sobbed for more.

'Bacon?' She blinked once, twice, then appeared to come out of whatever daydream she was in. 'Yes, thank you. I would like that. Bacon, I mean.'

Nicholas ate his breakfast in a state of mental turmoil that he had last experienced when he was seventeen. He had no idea what he was feeling, or, rather, he knew damn well what he was feeling, but he had no idea what it meant.

That kiss, that angry fight of a kiss—surely it could only have revolted and repulsed an innocent? But it had been mutual: Sarah had kissed him back with as much intent, as much furious intensity, as he had kissed her. He could still taste her if he closed his eyes, despite tooth powder and coffee and bacon. Could she still taste him? Was it possible that her dreams had been as disturbingly erotic as his had been?

A third cup of coffee brought some discipline to the speculation. Whatever the effect of that embrace had been on either of them, the fact remained that Sarah Parrish was a respectable spinster under his protection. He had no business thinking about her in any other terms and most certainly not the slightest excuse for acting upon those thoughts.

Miss Parrish was destined for a life of blameless gentility. No doubt she would buy herself a pleasant villa in an equally pleasant small town. The local doctor, a man of unimpeachable reputation, would court her and wed her. Or perhaps the local solicitor. To either she would prove an intelligent partner, an admirable mother to their resulting brood of infants...

At which point his fantasy juddered to a halt to be replaced with an image of himself, one hand spread protectively over the swell of Sarah's belly.

Nicholas shoved back his chair with a screech on the old boards and stood up. 'Excuse me.' He made it as far as the front door and stood there leaning against the door jamb, arms folded tightly across his chest, ignoring the bustle of the High Street. One did *not* get one's mistress pregnant. One took every precaution. One did not fantasise about taking respectable women to one's bed, let alone getting them with child.

What was the matter with him? Some men experienced a crisis in their middle years, he had heard, but damn it, he wasn't even thirty yet, let alone in his forties. Almost thirty. Time to think of things other than mistresses and steamships and enjoyably chasing villains with Fawcett and his band of ruthless sharpshooters. Time to look around for a suitable bride and start laying the foundations for the next generation of Terrells. That was why what passed for his brain at the moment was thinking about pregnant women.

There was nothing wrong with him except that he had reached an age where he should be thinking dynastically. Possibly he should grow an impressive set of side whiskers and practice the kind of poses that his forebears struck in portraits of them surrounded by their numerous chubby offspring.

'Good morning, sir. You seem in very good spirits, if I may say so.' It was Fawcett. He had apparently entered discreetly through the back yard of the inn and was now at his side, a step back in the shadows.

'I am?'

'You were, er, grinning, if I might use the word, Your... Sir.'

'Just recovering my sense of humour, Matt.'

A flicker of expression passed over his agent's

face and was gone. Presumably, Nick thought, he was not known for his sense of humour. Sarah had seemed surprised when he smiled. Something else that perhaps he should consider.

'I had a bad night for some reason,' he said with a shrug. 'Any news?'

'Andrews and Lake found Axminster's house— a very snug villa, apparently. They watched it all night and Lake came back to say no one entered or left other than servants who stayed within the boundaries of the property. The *Yarmouth Gannet*, which is now *Sea Diamond*, has not returned. Unless she circled around well out to sea, she is heading northward.'

'Then so will we. We'll meet on the Fakenham road. If the map is to be trusted there's a water mill and an inn at the foot of the first hill out of town.'

'Aye, sir. I'll get in a good supply of food so we can press on between changes.'

Nick went back inside to find Sarah, her face serious, talking to Millie at the foot of the stairs. 'Charlie is unwell,' she said as soon as she saw him.

'What with?'

'Nothing serious, my lord. Overexcitement and too much good food—he isn't used to it,' Millie said. 'He was casting up his accounts all through the night.'

'Is he still being sick?'

Millie shook her head. 'He just needs sleep. So does Pendell, if you hadn't noticed,' she added, half under her breath.

He hadn't: another good reason to pull himself together and concentrate on something other than adolescent erotic fantasies. 'I'll hire another vehicle. You, Pendell and Charlie take the carriage. There's room in that for two people and child to sleep fairly comfortably. I'll hire something here.'

'Who will drive it?' Sarah asked.

'I will, until we meet up with Fawcett and his men, then one of them can take over. Can you be ready in half an hour?'

He left them to go upstairs and went to find the landlord. He had nothing to hire, he said apologetically. 'Only the gig and the dog cart, my lord,' he said, waving a hand at the yard. 'There's nowhere near that can hire you a proper carriage; we mostly get asked for gentlemen's sporting vehicles for the shooting.'

'What's that?' Nick pointed to a shrouded shape.

'A gentleman's travelling carriage. I took it in

payment of a debt, more fool me. I haven't the horses for it, or the demand for hire if I did.'

'I'll buy it from you if you can find someone to sell me a team to put in the shafts.'

'Buy it, my lord? But—'

Nick named a price, the landlord blinked, then yelled, 'Bill! Get out here and fettle up that carriage. I'm off to see Mr Harris, see if he's still got that team of his.'

Chapter Fourteen

Half an hour later Sarah was driven out of town in solitary state in a somewhat musty vehicle from which two energetic chambermaids had removed one mouse's nest, a fine array of cobwebs and six months' worth of dust. Nicholas, clearly at home with a team, was on the box, trying the paces of a local farmer's impulsive purchase of a local bankrupt's livestock.

It was reasonably comfortable, she decided, after an experimental bounce on the upholstery, although the back of the seat facing her seemed to have slipped out of position. She moved across and gave it a tug and it came away in her hands in two pieces, leaving a large space under the driver's box.

Guilty at the damage she tried to fit them back, then realised that they had not broken, but seemed to be designed to be removed. On impulse she pushed one down between the facing seats and discovered that she had created a bed, long enough for someone to lie full-length with their feet sticking into the space at the front.

By the time they pulled up alongside the other two coaches and Nicholas had handed over the reins to one of the men she had the centre couch in place and the two sides as normal.

'Ah, one of those,' Nicholas said as he climbed in.

Sarah had thought she had discovered something rare and interesting. 'Should we let Millie, Charlie and Pendell have this one?'

'No need. I had a look and Pendell is out cold stretched along one seat, Millie along the other with her cap over her eyes and Charlie is snoring in a nest of blankets between the seats. We may need these for ourselves.'

'I thought you looked as though you had not slept well.' Sarah felt the blush rising to her cheeks.

'No, I did not,' Nicholas said curtly. 'Did you?' He did nothing to move the central squab that kept them neatly separated, one each side of the carriage.

'No,' she confessed, wondering if her cheeks could possibly be as heated as they felt. 'I suppose you have a great deal to think about and plan.' If only her treacherous memory would stop presenting her with images of the Nicholas of her dreams, then she might be able to look him in the face without blushing.

He nodded and Sarah fell silent, feeling snubbed. It was as though she had the chilly, distant Mr Smith of the London dockside back again. Had Nicholas decided that she was becoming too familiar, forgetting her place in the presence of a duke?

'What is wrong?' he asked after two miles had gone by in silence.

'Nothing.' She had been careful to keep any hint of a frown off her face. 'Your Grace.'

'What the—?' Yes, definitely Mr Smith had returned. 'What are you sulking about?'

'Sulking! I am not sulking. You did not appear to be in the mood for conversation and I am aware that I have become, that is—'

'Sarah, I do not require you to address me like that.' He still sounded irritable, but the frozen look had left him. 'I had a bad night, probably as a result of too much cheese at dinner.' The hint of a smile appeared, presumably as a signal that had been a joke.

'And I was probably too over-excited at having located Wilton,' she offered.

Silence fell again, but it was rather more companionable now. Nicholas leant over and lifted the squab, pushed it back into position and shifted so his back was in the corner and he could stretch out his long legs with a suspicion of a wince.

In that position he could look more directly at Sarah. 'Have you given any thought to where you would like to live when you have your money back from Wilton?'

She shook her head. 'It feels like counting my chickens when I do not even have any eggs in my basket yet. But I am not so certain that I would want to sell the ships if I can get them back.'

Where had that come from? It had never occurred to her until she found herself uttering the words.

'Run a shipping company? Yourself?' Nicholas sounded less mocking than bemused. 'A female ship owner would be…unusual.'

'Women run stagecoach companies,' she pointed out. 'Mrs Mountain, for example.' The little flame of excitement flickered and went out. 'But I have no ships yet, so it is only an idea.

Perhaps I should sell them and invest in your steam vessels instead.'

'And that, too, is only an idea: notes and sketches, some very vague estimates.' He shifted as though the seat was becoming uncomfortable. 'I have a few months to work on it before the Season.' He might as well have been referring to a visit to the dentist.

'Is that so very distasteful and time-consuming? Oh, of course—you will be looking for your duchess.'

She had the feeling that he regretted mentioning the Season and had no desire to answer her question. 'I might. I am almost thirty, after all. Time to be thinking of my posterity. My heir is a cousin who would be very surprised to be wrenched from his comfortable position as a cathedral dean if an accident should befall me.'

'Presumably you will be the biggest catch on the Marriage Mart. I cannot think of any other unmarried dukes.'

It wouldn't please Lady Farne, of course. However hopeless she must know her own position to be, it would be painful to see the man she loved wed to another. Sarah had not liked the widow, and it surprised her to feel this sneaking sympathy for Nicholas's sister-in-law. Loving a man you could not have must be hellish.

'There is one other available, a widower, aged eighty-seven, but I believe we may discount him.'

'I think so,' she agreed. 'You will not have to try very hard to attract a suitable debutante.'

'No,' Nicholas agreed. He did not sound particularly pleased about it.

Sarah held her breath, in case she jerked him out of this revealing, thoughtful mood with a sound or a movement to remind him that he was not musing aloud to himself.

'It seems… It seems to me that one *should* have to try hard, that this is a very important decision, one of the most important I will ever make, and that it should not be easy. That leads to mistakes that are painful to undo, misjudgments that last a lifetime.'

That was not abstract, that was the result of a real mistake, she realised. Nicholas had fallen in love with someone who did not return his regard? Lady Farne? But no, that could not be the case—he seemed almost to dislike his sister-in-law whilst Sarah remained certain that Lady Farne felt strongly for him.

He had fallen silent, staring out of the window

at the passing fields and coppices, so she ventured, 'I always imagined that a duke would have a list of all the required characteristics of a duchess and would use it to identify the most suitable candidate, then propose and be accepted.'

Nicholas gave a faint huff of laughter and turned back to look at her. 'Yes, I suppose that's the way it is done. It would be refreshing to find someone who would turn me down, I think. The title has the effect of shining a strong light in someone's eyes: they do not see the man standing behind it.' He shrugged, almost as though he was giving himself a shake. 'What a coxcomb I sound, lamenting feebly that nobody could love me for myself when love is the last thing I should be looking for.'

'It is? But why? Do we not all wish to be loved? To share our lives with someone who sees us and knows us and cares for us?'

She shivered at his expression and those blue eyes seemed to look straight through her like shards of ice.

'A snare and a delusion. A pretence to secure what the lover wants, that is all. Love can grow, I will give you that, but to fall in love with someone I do not know? Impossible.'

'You believe—'

'I know,' Nicholas said flatly.

Sarah fell silent. That sounded like bitter experience, not theorising. She could only conclude that Nicholas had loved once and had been disillusioned, hurt and left with no faith that love was possible. She was certainly not going to argue with him. She had never meant to see into his heart so intimately: this was far too personal and exposing.

'I should have thought to buy a book or a journal,' she said brightly. Too brightly, she thought with a wince at her over-jolly tone. 'Never mind, the countryside is interesting.'

Nicholas raised an eyebrow and she shrugged. 'Oh, very well. It is not particularly fascinating, I must admit. A great deal of sky, some undulations, a lot of fields. It looks quite prosperous.'

'Yes.' Nicholas stared at the passing scene with what she assumed was a landowner's knowledgeable eye. 'Well kept, in good heart.'

'Your land is in Gloucestershire, is it not?'

He nodded. 'Mainly. I have other estates around the country, of course. We have dairy and beef cattle and orchards in the Vale and sheep and cereals on the hillsides. I would not change it for any other land.'

Sarah thought he had relaxed, his whole body

less tense now he was talking about something he loved. There was that word *love* again. He would marry someone suitable in order to give that land heirs to cherish it as he did.

But what about yourself? she wanted to ask. *Don't give up, there must be someone who would be perfect for you.*

Nick told himself that he had perfectly good social manners and brooding in his corner was ill-bred and selfish. He made conversation and kept them both awake while their little convoy stopped to change horses, to swap the drivers around and, at just past noon, to eat.

Sarah was very quiet after that and, when he leaned forward to look into her face, he saw her eyes were closed. He wished his were, and then recalled that the carriage would convert to make a bed.

'Sarah.'

'Mmm? What? Oh, I am sorry, I dropped off to sleep.'

'And I am beginning to doze. Shall we try converting these seats and see if we cannot get some rest to make up for our disturbed nights?'

They wrestled all three central squabs into place. Sarah rolled up her cloak and he folded his greatcoat to make pillows, then pulled down the window shades.

'You see, it makes a good, wide bed.' He lay down and stretched out his legs. 'Almost long enough for me.' By dint of curling up on his side with his bad leg uppermost he found it was positively comfortable, if rather firm.

Sarah lay down too, twitched her skirts decently over her ankles, shook out a shawl over herself and curled up too, one hand under her cheek. She smiled at him in the dim light. 'Sleep well.'

Nick was conscious of the carriage stopping, of the door opening a crack and then closing softly and then they were off again. It would have only been Pendell or Millie, he thought, squinting to see if Sarah had been disturbed. No, she was still where she had fallen asleep, tucked up respectably a good eighteen inches away from him.

He closed his eyes, too sleepy to even feel more than a sense of comfort at her nearness, the soft sounds of her breathing. Despite the occasional lurch and bump as the carriage wheels hit potholes and ruts she was profoundly asleep and he slid into darkness within seconds.

* * *

This dream was gentler, sweeter, than the one the night before, Sarah thought as she curled herself around the warm, solid male body beside her. They had their clothes on, which was easier, because last night her fantasy had been shot through with anxiety about her own body and her own inexperience.

The skin under her lips was firm and soft at the same time, and smelt of Nicholas's soap and, indefinably, of him and she nuzzled against it, feeling the thud of the big artery in his neck, the prickle of afternoon stubble along the edge of his jaw.

His arm came around her, pulling her in close to his body, then up, so she was sprawled over him. It was comfortable and disturbing, all at once.

At which point it occurred to Sarah that her thoughts were exceedingly coherent for a dream and that she was, in fact, awake and kissing Nicholas's face.

She opened her eyes, found herself nose to nose with him, staring deep into his eyes which were wide open. Nicholas was as awake as she was. A bump in the road drove her body into his and the impact brought with it the fact that not only was she *lying* on a man, she was wantonly draped over an aroused man. She might be inexperienced, but it did not mean she was ignorant.

Nicholas froze. 'Hell. I am sorry—'

'No… I mean, no, it isn't your fault. I woke up and I was kissing your neck. Or rather, I thought I was dreaming that I was and then you put your arm around me and you were asleep too. It was lovely and so I just drifted and then the carriage bumped and I ended up on top of you like this.' She ran out of breath.

'It was lovely?' Nicholas asked, his breath a caress across her lips.

'I thought so. It was nice to be kissing when we weren't angry with each other.' But he hadn't wanted her to kiss him. He had said, *Hell*, when he woke. 'I'm sorry, I shouldn't have…er…taken advantage of you.'

That provoked a huff of a laugh. 'I do not feel taken advantage of. But it was rather a one-sided kiss. Should we try it together?'

The carriage lurched again, their noses bumped and she said, 'Ow!' and then their lips met and everything changed. The jolting carriage vanished. The air darkened and swirled, even though her eyes were closed now. There was the familiar taste of Nicholas, subtly different now that he wasn't angry; there was the strength of his body supporting hers and the feel of his muscles shifting beneath her and there was the consuming, aching awareness of him, of the movement of his lips as if their mouths were holding a silent conversation and the clamour of her body that wanted things she only half understood, half guessed at.

Sarah came to herself to find she was lying on her back again and that Nicholas was beside her, propped on one elbow. She blinked up at him and smiled. It felt rather wobbly.

'That was very pleasurable and probably a thoroughly bad idea,' Nicholas said. He sounded grim.

'It was—'

'Don't you dare say *interesting,*' he warned. 'I am not in the mood to be calm and rational and sensible about this.'

There is a 'this'?

'I suggest we restore the seats, raise the blinds and drop the window glass. I feel the need for some cold, fresh air.'

'It isn't very cold.' Sarah scrambled across to the nearest window, lifted the blind and opened it.

'Better than nothing.' Nicholas was restoring the squabs to the backward-facing seat with some force. When they were seated again, with a strong breeze blowing through the carriage and making her eyes water, he cleared his throat. 'This is a difficult situation.'

'No, it is not,' Sarah interrupted before he could get launched into some speech about compromising her. 'We found ourselves in a…in a somewhat intimate position through chance. We wanted to kiss, so we did. There is no need to make a fuss about it. It isn't going to happen again, is it?'

'I sincerely hope not,' Nicholas said, with unflattering promptness. 'But even so you will feel—'

'Please do not presume to tell me how I feel,' she retorted, suddenly angry and embarrassed. Goodness knew what Nicholas's sense of what was right and proper would prompt him to say. She certainly did not want to listen to excuses about how he respected her and had no intention of seducing her or making her his mistress. 'I do not want to discuss it. It was just one of those things. Let us change the subject, please. Where are we?'

Nicholas gave her a look that reminded her that he was a duke, and an irritated and possibly embarrassed one at that, then looked out of the window as the carriage slowed on a slight hill. 'The King's Lynn road,' he said. 'I think that milestone said seven miles.'

'Excellent. Where do you expect to stop for the night?'

Nicholas studied the road book. 'Boston, I imagine, unless we have any problems on the road. We will be crossing the Fens, although at this time of year I doubt there will be flooding.'

They proceeded to make careful conversation about land drainage, King John, who had lost his treasure and crown jewels in the Fens, what Boston's inns might be like and how much longer it would take them to reach Lockhart's safe haven of Saltfleet.

By the time the tower of St Botolph's church, the famous Boston Stump, was looming on the horizon, Sarah thought she would scream if she had to continue to spout platitudes, make interested noises and refrain from blurting out what she really felt.

I think I have fallen in love with you, Nicholas Terrell. And I know it is hopeless and I have no idea how I am going to manage if I have to spend any more time shut up in a carriage with you.

Chapter Fifteen

'Good evening.' Nick got to his feet warily, conscious that he was alone in the private parlour in the Boston inn and that he had not had any meaningful conversation with Sarah since they had woken in each other's arms that afternoon.

'Oh, good. I was hoping you'd be here.' She came in and sat on the chair on the other side of the table. 'I wanted to ask you something.'

She looked serious and thoughtful. Nick braced himself for a discussion about that kiss. He was not certain what he most feared—that Sarah had come to say that she wanted them to be lovers or that she was shocked and appalled and demanding some redress.

'Yes?' he said. It did not sound too defensive, he thought. On the other hand he was rarely in a position to be defensive, so it was hard to judge.

'What I want—what I *need*—is a schoolroom slate and some slate pencils or chalks,' she said earnestly. 'I looked out of the window as we came into the town, but I didn't see any shops that looked as though they would stock such a thing.'

'You want a *slate*?' He stood up and no, it was not his imagination, Sarah moved back slightly in her seat, then checked the movement and clasped her hands together tightly in her lap. 'It is quite all right: I am not going to pounce on you,' he said and could have kicked himself when she bit her lip and looked away.

'I am quite well aware of that,' she said coldly.

'Yes. Well. I'll send Pendell out for them. Just the one slate?'

'No, better make it two. Millie and I are going to teach Charlie to read and write. He was so interested in the book I showed him today that he said he wanted to try to read it and he was so frustrated when he could not.'

'That is admirable, but do you really wish to spend your time teaching a troublesome brat to read? If I find him a position as gardener's boy he will be able to go to the dame school in the village.'

'He will settle in more quickly and be happier

if he already has skills and is not behind children younger than he is.' Sarah seemed to have recovered her poise. 'Besides, what else am I to do? There are limits to the pleasure one may gain from gazing at thousands of acres of flat farmland.'

Spend tomorrow in that carriage with me? Make love to me? That would pass the time.

Nick moved away abruptly to stare out of the window onto the street below, still busy despite the fading light. This was ridiculous and he simply could not—must not—get involved with an innocent young woman. Dukes did not marry ship owner's daughters and neither, if they were gentlemen, did they seduce them. He turned, frowning at her, confused by his own feelings. It was not even as though Sarah was a beauty, he thought, forcing himself to be critical, distanced. If they did... If this went any further, she had none of the attributes that would launch her into a career as a courtesan after the affair came to its inevitable conclusion.

'It is only another forty miles to Saltfleet. You wanted to come with us,' he said flatly.

'I did, and you would think me an absolute ninny if I pretended there is anything pleasurable in a journey of this nature, in such haste and for such a grim purpose as bringing a murdering thief to justice,' she retorted, pushing back her chair and standing. 'If I may send Pendell out, then I had best go and find him before it gets any later.'

'I will talk to him,' Nick said. 'And leave you in possession of this parlour. There appear to be some recent journals in the rack.'

When he came back, almost an hour later, Sarah and Millie had a stack of ladies' magazines open on the table and were laughing over one of the fashion plates. 'Have you ever seen anything so preposterous, Millie? Really, if waists become any higher I fail to see where a lady is expected to put her bosom. This one seems to have hers on a shelf: one might almost add a mantel clock and a vase of flowers.'

A tactful man would back silently out of the room before he was noticed. Unfortunately the image Sarah's words conjured up was too much for Nick.

Both women looked up at his gasp of laughter and for a fraught moment he wondered if they were both going to retreat into embarrassed flight. Then Sarah met his gaze and, after a visible struggle with herself, collapsed into giggles.

Nick cleared his throat, then came into the room and placed a brown paper parcel in front of her. 'Two slates, half a dozen slate pencils because I seem to recall losing and breaking them at a great rate myself, and three books with pictures.'

Sarah stared at him, her face wet with laughter tears, and he passed her his spare handkerchief. 'Quite clean. Pendell doesn't let me out without at least two.'

'You went and bought these yourself?' She unwrapped the parcel as she spoke. 'Oh, they are perfect! Look, Millie. This book has all kinds of things to do with soldiers, this one has farm animals and this one is about gardening. Thank you, Nicholas.'

It seemed he was forgiven.

The next morning Sarah announced that as Charlie was still looking a little unwell, he would be better in the coach she and Nicholas had been in the day before and moved herself, Millie and a faintly protesting small boy into it, saying that she expected that the Duke and Pendell would be glad of some masculine conversation with Captain Fawcett.

She was quite certain now that Nicholas would

not presume on that incident yesterday, but she was not at all sure how comfortable she would feel shut up alone with him when all she wanted was to be in his arms again, kissing him.

Could he tell? Perhaps she was looking at him with her heart in her eyes and he, an experienced man, would recognise her feelings. That was enough to make her want to sink through the floor. Bad enough that Nicholas thought her ineptly wanton, but his reaction if he realised she was falling in love with him did not bear thinking about.

She closed the carriage door firmly behind her and sank down with a sigh while Millie quelled Charlie's protests that he was in plump currant and didn't need to be mollycoddled by a brace of morts. He wanted, he grumbled, to listen to Captain Fawcett, who had some right good tales to tell, or to sit on the roof with the men.

'They'll be loading their rifles, and I want to watch and then there'll be a big fight and—'

'You may sit on the roof tomorrow going back if you are good today,' Sarah promised. 'And if you make a nuisance of yourself, then I expect the men will drop you off the back. But I do have some books in here, with pictures.'

'Can't read,' Charlie mumbled.

'Well, I couldn't once upon a time. Neither could Millie. You have to learn. I could read the book to you, if you like. And there is a slate and some slate pencils and you can learn to write your name.'

She took out a slate and pencil and wrote *Charlie* on it. 'What is your second name?'

''iggins, miss.'

'Charlie Higgins. There.' She held the slate up for him to see. 'What shall we do? Read a book or write your name?'

The land was very flat for the first two hours and Charlie, who kept eyeing his name on the slate, was very happy to be occupied with the books Nicholas had purchased in Boston. Sarah read out loud, following the words with her finger and they played at finding words that began with *C* and *H*, like Charlie Higgins.

It served excellently at keeping her mind off Nicholas and the day before and also allowing her to forget the forthcoming encounter with Lockhart and his crew which nobody had discussed with her.

After almost three hours the land was beginning to rise a little, with low hills and valleys to make the prospect more interesting. Just when both Millie and Charlie were beginning to speak longingly of food they drew to a halt in the market square of a little town. One of Captain Fawcett's men went across to the Windmill Inn and Nicholas came across to them.

'I suggest we eat here in the carriages and have the food brought across to us. We are about fifteen miles from Saltfleet and I do not think it wise to stop any closer to Lockhart's home ground. We will finalise our plans here when we have eaten.'

'I have been thinking—there are no natural harbours on this stretch of coast, I am sure, not until the Humber, so the *Gannet* must be moored offshore. How are we going to get to it?' Sarah asked.

'*We* are not,' Nicholas said, with emphasis. 'Look, here comes food and drink; we will talk later.'

Ale and pies were brought by three maids who giggled at the sight of so many men and then ran back to fetch fresh supplies. Captain Fawcett and Nicholas ate standing by one of the carriages with the road map open on the floor of the vehicle. Sarah strained to hear, but all she could make out was the occasional, 'That'll be best,' and, 'Need to stay small.'

Eventually Nicholas came over. 'None of Lockhart's men have seen this carriage so two of the men looking as much like coachman and groom as possible will drive Fawcett, dressed in his best, into the village. He will stop at the New Inn to ask about sea bathing.'

'Sea bathing? Here?'

'Apparently yes. Luckily Harris, one of the Riflemen, comes from a bit north of here. The New Inn is famed hereabouts for its fresh fish and accommodation for local gentry who want to bathe. Fawcett will take a room if there is one and can then stroll about the village, behave like a tourist and generally poke about. Driving to the seashore will arouse no suspicion.'

'What will we do?'

'The rest of us will hide away as best we can in the nearest copse or wood we can find and await developments.'

It sounded a very sensible plan. Sarah had assumed that she, Millie and Charlie would be stowed away somewhere and made to wait while all the men rushed off to engage the enemy, leaving them in total ignorance of what was happening.

'I have no idea how long it will take,' Nicholas

admitted. 'If we find ourselves still sitting there at midnight we will have to rethink our strategy.'

As it turned out, finding Lockhart and his crew was so easy it was almost dangerous. Two hours after he had been driven off, leaving them in a somewhat dank and ill-drained copse, Captain Fawcett returned, riding a hired hack.

'I as near as damn it—apologies, ma'am—almost collided with Lockhart in the doorway of the inn. He was on his way out in company with a very smooth-looking gentleman, the pair of them with the air of just having business to discuss. I have a room at the inn, was told the way to the nearest beach for bathing and hired this horse.

'Timms and Worth are back in the village taking a stroll to locate Lockhart and his friend and I rode to the beach. Sure enough, there is the *Gannet* with her new sails furled, lying quarter of a mile offshore and a rowing boat pulled up on the beach with three sailors lounging around it smoking and yarning. I rode past with my superior nose in the air, they stared hard, then went back to their talk.

'I had a word with a fat squire who was emerging from the waves in a state of nature and established the best place and time to swim, then rode back to find my men had seen Lockhart and his companion enter a very down-at-heel ale house at the other end of the village. I've left them keeping an eye on things and complaining to any locals who'll listen about having an employer who fancies taking the waters on a desolate bit of coast instead of behaving like an honest gentleman and going to Brighton where they could enjoy themselves.'

'What will you do now?' Sarah asked Nicholas.

'Seize Lockhart and his friend and secure them, then tackle the sailors on the beach and row out to take the ship. The crate with the silver will be on board until Lockhart's finished his transaction, we're assuming.'

'This is his base—goodness knows how many of the local people will turn out to support him,' Sarah protested. 'And even if you capture the ship, how are you going to sail her?'

'Two of my men were fishermen before they joined the army,' Fawcett said. 'We've enough muscle to act as crew if they give orders. That will get us back down to Lynn and the authorities.'

'But—'

'The longer we talk about it the more chance that Lockhart and the man he is meeting will move out of the ale house. Pendell and two of the men will stay with you until we have it all secure: you will be quite safe.'

'I am sure we will! It is you and the others I am worried about—'

But Nicholas was already walking away. Captain Fawcett rode back towards the village and the other carriages moved off after him.

'I'll sit up on top, keep a lookout, Miss Parrish,' Pendell said after one look at Sarah's stormy expression. The two Riflemen moved away and quietly vanished into the undergrowth.

'Of all the reckless, arrogant, infuriating men,' she fumed. 'Goodness knows how many men Lockhart can call on in the village, all armed to the teeth with shotguns, or billhooks, or pitchforks. They'll get themselves killed. Or drowned. They should have taken those two with them, as well.' She waved vaguely at the clearing outside.

'His Grace will be worried about you,' Millie ventured.

'I am worried about *him*. About all of them, of course,' she added hastily.

'Yes, miss,' Millie said, with a betraying twinkle in her eye.

'I'll go and see what's happening,' Charlie offered. 'I can sneak along an' report back, like.'

'You'd never get past our guards,' Millie said, 'but it is a very brave offer.'

'I can't hear anything. How long do you think we will have to wait before the shooting starts?'

'I don't know, miss.' Millie dropped the glass in the window on her side of the carriage and they sat there silent, ears straining.

Sarah made herself stay still, without fidgeting. Nicholas was courageous and intelligent— even if he was like all men and just threw himself into a fight. The ex-Riflemen were skilled and ruthless. There were enough of them... Weren't there? But why was it so quiet? Had Captain Fawcett been recognised? Had they walked into a trap?

Very well. Assume that they have. Think of a plan to get them out. I have two Riflemen, Pendell and a small, tough boy. And Millie. They won't be expecting us. We could get there before Lockhart starts cutting pieces off Nicholas. He's too valuable to kill out of hand...

She could only hope the same could be said for the others.

How much longer?

But the silence endured.

* * *

'They have been captured,' Sarah said. 'They have been gone over an hour. We have to do something—'

'Someone's coming,' Charlie said. 'A horse.'

They all stared out of the window. One of the shadows at the edge of the clearing moved slightly and revealed itself as a man with a rifle to his shoulder. He whistled, three notes. Three answered him, but he kept the weapon raised until the rider came into the clearing and dismounted. It was one of Fawcett's men.

Sarah pushed open the door. 'What has happened? Is anyone hurt?'

'We have Lockhart and his men, ma'am, and the ship. My orders are to see you down to Lynn to meet them when they arrive. The other two carriages are being driven down empty.'

Sarah sat down abruptly on the step of the carriage. 'That is wonderful news.' Then she realised he had not answered her other question. 'Was anyone hurt?'

'I couldn't say, ma'am.'

Sarah didn't know him except by sight, but instinct told her that he was concealing something. 'Cannot or must not?' she asked sharply.

'You'd best be on your way, ma'am, away from

the village before anyone realises what's been going on.'

'I will do no such thing.' She stood up and turned to face the coach. 'Pendell, can you drive this thing?'

'Pretty well, Miss Sarah, provided it's just at a walk.'

'Right. Then take us to the beach. You—lead the way.'

'Miss, my orders are to see you on your way.'

'You are not in the army now. If you stop the carriage, then I will walk—or are your orders to hurt me to stop me?'

'No, ma'am!' He sounded alarmed at the very idea.

'Right. Lead on, then.'

She got back into the carriage, wondering what she would do if they forcibly removed Pendell from the driver's seat and drove off at speed, but the carriage moved out of the clearing and turned towards the village and she heard the sounds of the two Riflemen climbing on behind.

It took only minutes to get to the beach by a turning before they reached the church. Sarah jumped down, Charlie at her heels, and saw some of their men about to get into a large rowing boat. The other two coaches stood nearby.

'Wait! We are coming with you.'

It was a tight fit to get three more adults and a boy packed in, but they managed it. Their two guards pushed them off and went back to the carriage.

'See you in Lynn,' one of them called, and the three vehicles bumped off back along the track.

Sarah sat rigid, one hand clenched on the gunwale, ignoring the water slopping about her feet. Someone had been hurt, the man had not wanted to answer her question.

Nicholas. His name kept circling, repeating in her head, and she craned round to watch the *Gannet*. They seemed to be crawling towards the ship but finally the rowing boat bumped against the side and she grabbed for the ladder, scrambling up it before any of the men could help her.

There was no entry port on the little ship and Sarah tumbled gracelessly over the side in a flurry of damp skirts and stared around the deck, searching for a familiar dark head amongst the men moving purposefully around.

There were men lying down too, with their hands tied behind their backs and blood on the deck.

And then she saw him. Nicholas stood up unsteadily, holding on to the foremast to help himself. The front of his shirt was stained crimson with blood.

Chapter Sixteen

'Nicholas!' Sarah ran, dodging between the men, pushing them aside, until she was in front of him. 'Where are you wounded? Sit down, let me see.' She took his arm, tried to urge him towards the nearest hatch cover.

'It isn't my blood, Sarah.' He had to say it twice before she would let go of his arm.

'It isn't?' Her heart was pounding as though she had run a race, a race from a monster, a nightmare.

It isn't his blood. Breathe...

'No.' Nicholas gestured to the sprawled figure at his feet. 'He kept coming with that great knife in his hand. I suppose he would say it was a better end than the gallows.'

'Captain Lockhart,' she said blankly. 'He is dead?' Of course he was. No one could live with that knife in their chest. They must have been struggling hand-to-hand. That could so easily have been Nicholas lying at her feet. So easily have been the man she very much feared that she loved.

'Is anyone else hurt? Are all our men safe?'

'A few cuts, bruises, a broken arm and a torn ear. Nothing serious. Why are you here?' He asked it almost roughly. 'I gave orders that you were to go to Lynn.'

'They wouldn't tell me anything. I had no idea what had happened. I did not know if you were safe. All of you, I mean,' she added, rather belatedly.

'They are army men, used to obeying orders and to seeing orders obeyed without question. You, I imagine, are somewhat outside their experience.' He looked around the deck to where the rowing boat was being hoisted on board. 'I should send you back, but the carriages will have gone now and the village will probably have woken up to the fact that something is amiss.'

He turned to where two of the men were ordering the others to various positions. 'Time to go.'

'Aye-aye, Captain,' one of them said with a grin. 'Come on, lads, lively on those capstan bars now or we'll never get the anchor up.'

'Have you found the silver?' Sarah asked as

they moved out of the way of the men towards the mainmast.

'We have. Still in the hold below, locked up with a certain Mr Brown of no address he is willing to give us, who was in earnest conversation in the ale house with Lockhart. He was all bluster until I promised him we would deliver him to Bow Street along with Mr Axminster, at which point he became very quiet indeed. Lockhart's crew are keeping their lips shut too, but I suspect that once they realise that he's dead they'll be willing to talk rather than to take the blame for it all.'

There was the crack of canvas as the wind caught the sails, then the little ship was moving, heading south again. The breeze caught at Sarah's hair, played over her face, fresh and cool, but she put her hand to her forehead. It seemed strangely hot and the deck was, surely, moving more than it should be.

Shock and relief, she realised, putting out her hand to steady herself. Shock, relief and anger.

'Sarah? Are you all right? Come away and stop looking at that blood.' Nicholas caught her in his arms. 'Are you feeling faint?'

'Faint? No, I am not feeling faint. I am furious! You would have sailed away without telling me a thing, left me in suspense until we got to Lynn. I am part of this, Nicholas. I have a right to know what is happening.'

'It was not safe to delay.' He had stiffened at the anger in her tone and there was that cold expression she had come to hate. The ducal, male, master of the universe expression that hid the kind man who had a sense of humour and courage and intelligence and who had talked with her as though he recognised that she had those qualities too.

'Poppycock,' she replied sharply, making a passing Rifleman jump. 'I made it back in time, even with wasting minutes arguing with the men.'

'You are my responsibility,' he said and something changed as he looked at her, something shifted, as though the ice was cracking over his mask of authority. 'Sarah, don't make this so hard for me—'

'Hard for *you*? It was my father's old bosun who was murdered at the start of this. It is the man who ruined my life behind this. Now I have to live through everything that happened again if we can bring him to justice at last. This is hard for me and it does not help in the slightest if I do not know what is happening and then I come on board and there you are covered in blood and I thought you were… I thought…'

She was crying, she realised, appalled, and turned, stumbling for the hatchway down to the lower deck.

'Sarah.' Nicholas caught at her arm but she shook him off violently.

'No. Leave me alone.'

There was one of Fawcett's men at the foot of the companionway. 'You can't go down to the saloon, miss, we've got them penned up there.'

'I just want to go to one of the cabins,' she muttered, head down so he could not see her wet cheeks. 'Is that all right?'

'Yes, miss. There's nobody in any of them now.'

She found the one that she had shared originally with Millie, shut the door and threw herself on the bunk. But the tears had stopped, leaving her feeling shaken and sick and very tired.

Sarah curled up with her back to the door and closed her eyes. If she could just rest for a few moments, regain her composure, she would be able to go back on deck, pretend none of that had… She was asleep before the thought was finished.

* * *

Nick caught himself after two steps towards the open hatch. Chasing Sarah down below decks would not help matters; she was in shock, that was all, and she needed to be alone.

It had not occurred to him that she would be anxious, or that any worries would persist beyond the message that the ship was taken and she should go south to Lynn. He had acted for the best, to keep her safe, but he made himself try and see things from Sarah's perspective.

There had been nothing to do but wait. No action to distract her, no clue at all as to what was happening. That was enough to prey on anyone's nerves, he acknowledged. He, after all, had the plan to put into effect, the exhilaration of the fight, the triumph of success.

But she is a woman; it is her place to wait, to be protected and directed, the conventional part of him argued.

But Sarah had courage and intelligence and waiting in ignorance would be intolerable for her, he recognised. He had not thought about what she might want, might need, only what suited his opinion of what was the proper way to proceed.

Nick paced back down the deck, cursing under

his breath. He would apologise, of course. He stopped where two of the men, released from hauling on ropes, were stitching Lockhart's body into a piece of sailcloth. There was the bulge of some kind of ballast at the feet.

'I assumed you'd want to bury him at sea, sir,' Fawcett said, looking up from cleaning the knife in a bucket of water. 'Can't see any reason the coroner would want to be bothered with him. I'll say a word or two over him and we'll slip him in out here.'

'Yes,' Nick agreed absently, his thoughts still on Sarah. Her face as she had run towards him across the deck, the horror and the fear in it. Fear for him. He looked down at himself and saw for the first time what a gory mess he was. No wonder she had thought it was his blood. And then her sudden collapse into tears, then anger—anger directed squarely at him. It was the reaction to the worry, he realised that. But that she should care so much, should react like that, shook him. Surely Sarah was not falling—

His speculation came to an abrupt halt. He did not want to think the word because he had no idea how to deal with the situation.

Yes, he had enjoyed kissing her; he found her attractive, disturbingly so under the circumstances. He liked her more than any other lady of his acquaintance. But it was impossible, of course, that there should be any more between them.

'Sir?' Fawcett was standing next to him.

Nick had the feeling that his agent had been talking for some time. 'I'm sorry. I was thinking of something else. What did you say?'

'I think Pendell is hoping to catch your attention.'

His valet was, in fact, regarding him with undisguised horror.

'Pendell, it is not my blood,' he said when he reached him.

'I apprehended that, Your Grace, seeing that it is probable that life would be extinct if it was.' Pendell had reverted to exceedingly proper London valet as instructed by his uncle. 'I have water heating for you to wash and clean garments ready. It appears that someone had the foresight to bring all the baggage on board.'

That had been Fawcett, presumably. The provision of clean linen had not been uppermost in Nick's mind at the time. 'Miss Parrish has gone to a cabin. Please make sure that Millie knows where she is and that they have all their luggage.'

'Yes, Your Grace. I have selected the first cabin on the right for you, if that is acceptable.'

'If that is the one with the four-poster bed, the large bathtub and the Gobelin tapestries, then I am sure it will be adequate,' Nick said, amused by the efforts Pendell was making not to grin.

'Naturally, Your Grace.'

Judging by the murmur of voices from across the passageway, it seemed that Millie had found Sarah. Nick dropped the ruined garments on the deck and did his best to get clean in warm salt water while he listened to the rise and fall of feminine voices.

He had to think about Sarah and about his own feelings and he needed to be alone and to have some peace to do it, because here and now his thoughts were a jumble of surprise: eagerness, desire and denial, heavily laced with apprehension.

Damp, sticky with salt, but mercifully free of bloodstains, Nick dressed and made his way along to what had been the saloon and was now a prison for the *Gannet*'s crew. 'Mr Brown' had been put in the hold to ensure he had no opportunity to talk to the men.

Three of the ex-Riflemen stood guard and the prisoners were tied. They looked at Nick with a mixture of defiance, resignation and apprehension.

'You will be handed over to the Justices at Lynn and transported to London to face charges of piracy, theft and accessory to murder. There may be other charges. Think carefully about the position you are in. When we reach the port you will be questioned separately and there may be leniency for those of you who give information.'

There was a rumble of comments, most of them foul, and someone spat on the deck.

Nick shrugged and turned away. Let them sweat for a while with thoughts of the noose and they might well be more forthcoming in a day or so. He was in no mood to waste his time questioning them yet; he had more important things to think about.

He made his way up on deck, found a space in the bows away from the cursing ex-soldiers whose comrades were trying to turn them into sailors and set himself to think about what he wanted, what he needed and what his duty told him he must do.

Sarah woke when Millie entered the cabin and lay drowsing, too weary to stir herself to get up and too restless to go back to sleep.

'The bags and the trunk are outside the door,' Millie said. 'I'll bring them in. We may as well get comfortable, I suppose, miss. They say we won't dock at Lynn until the morning, early.'

She moved about, tidying and finding what they would need overnight while Sarah strained her ears to listen to the sound of Pendell and Nicholas across the passageway. After a while she heard them go out again. Up on deck, she supposed.

The storm of emotions that had swept through her had left her feeling as though she had just recovered from a fever. Anxiety and then the horror of seeing Nick, covered in gore. The relief, then the reaction, the anger and the frustration that she could not tell him how she felt, that she had no right to take him in her arms and show him.

Sarah sat up and pushed back her hair. Everyone else was doing their part, guarding the prisoners, sailing the ship, making plans. She was not going to lie here like a weak, feeble female and give Nick something else to worry about.

'I shall get up,' she announced. 'Have you found my hairbrush? I feel like a gorse bush after a hurricane.'

She put herself to rights and they left the cabin

only to almost run into Charlie, who was carrying a rough plank tray with several mugs on it.

'I went in the galley and I found Cap'n Lockhart's cocoa,' he announced. 'He thought nobody knew about it, but I did—saw Cookie making it one day. Cor, it do smell good, don't it? I reckon I've made it right.'

'How much is there?' Millie asked.

'I reckon enough for a mug for everyone—us, I mean. Not them.' He jerked his tousled head towards the saloon and the prisoners.

'I'll take one of these to the Duke,' Sarah said. 'You find Pendell and give him his, Millie. Well done, Charlie, it was a brilliant idea.'

She was smiling as she climbed carefully up the companionway, setting the mugs several steps up, climbing, moving them again until she could look out of the hatch and see where Nicholas had gone. Her sea legs appeared to be returning, she thought as she negotiated the deck without a splash to mar the white of the planking. Whatever his failings, Lockhart had ensured the external appearance of the *Gannet* was that of a smart little ship.

Distracted by the delicious smell of the chocolate, and the need to concentrate, it was not until she was a few steps away from the bow that Sarah realised how awkward this encounter might be.

Nicholas reached out to catch hold of the mugs as her hands shook, held them around the middle and put them down hastily on the deck, blowing on his fingers. He picked them up again by the handles and passed her one. 'Hot chocolate? Where did that come from?'

'Charlie made it from Lockhart's secret hoard. They must have brought fresh supplies aboard, because Charlie even managed to find some milk.' She sipped. 'And sugar. Goodness, this is good.' She was babbling, she knew. 'Nicholas. I wanted to say—'

'You said it, very eloquently.' She could not tell whether he was angry or not; the expressionless mask that seemed to come so naturally to him was in place again.

'And I meant what I said.' She was not going to grovel. 'But I should also have realised that you only wanted to protect me and not to have to worry about anyone who was not part of the attack. So I apologise for that.' She put up her chin, determined to look reasonable, but firm.

Nicholas's lips twitched. 'You have a chocolate moustache.' He took out his handkerchief and wiped it carefully along her upper lip. 'Very dashing.'

Sarah found her sense of humour had deserted her. It was worse when he was kind to her, when that rare smile made its appearance, when it hit her like a blow in her stomach that she loved him and she was going to miss him for the rest of her life.

'It amuses you to make fun of me.'

'No.' He shook his head. 'It looked charming and a moment of humour, just now, is very welcome.'

'Why just now? Everything is going exceedingly well, is it not?'

'Certainly, so far as bringing this gang of pirates to justice is concerned, and, I hope, putting right as much of the wrong done to you as is possible.'

'And so?'

'And so I should have thought more carefully before agreeing to allow you to accompany me on this part of the journey.'

She had threatened to follow by herself if necessary and he could not have done much about that, short of locking her up, but Sarah did not feel inclined to argue about that just now. 'Go on.'

'It now appears to me that you have spent a great deal of time in my company unchaperoned. There have been passages between us that were… That should never have occurred between a gentleman and a lady under his protection.'

'You said that your sister could provide me with references,' she began, hardly able to believe where this appeared to be leading.

'When you were simply looking for employment in a genteel household, away from society, that would have served. Now there is every chance that your position can be restored. There is a strong likelihood that a reward for the return of the silver will be given which will further enhance your resources. You will be an independent gentlewoman and it is essential that this position should be protected and be untouched by any risk of gossip.'

Nicholas set his scarcely touched mug down as though preparing for something formal, something difficult. 'I believe you would not be averse to what I am about to suggest, that you may, in fact already be expecting it.'

There are moments in dreams where the ground disappears from under the dreamer's feet, plunging them into the void. For the blink of an eye Sarah felt that sensation of falling, then the lick of hot liquid on her hand brought her back to reality. She reached out and put the mug on the nearest hatch cover. 'I am expecting nothing.' It came out as a croak.

'Sarah, I am asking you to marry me.' Nicholas sounded anything but romantic.

He might as well be asking me impatiently to pass the salt for the second time, she thought.

It was difficult to articulate with such a dry mouth, but she did her best. 'You cannot possibly do such a thing.'

'I am of age, I may do as I wish.'

Yes, that is definitely impatience. But say yes—this is your dream.

'No,' she heard herself say clearly. 'It is ridiculous.'

Chapter Seventeen

Nicholas stared at her. 'Ridiculous? Of course not. Unconventional, of course, but I may wed who I wish and, although you come of merchant stock, you have been raised as a lady. You are intelligent and determined and I am certain that you will master the requirements of your new station in life very quickly.' He must have taken her stunned silence for agreement, because he said, 'It is a pity that my mother is not alive to teach you how to go on, but I am certain my sister will help you.'

'No,' Sarah said again. It became easier with repetition. 'How could you even think I would accept such an unequal match? Only a few days ago you were talking of the next Season, of finding a bride.'

'And now I will not have to,' he pointed out, apparently unaware of the danger he was in, standing so close to the rail while provoking a woman to the point of violence.

'Naturally, the thought that I might save you some trouble must weigh with me,' she observed as sweetly as possible between clenched teeth. 'However, I have no desire to marry you.'

Not when you propose like that.

'I believed you were not averse to me, that you felt some liking, that there was some attraction between us,' Nicholas said, the impatience audible now.

'Do you imagine that I am coyly refusing because that is what is expected of me on receiving such a flattering, eloquently worded, heartfelt offer? Do you think that because I have enjoyed kissing you and do not actually find you physically repellent that I will fall into your arms sobbing out my gratitude for your most condescending proposal?'

The relief of actually saying what she thought, of releasing her pent-up feelings, was almost physical. Sarah found she was standing tall, head up, chin raised, glaring at him. This was the man she had fallen in love with and she could not believe she had been such a fool.

'I can assure you, Your Grace, that I have not the slightest desire to marry you. You have just insulted me and patronised me. You have wounded me, because I believed that we had reached a position of friendship and I see how wrong I was to presume such a thing. You will have to excuse my merchant blood for that vulgar error.'

Sarah spun around and stalked towards the hatch to the companionway, furious that the motion of the ship reduced even an attempt at a dignified retreat to a clumsy stumble.

There was no sound of pursuing footsteps. She was not certain whether she had expected them or what she would do if Nicholas came after her. Hit him, probably.

Nicholas drained his mug of chocolate. It was still warm. How could it have taken so little time for things to have gone so utterly awry?

What was the matter with Sarah? Despite her anger at almost being left behind when they sailed, which he could comprehend, he had seen no hint that she disliked him. She had kissed him with passion, talked with him readily and easily. Why the devil had she reacted as though an honourable proposal of marriage had been a mortal insult?

She had spoken of it being an unequal match,

and it was—she could never have hoped for the title of duchess, of a standing in society immediately below the consorts of the royal dukes. But that was for him to worry about, not for her.

What had she called his offer? *Flattering, eloquently worded, heartfelt*—and Sarah had clearly intended that sarcastically. Nick was beginning to be aware of a sense of grievance. He had been honest, damn it. He had not lied, pretended he was in love with her. She knew perfectly well that dukes did not marry for love.

And he knew all too well that love took second place to rank and fortune. He had given his heart in the past, had been made promises in return and had been betrayed, simply because the status and wealth and ease which he could have offered along with his heart were not enough. Not when weighed against a dukedom without love.

He had offered Sarah marriage out of an honourable concern for her reputation and well-being, but it seemed that if it had not been dressed up in trappings of high romance and deep feeling, then it was not enough. It almost felt as though Sarah was the opposite of Marietta. Sarah wanted the pretence of love and romance and would sacrifice a duchess's coronet for that fairy tale, whilst Marietta had spurned love to get her hands on the same bauble.

Nick realised that he understood Marietta's motives far more easily than he did Sarah's.

And now, after that slap in the face, he had to remain civil to her. He had promised his help in retrieving her stolen property and he was honour-bound to do so. When they had located this Axminster character and she had positively identified him as Wilton, then he could hand her over to his lawyers and they could pursue his ill-gotten gains for her. It would hurt her pride to accept his help, he imagined. Well, that was not his problem. He would do the right thing and then he need never set eyes on Miss Sarah Parrish again.

That this conclusion left him feeling hollow inside was doubtless due to the after-effects of violent action followed by a thoroughly disagreeable interview. Now felt as good a time as any to begin questioning their prisoners.

Nick located Fawcett and went down below decks.

'We had best have them one by one in a cabin,' Fawcett said. 'My men have stopped them talking to each other, this way we've our best hope of gathering as much information as possible. What do you want to do with Mr Brown?'

'Leave him to think about things. I doubt he is used to the level of discomfort and squalor of life just above the bilges—it should help concentrate his mind on being helpful when we get him out tomorrow.'

Fawcett opened a cabin door. 'This one should do. I'll go and get two more stools. It won't do our dignity much good to be perched side by side on the bottom bunk.'

It was the cabin that he and Sarah had shared, Nick realised. It ought to carry some lingering traces of her scent, an indefinable, subtle trace of flowers and spice. He had never been certain whether it was from her soap or a rinse for her hair, or whether it was her skin, but its absence felt like a loss in this space. There should have been some trace left of the time they had spent here—arguing over cards, learning to trust each other. Learning to know each other.

Only it seemed he did not know her, after all.

'Sir?' It was Fawcett behind him. 'I found two chairs in Lockhart's cabin. I've got some paper and writing implements so I can note down what they say. It is too much to hope that they know the name of the person the silver was intended for, but we may get some clues.'

Nick moved aside to let him into the cabin and waited while he set the chairs down, sorted out his note-taking equipment and stepped back out into the passageway to call for the first prisoner.

Nick sat, set his face into his most severe expression—no great difficulty with that, he found—and prepared to extract some facts.

'Is everything all right, Miss Sarah?' Millie was perched on the edge of the bunk whipping stitches along a length of torn hem on one of Sarah's petticoats. 'Only you look as though you've eaten a wasp, if you don't mind me saying so.'

'I suppose the good Lord had, in his infinite wisdom, some reason for creating men, but I am afraid that I cannot comprehend it just at this moment.' Sarah paced across to the porthole and glared through it at the waves surging past. 'And I suppose that was both blasphemous and irreverent and I should be ashamed of myself.'

'I've felt the same myself, often times,' Millie said. She bit off the end of the thread and shook out the petticoat. 'Then you forget and they do something to get themselves back in your good graces and off you go again, trusting them. My ma, she said it was like having babies: you have one, swear you will never go through that again so long as you live and, a few months later, there you are with a bump under your apron.'

'Do you have many brothers and sisters, Millie?' Sarah came away from the porthole and sat down on the bunk beside the maid. 'You've never said anything about your family before and I didn't like to pry.'

'Four brothers and three sisters—eight of us that was that lived until we were toddling about. Ma took in washing, Pa did a bit down at the docks. Some thieving on the side, as well. A bit of this, a bit of that.' She shrugged. 'Then he upped and went off with this doxy down at Limehouse and Ma got sick and died and so did the two youngest girls. The rest of us ended up in the workhouse.'

'That's awful. What happened to the other five?'

Millie shrugged. 'My sister died too. The boys ran away; I never heard from them again.'

'I'm so sorry, Millie. And I am so glad you got away. I hope you will stay with me after this. If I can get some of the money back from Wilton, then I will not have to work for anyone and we could have a nice little villa somewhere.'

Millie nodded. 'Of course I'll stay, Miss Sarah. I would anyway.'

'Unless of course… Are you and Pendell… um…friends?'

'Jimmy?' Millie laughed. 'He's all right for a kiss and a cuddle and to tease, but he's not man enough for me. Too full of himself about being a duke's valet, he is.' She slid a sideways glance towards Sarah. 'Maddening, ain't it, when they're so full of their own importance?'

'It is indeed.'

Could Nicholas help it? she wondered. If you are brought up to think you are almost at the top of the tree, if everything in your world revolves around you and what you want, can you help not understanding those below you? And yet he was not unkind, not when she considered how he had tolerated Charlie, how he had treated her when they had been prisoners together. Or was that simply *noblesse oblige*? Did Nicholas act in a certain manner because not to do so would lower himself in his own estimation?

'Can I ask, miss? Has the Duke done something to upset you?' Millie was biting her lower lip as though frightened of her own daring in asking such a thing.

'He made me an offer,' Sarah said. If she couldn't trust Millie, who could she trust?

'He didn't! The cheeky—' Millie expressed herself freely in language that Sarah thought would probably have been perfectly intelligible to a docker but not, thankfully, to her. 'Sorry, Miss Sarah. But honestly, the nerve of the man. He knows you're a respectable lady. I thought better of him, I did.'

'No, not that kind of offer. He asked me to marry him, Millie.' The fierceness of Millie's defence warmed the cold core of her, just a little.

'Wot?' All Millie's carefully learned elocution deserted her. 'You a duchess? That's bl— But why are you angry, miss?'

'He made himself do it because he thinks that once I have my father's money back, and perhaps the ships too, then I will be a respectable young lady and he has compromised me. Before it didn't matter—I was just a paid companion and his sister could find me a post, sweep me under the carpet, as it were. He is gritting his teeth because he knows as well as I do that he would never, in a decade of blue moons, have made me an offer if he didn't feel honour-bound to.'

'And Sarah Parrish the paid companion didn't

have a good name worth saving: it'd be like they say. He'd be a man who'd made his dishcloth his table napkin. But Miss Parrish who can afford her own house and carriage does, otherwise it makes him look bad?'

'Which would be bad for his self-esteem. Yes, exactly.'

'Must've stung.' There wasn't much answer to that. Millie fiddled with the cotton reel. 'Especially as you're in love with him, Miss Sarah.'

'I—' Really, there was no point in denying it. Not to herself, not to her perceptive and constant companion. 'Yes, more fool me.'

'Even now?'

'Even now, when I could cheer at the thought of him landing face down in the mud next time he goes ashore and the entire crew and all the prisoners using him as a gangplank.' She took a moment to relish the idea, then realised that it didn't really help at all, and said so.

'I know,' Millie said gloomily. 'You want to hurt them like they hurt you, but you can't stop thinking about them and wishing...' Her voice trailed off.

'You too. Oh, Millie, I am sorry. Who is it?'

The maid shrugged. 'Nobody I think about now, not often anyway. It was before I went to

Miss Trotter's. He was a local lad. Cor, but he was good-looking and the shoulders on him were enough to make a girl weak at the knees. But he had as much idea of treating a woman decent as an old tom cat, did Josh Fenn, and I told myself not to be a fool and, luck would have it, along comes Miss Trotter, else I'd have probably done something daft like getting myself in the family way with him.'

There wasn't much to be said to that. Sarah took Millie's hand in hers and squeezed it and they sat in silence for a while.

'Is it going to be awkward, Miss Sarah? I mean, what did you say to him?'

'I refused him and left him in no doubt that I was insulted by his offer.'

Millie made a sound between a gulp and a groan.

'Yes, quite. We will just have to be on our best behaviour, both of us, and pretend it never happened.'

'Does he know you... I mean, does he know how you feel about him?'

'I hope not,' Sarah said fervently. 'He knows I am not averse to him, of course, but he just assumed that an offer from a duke was irresistible.'

The rumble of masculine voices penetrated the

wooden walls separating the cabins. 'I think he's across the way interrogating the prisoners,' she said. 'I hope that will cool his temper.'

'We'll be in Lynn tomorrow and then we've got the three coaches, so you can keep out of his way,' Millie said. 'We can carry on teaching Charlie and he won't want to have to sit through that—it will give him an excuse to go in one of the other carriages.'

Sarah could only hope so. Under all the hurt and anger there was the tattered remains of her daydream, her impossible fantasy, that Nicholas had come to love her for herself, had wanted to marry her despite her birth and her station in life. Like an injured bird hiding in the deepest shadows at the foot of a hedge it fluttered its damaged wings, fanning the misery in her heart.

They sailed into the mouth of the River Ouse early the next morning and it was coming up to eight o'clock when they passed the ferry plying the wide river between North Lynn and the port of Lynn Regis, King's Lynn, or as everyone always called it, simply Lynn.

Sarah found an unobtrusive corner on deck while Nicholas and Fawcett set out their plans. They would report to the local Justices and hopefully secure the loan of some burly men to assist in guarding the prisoners and the silver on their way down to London with two of Fawcett's men.

'The theft of both the ship and the silver was from the Port of London. The silver needs to be returned to Rundell, Bridge & Rundell for them to assess whether there is any damage or losses. The rest of us will continue on the *Gannet* to Blakeney, where we will hope to apprehend Wilton, who can be identified by Miss Parrish.'

He did not seek her out in the crowd, Sarah noticed. His gaze remained on the men in front of him.

'His crimes also took place in London and we will take him directly there by ship to hand him over to the authorities to stand trial. Before leaving we will search his house thoroughly for all incriminating documents, ledgers and so forth. It may be necessary to seek help from local Justices if we need to attach any assets in local banks, but I want to secure Wilton and attempt to establish who his local allies are before doing that.'

'We want to do this as discreetly as possible,' Fawcett added. 'We'll change the *Gannet*'s sails again, give her new name boards and we'll land dressed as sailors. Is that clear?'

'This man Wilton is not going to escape us,' Nicholas said, and this time his gaze swept over the group and settled on Sarah. 'I will be greatly displeased if he does.'

Chapter Eighteen

'I am coming ashore.'

'You most certainly are not. It is not safe and, besides, we are landing in the guise of common sailors.'

It was dawn and they were about to navigate the tricky mouth of Blakeney Harbour which involved sailing between the tip of the long Point and sandbanks. Fortunately they had been able to pick up a new skipper at Lynn, a man who knew the coast and was vouched for by the coastguard as reliable, but he was not prepared to enter in darkness.

The dawn light was pearly on the sea. The wind had dropped to a light onshore breeze and the little ship's set of white sails filled as she was turned towards the buoys marking the channel.

Sarah watched seals humping their way from the Point into the surf and then bobbing in the water to watch them with wide, dark eyes. 'Women sail on working vessels, don't they?'

'Women automatically attract more attention.'

'And whose fault is that?' Sarah muttered.

This was the first significant exchange with Nicholas since that ill-fated proposal and it was proving about as successful. Sarah had decided that the safest way to avoid confrontation with Nicholas was to avoid him—not the easiest thing to do on a small ship without becoming a prisoner in one's cabin, but they had managed because it seemed he had the same idea. An exchange of frigid bows at mealtimes was the extent of their mutual unbending.

But that had not stopped Sarah from listening as plans were laid. Two boats would be going ashore first, the passengers including Nicholas, Fawcett, the two men who had located Axminster's residence and four of the ex-Riflemen. They had all dressed themselves from the original crew's sea chests and presented a convincingly scruffy appearance. A third boat, a little later to avoid the appearance of a small army disembarking together, would follow ten minutes later, armed with a sketch map and with instructions to form a rear guard.

As Nicholas moved away, clearly satisfied that

the briefing was at an end, Sarah looked around. Virtually everyone was on deck except Pendell, who was presumably doing whatever valets did at that point in the day, and Millie, who was tidying their cabin. Sarah strolled across to the hatch and went down.

'We need to look through those sea chests,' she announced when she found Millie. 'The Duke is being pig-headed and will not allow me to land. If I dress in men's clothing, then I can get on board the third boat.'

'Me too.' Millie was already half out of the door. 'They carried the sea chests to the saloon now the prisoners have been taken off and they are still there.'

They were sorting through what Fawcett's men had left when Charlie joined them. 'Wondered where you were.' His lower lip was stuck out in a sulk. 'They won't let me go with them.'

'Nor us,' Sarah said, locating a more or less clean shirt and holding it up against her. It seemed small enough. 'So we are dressing up as men and going in the third boat.'

'Me too. I'll come an' guard you,' Charlie said, suddenly all smiles. Sarah made a mental note to buy him a toothbrush.

She met Millie's gaze and could see the same

question there—should they allow him to go? Sarah had a strong suspicion that if they said *no*, then he would get himself ashore somehow. At least, if he came with them, they could keep an eye on him.

Some digging about located enough clothing that was small enough to take and try on. They plaited their hair tightly to bind up under neck-erchiefs, then topped them with battered hats and agreed that the effect would deceive anyone from a distance. They were not, after all, trying to pass as men close to. Shoes were a problem, then Millie suggested going barefoot and putting their own stoutest shoes in a sack to change into once they were ashore and away from the quayside.

'Now all we have to do is get ourselves on board the third boat.' Sarah consoled herself with the thought that it probably hadn't occurred to Nicholas that he might not be obeyed and therefore he'd not have told the remaining crew not to take them.

In the event, it proved surprisingly easy. The *Gannet*, renamed *Diana*, anchored in the wide pool just outside the harbour and the first two boats pulled away.

Sarah watched the men land and saunter off,

some to buy fish, a couple into the chandler's shop and the others splitting off in different directions. Some looked purposeful, some seemed just to be wandering, a few were skylarking. They certainly did not look like a group of highly trained marksmen accompanying a duke.

The crew was getting the third boat ready. Sarah, Millie and Charlie sauntered over and joined the queue at the ladder.

The ex-fisherman from Fawcett's group who had been helping sail the *Gannet* stared. 'Er… miss? Captain said nothing about you going ashore, miss.'

'Did he not? How careless of him,' Sarah said casually. 'Never mind, there seems to be enough room.' She swung a leg over the rail, found the ladder with her bare feet and was down it before the man had a chance to object. Millie and Charlie were right behind her.

When they landed she kept an eye on the man with the sketch map in his hand and they followed him up the main street, climbing away from the harbour up to the coast road.

It did not take very long to be out of sight of the last straggling cottages and the group closed up more.

Green Lodge proved to be a charming villa

half a mile inland with a sea view in one direction and, doubtless, a pleasant rural vista from the other sides. The men began to fan out and one after another dropped behind making a chain of lookouts. Sarah pressed on with her companions and then had to stop sharply to prevent herself running into Nicholas, who had clearly just changed into his own clothes and now presented the picture of a gentleman out for a country walk.

She could hear him running over the description of Wilton with the men who had not already glimpsed him. 'About five foot ten, slim, brown hair greying at the temples, grey eyes, large mole on left cheek, slight stammer. Wears spectacles, looks like a clerk.'

He adjusted his hat at a rakish angle, swung his cane and stepped back into the lane. In a few moments he was knocking on the door of the lodge. A conversation took place, presumably with an unseen servant.

Sarah edged closer as Nicholas stepped inside. The movement must have caught Captain Fawcett's eye, because he turned and came across to her. 'Miss Parrish? What are you doing here? Keep out of sight, please. His Grace will be out in a moment having discovered whether the occupant is actually—'

There was a shot, a shout, the sound of splintering glass and a figure burst through the long window overlooking the garden. The man swung around, saw the group near the gate and made off at an angle to them, sprinting across the lawn towards where Sarah, Millie, Charlie and Captain Fawcett were concealed by the hedge.

'Is that him?' the captain began as Nicholas came out onto the lawn.

'Oh, yes. That is Wilton.' She stooped and took off her shoe.

He was a yard away now, heading for a gap in the hedge. Sarah stepped through it and he stopped dead, a look of stunned recognition on his face as she swung the heavy shoe and hit him squarely on the chin, then kicked him in the groin with the foot that was still shod and gave him a hard shove with both hands. He went down, flat on his back, and Charlie, like a small, fierce terrier, leapt on his stomach, knocking the remaining air out of him.

'Get that boy off him,' the captain snapped, levelling a pistol at Wilton.

Millie, who had been yelling encouragement to Charlie, took his arm and pulled him away.

'Well done, Charlie, but you're in the way of the captain's shot.'

Sarah glanced up as a shadow fell across the man at her feet. Nicholas stood looking at her. 'He apparently recognised me from Lockhart's description. I walked in, got the study door slammed in my face and a bullet through the panels, which slightly impeded my progress. You were rather more effective than I was, Miss Parrish. You are not hurt?'

'Thank you, no.' She wanted to look away from him, focus on Wilton, who was still sprawled at her feet, but there was something in Nicholas's expression that did not let her. Anxiety, admiration, annoyance? She was not certain, but whatever he was feeling it was intense and it was focused on her.

'I should have known that you would not obey my request to stay on board,' he said.

'Yes, I think you should, given that I had made it clear how very important this was to me,' she replied, her voice level.

'This is assault.' Wilton had recovered his voice. 'I will see you all before the magistrates!'

'You most certainly will,' Nicholas agreed. 'The Bow Street magistrates where, I have no doubt, you will be committed to prison to await your trial for fraud, theft, conspiracy to kidnap, assault and piracy. I am sure we can think of a few other charges when we have investigated your study.'

There was movement at the front door and one of the men came down to report. 'One butler, a footman, a valet, a cook and two maids all under guard in the kitchen.'

'Get Wilton down to the ship,' Nicholas told Fawcett. 'Make certain he can't be identified as you go through the village. We'll search here.'

He watched them go, then turned back to Sarah. 'I suppose you wish to take part in the search?'

'Of course. His study first, I think.'

Nicholas let her lead, watched as she sat at the desk, handed her the keys that Fawcett had taken from Wilton's pocket, then turned away and began to search the rest of the room, looking behind pictures, moving books on shelves, tapping panelling.

Sarah watched him and wondered why she felt so very blank and empty. She should be overjoyed to have found Wilton, to see him hauled off to face justice, but all she was conscious of was a vacuum where her emotions should be.

She unlocked the first of the desk drawers.

Within minutes she was absorbed, sorting the papers into piles, scanning each for any evidence.

'I made a sad mull of my proposal,' Nicholas said, so suddenly that she jumped, toppling a neat pile of household bills.

Sarah took a moment to tidy them again while her breathing got back to normal, then said, 'Yes. You did.'

He was behind her, still searching. She heard the scrape of books on a shelf, the rustle of paper. 'Marriage is not a matter of affections, of emotion—'

'Not for dukes, it appears. The rest of us lower ranks of humanity may, perhaps, hope for such things.' Surprisingly she found it easy enough to keep her voice level. Perhaps the fact that they were both engaged on a task and not looking at each other made this easier. It seemed oddly impersonal, as though they were discussing a theoretical case, not two people with feelings, hearts to wound.

'Do you honestly believe that such a thing as love between a man and a woman is real—or, perhaps I should say, realistic? Infatuation withers and dies after a while. Self-deception can only last for so long.'

'How very cynical you sound.' Sarah opened another drawer and lifted out the papers within it. 'Anyone would think that you had been disappointed in love.'

She jumped as a book hit the floor behind her chair. Nicholas's voice sounded muffled as he bent to retrieve it. 'I was speaking theoretically and from observation.'

'I think it very sad, whatever causes you to have that opinion. I agree, it is a miracle when two people find each other and fall in love, but it does happen and it should make for great happiness.'

'And without love one is doomed to unhappiness?' Nicholas sounded scornful. He worked around to the left of the desk now and she could see him out of the corner of her eye.

'Not at all. But I believe there must be an equality of feeling, of liking, of desire, between a couple. Oh, I have found it!'

'What? True love?' Nicholas drawled, but he came to stand beside her as she spread out a document that had been tied up in red tape.

'No, of course not. A list of the ships he stole from us—see?' She ran her finger down the neat columns. 'The name, what he has changed it to and where he has based each one. *Dawn Wind*,

Sally's Song, Portugal Lass… All of them. Ports, captains. Oh, Nicholas, I can find them all again. Papa would be so happy.'

She had not realised that she was weeping, not until she found herself in Nicholas's arms as he knelt beside the chair. 'I'm sorry,' she managed to sob against his lapel.

'There is no need to apologise.' His hand, flat against her spine, massaged soothing circles until the sobs subsided into sniffles and she sat back.

'Oh, what a watering pot I am.' Sarah scrubbed her hand across her eyes. 'I have made your lovely coat soggy now.' She took the handkerchief he passed her and mopped at the broadcloth.

'That isn't why I gave it to you, you foolish female.' He took it back and applied it to her face. 'You look a complete ragamuffin in those clothes and with your nose all red and your eyes watery.'

'You— Of all the unkind things to say!'

That elusive smile twitched at the corner of Nicholas's mouth. 'But true. What else is in that drawer?'

'There's this ledger.' She opened it. 'Oh, yes. See—sailing schedules and cargoes and profit and loss calculations. This will be excellent evidence, will it not?'

'It will. See what else you can find. We need to discover where he has hoarded his assets so they can be seized.' Nicholas stood up and went back to examining the paintings on the wall. 'Ah, here we are. Now all I need is the key.'

She turned to look and found he had taken down a large oil painting. Behind it was a cupboard door. 'Can't you break it?'

'I prefer not to do any damage at this stage and, besides, it appears to be iron.' He tapped it with his knuckles. 'Yes, painted metal.' He took the ring of keys and sorted through them. 'This one… No. Here we are.' The door opened with a squeal of hinges to reveal a space stacked with ledgers and canvas bags.

Half an hour later Nicholas, seated on the other side of the desk, threw down his pen and sat back. 'Thank goodness for organised and educated criminals. A nice neat list of banks and deposits and of investments.'

Sarah, who had been counting the contents of the canvas bags made a final total and showed him. 'Far more than he stole from Papa in cash.'

'I will make a list of everything we are removing and put that in the safe and lock it. I am hoping that we can get Wilton to London before anyone realises what has happened and some shifty lawyer or corrupt justice starts emptying the bank holdings.' He began to stack up the paperwork and bags.

'I'll see if I can find a trunk to put it all in and look in the other rooms, although it seems as if he kept everything to do with his business in the one place.' She paused past the door. 'What are we going to do about his servants?'

'They appear to be normal domestic staff—no sinister secretaries or cunning clerks. We can hardly detain them with no cause. I shall tell them he has been arrested for assault and make no mention of anything else, so if we lock it all up again here and we can remove a trunk that they won't miss, they may not suspect anything more.'

Sarah found a small trunk in a shabby box room and brought it down. 'They won't notice this has gone.'

Between them they packed it and Nicholas dragged it out to the garden. Half an hour later, with the servants released and pacified with a significant *douceur* in coin, they were on their way back to the harbour, the trunk carried by the last of Fawcett's comrades.

'London now,' Nicholas said. 'London and I can unleash my lawyers. It will give me great pleasure to see them pick apart Mr Wilton's little empire.'

'You will still set your own people on the case?' Sarah asked, suddenly seized with doubts. 'I mean… After I…'

'My offer to help secure the return of all your assets was not conditional on you marrying me,' Nicholas said. There was an edge to his voice that did not invite discussion.

'Thank you,' Sarah said.

At least once we are back in London I need not see him again.

That was the right thing, the sensible thing, and she should be pleased. Surely this would become easier if she was not seeing Nicholas every day, talking to him, touching him? Surely?

Chapter Nineteen

London. Sarah leant on the ship's rail and looked out over the familiar turmoil of the Pool of London ahead. London was the only home she had known, but now there was no roof here to call her own. A disturbing thought had just struck her and she could have kicked herself for not considering it earlier. It hadn't occurred to her that she would have to find lodgings at once, but of course, the *Gannet* was not their ship; it had been stolen, and she could not simply stay on board while she took her time over accommodation.

A nostalgic homecoming, watching the wharves and warehouses come closer, seeing the White Tower loom ahead: that had to wait until she checked how much money she had and calculated what lodgings it would buy her.

'Where do you intend to stay?' Nicholas asked.

She had not heard him approach and the question, and his nearness, made her stammer.

'Er...lodgings. Yes, lodgings.'

They had hardly spoken since the *Gannet* had put out from Blakeney and headed south, except to finalise listing all Wilton's assets and to tabulate how they compared to what he had stolen from her father. When they had done that they had been in the saloon, with Pendell helping with the note-taking.

She had not seen Wilton, although she had heard his voice raised in complaint, uttering threats, making excuses.

Now Nicholas stood squarely in front of her. 'What lodgings, where?'

'I... I haven't decided yet. I will go to a library, look at advertisements in the newspapers. I will soon find something suitable.'

Nicholas made a sound suspiciously like a snort. 'How much money do you have?'

'I—I was just about to go and check. Enough.'

'It will be months before we can hope to reclaim all your stolen assets. How do you intend to live until then?'

'If your sister Lady Wellingfield would be kind enough to give me a reference I have no doubt I can find employment.'

'That would be quite unacceptable.'

'Oh.' She felt ready to sink through the deck. 'Of course. My refusal of your offer. Yes, I can see that would make the situation impossible.'

'That has nothing to do with it,' he said impatiently. 'We discussed this before: your status when you do have independent means will be quite different and as much distance should be put between your former life as a paid companion and your new one as is possible.'

'Ideally, that may be the case,' Sarah said. She sidestepped and walked past him towards the hatch. 'However, this is reality. I will approach employment agencies just as soon as I have found lodgings. I have no intention of starving in genteel poverty, Your Grace.'

'I have another sister.' Nicholas was in front of her again.

'May I felicitate you on your good fortune?' she said politely.

'Sarah.' He stopped.

She sidestepped again. 'We could set this to music and dance, I suppose.'

'Will you stand still for one minute and listen to me, you maddening woman? She lives in London. You can stay with her. Anna Beale, Lady Grassington.'

'Why on earth should she accept a complete stranger into her home for an indefinite period of time?'

Maddening woman, indeed! I am not the maddening one here.

'Because I ask her to,' he said simply. 'Anna is very sociable and very domestic too. She adores company; she is rattling around in a large house while her husband is on a diplomatic mission to Turkey—you would be doing her a favour.'

'I do not wish to be beholden,' Sarah said. It was difficult to express herself honestly about this. 'You are already doing a great deal for me by helping retrieve what Wilton stole.'

He waved it away. 'I have to do nothing except instruct men who are already on a retainer. Their expenses can be reclaimed if you insist. It costs me nothing to ask Anna if she will give you houseroom.'

'And Millie?'

'Yes, of course.'

Should she agree? It sounded so tempting, so safe compared to the prospect of tramping the streets searching for decent lodgings. But nothing involving Nicholas Terrell was safe. She played for time to think. 'What about Charlie?'

'If he wishes to try life as a gardener's boy, then I will employ him at Severton. The head gardener is a good man and the boys lodge with him and his wife. I will send him down with Fawcett, who is returning there in a few days. Now, are there any other stray souls you wish me to accommodate?'

'You make it sound as though I am making demands.' It sounded petulant, even to her own ears. 'I am sorry, I did not mean that. I am causing you so much trouble, Nicholas.'

It was on the tip of his tongue to agree with her. Yes, Sarah Parrish was a most troublesome female.

She is too independent, too opinionated, he had been telling himself for days. Now he thought, *Too intelligent, too courageous? Too attractive?*

All his instincts, all his poise, seemed to desert him when confronted with Sarah. He should have been able to make that proposal with grace and tact: instead he had blundered into it like a green youth in the throes of his first infatuation, when actually he had no idea of his own mind. He wanted her in his bed, but a gentleman spent his life ignoring sensual urges towards respectable young ladies. He wanted to help her, to protect her, and yet she made it quite clear that whilst his help and his ideas were welcome—even if she felt at liberty to argue with those ideas—his protection was not required.

He had come on deck now intending to suggest that she went to a hotel of the kind approved of by his aunts and elderly cousins whilst he roused his secretary from his comfortable study at the town house and sent him off to find modest but decent lodgings for Sarah. She would protest, he knew, but he would point out that he could afford to wait for repayment until her funds had been restored to her.

Where had the idea of sending her to Anna come from? The explanation hit him with unsettling clarity. If Sarah was staying with his sister, then he could call with perfect propriety, whereas a duke, or any gentleman for that matter, descending on the kind of lodgings fit for a respectable single lady would cause all manner of comment.

He wanted to continue to see Sarah, Nicholas realised.

I want to court her.

'Nicholas? What is wrong?' Sarah was staring at him as though he had spoken out loud. Surely he hadn't? What the hell *was* wrong with him? 'Have I got a smudge on my face or something?'

'I am sorry. I…' He found a smile. 'No smudges. I just realised something. Something very important. Now, are we agreed? You will stay with my sister Anna?'

Sarah blinked at him. Perhaps the smile was overdone. He got his face under control and raised an interrogative eyebrow.

'Thank you. If Lady Grassington agrees—and you must ask her when I am not present or the poor soul will feel obligated—then I would be most grateful for her hospitality.'

She was still regarding him a trifle quizzically and he could hardly blame her.

I probably looked like a stunned cod, Nicholas thought savagely.

That was no way to make her change her mind about him, although how one went about courting a lady who had already been insulted by your inept offer of marriage, he was not certain. Perhaps he could ask Anna's advice, although he could almost hear her now.

The Duke of Severton unable to woo a ship owner's daughter? Really, Nicholas, you must be losing your touch…

And she'd laugh at him, Nicholas thought

gloomily. Anna never would take him seriously, nor let him get too top-lofty, either. She was his favourite sibling of the three of them and the most intelligent.

But if he really was in love with Sarah, then he was prepared to withstand any amount of affectionate teasing if it helped undo his clumsiness.

In love? He tried to compare what he was feeling now with his emotions when he had asked Marietta to marry him and could find no comparison. Marietta—

'Nicholas.' Sarah was regarding him quizzically. 'You look like—'

'A stunned cod. Yes, I know. I'm sorry.'

'I wouldn't go as far as that,' she said with the first laugh he had heard from her in days. 'A poet in the throes of composition, perhaps. Misty-eyed. Most romantic.' Then she was gone, leaving the echo of a giggle behind her.

Nicholas wanted Sarah off the ship before they removed Wilton. He sent messengers to Bow Street and to Rundell, Bridge & Rundell and then escorted her and Millie to a hackney carriage.

'We will make certain my sister is at home

and then I will send for your luggage,' he said, climbing in.

The motion of the vehicle felt strange after days at sea and he wondered whether that accounted for the strain that he could discern under Sarah's determinedly calm expression. He was coming to be able to read her face. Was that familiarity, or the insights of love? It was still difficult to come to terms with the notion that he was in love at all, let alone with this woman, but there was no other explanation he could think of for why he felt both happy and terrified, aroused and yet respectful, anxious and somehow at peace. Or why, when he caught sight of Sarah, he felt hollow inside as though all the breath had been sucked out of him. Oddly, that was not unpleasant.

Lord and Lady Grassington's town house was in Mount Street, just to the east of Hyde Park. To his relief the knocker was on the door—Anna had not gone to the country or the seaside.

As Sarah had requested, he left her waiting in the carriage while he went in.

Handley, the butler, greeted him with his usual smile. 'Your Grace. Her Ladyship—'

'Is that you, Nicholas?' Anna, sudden as always, rushed out of the drawing room and flung her arms around him. 'Darling man! I was quite beside myself with boredom and completely unable to make up my mind what to do about it and here you are, like a good angel to cheer me up with tales of steamships. Come along and tell me all about your adventures. Is it too early for sherry?'

'Far too early.' He bent to kiss her cheek, soft and scented with something discreetly expensive. 'You smell like a Persian garden. I have come to ask you a favour—shall we sit down for a moment while I explain?'

He did so, as concisely as possible, leaving aside any mention of proposals and the state of his emotions.

'And you left the poor soul out in the street in some ghastly hackney carriage? Of course she may stay—go and fetch her this instant, you provoking man!'

When Sarah came back with him she was composed, polite and self-effacing. 'I am so grateful for your hospitality, Lady Grassington. I beg that you will not look on me as someone who has to be entertained in any way—I am used to London and quite at home here. And I have my maid, so I hope I will not create extra work for your household. If there is anything with which I can assist you, I would be very happy to do so. I have been, until lately, a lady's companion, you see.'

'Then we will be companionable, I am certain. I cannot tell you how much I look forward to having a friend in the house. And you will call me Anna and I hope I may call you Sarah.'

She smiled at Nicholas, the rather ambiguous, sisterly little smile that always made him feel slightly uneasy. 'You will have Sarah's luggage sent as soon as possible, Nicholas?'

It was a clear dismissal. He stood, kissed Anna on the cheek and shook hands with Sarah in a very proper manner. That did nothing to stop the shivers that ran up his arm, despite the fact that there were two layers of glove leather between their bare fingers.

'I will keep you in touch with the progress of the prosecutions and of your claims,' he said.

'Thank you. I am most grateful.' She met his gaze frankly and smiled. 'I feel very safe now, although I would not have admitted to feeling unsafe this morning. And I am very eager to hear how everything progresses.'

'You may become weary of my daily reports.'

'Oh, I do not think so.' And there was that smile again, and his pulse was doing the most remarkable things.

Anna cleared her throat in a meaningful manner, and he realised he was still holding Sarah's hand.

He found himself out on the pavement with no very clear memory of Handley letting him out, and dismissed the hackney. Today he felt like walking and to hell with his leg.

Sarah looked at her hostess, who had a decidedly mischievous smile on her lips. It changed to an uncomplicated, friendly expression as she turned fully to face her unexpected guest.

'I imagine that you would like to see your room and to have a bath? I cannot imagine that such a thing was available on board a little sailing ship. And, of course, your maid will welcome the opportunity for one too, and the chance to sort out your wardrobes.'

'Indeed, yes, if it is not too much trouble. Hot, fresh water was in very short supply.'

Lady Grassington reached out for the bell pull. 'Ah, Handley. Please ask Mrs Wilson to prepare the Blue Bedchamber for Miss Parrish and send

Smart to run a bath and look after Miss Parrish. Her maid will need a room and please have a bath and hot water sent up for her.

'Smart is my maid,' she explained as Handley bowed and removed himself. 'I will take you up in a moment. Now, what is the state of your wardrobe after your adventures? We are much the same height, I think, so I can lend you whatever you need until you can go shopping.'

She cocked her head to one side, considering Sarah. 'You are a brunette and your hair is fairer than mine, but our colouring is much the same. All my favourite colours would suit you.'

'Thank you, my lady. Anna. Everything needs laundering or pressing, I imagine, so I would be very grateful for the loan of a nightgown and perhaps a day gown.'

'But of course. Smart will find you everything you need. Then we can plan what shopping you need to do.'

Anna seemed pleased at the prospect. Time, Sarah thought, to make her circumstances very clear.

'I cannot afford to buy very much, just fresh linen and some shoes, in fact. The case is, until it is possible to retrieve what Wilton stole from my father, I have very little money. If it takes a great deal of time, or the Duke's lawyers cannot secure it, then I must seek employment again.'

'How tiresome for you. We must give this some thought. The Pantheon Bazaar is the place for us, I think. You must put your head together with your maid and Smart and make a list and we will have a delightful time seeking out dagger-cheap bargains. Now, here is Mrs Wilson, my housekeeper. Mrs Wilson, this is Miss Parrish, who, I am delighted to say, will be staying for several weeks. Now, off you go and have a lovely long soak.'

'We've fallen on our feet here, Miss Sarah,' Millie whispered. 'I've got ever such a nice room, all to myself, and they sent me up water for a bath and everything. Isn't it good not to feel sticky with salt again?'

She came into the bathroom, a luxurious little chamber off the dressing room attached to Sarah's large, very blue bedchamber. 'Smart's gone to find you some clothes. She's taken everything away for laundering and all mine too. This is hers.' She did a twirl to show off a pale blue cotton gown with a narrow lace trim at neck and cuffs, a crisp little white apron and a smart lawn cap with floating blue ribbons.

'Very chic,' Sarah said, looking over the edge of the large porcelain tub. 'Doesn't this smell gorgeous?' She waved a hand, wafting scented steam about. 'Bath oils and soap to match. Such luxury.'

There was the sound of the bedchamber door opening and closing, then a tap on the bathroom door.

'Excuse me, Miss Parrish, but I have brought a wrapper for you and some slippers.' Smart, Lady Grassington's aptly named maid, looked in. 'Greene, if Miss Parrish does not require you for a moment, you can look over what I have brought that might suit Miss Parrish.'

'Greene!' Millie mouthed at Sarah. 'Just as if I was a proper lady's maid,' she whispered.

'You *are* a proper lady's maid,' Sarah whispered back and grinned as Millie rolled her eyes and went out.

The warm water embraced her as Sarah lay back again. There was a terrible temptation to stay here pretending that she was the kind of young lady for whom this was normal, the kind who might stay with the sister of a duke as a matter of course, the sort who might love that duke and have a realistic hope that he might return her feelings and not propose simply because he felt honour-bound to do so.

She forced her unwilling memory back to that humiliating proposal. It was hard to believe that anyone as confident and articulate as Nicholas could have made such a clumsy fist of it. She supposed it was because he was so very reluctant to ask her, otherwise the only other explanation was that he was deeply anxious that she might refuse. Or he was in two minds about whether he wanted her to accept or not. Yes, that was most likely what it was. His sense of honour told him to propose, his natural inclination was to hope that she would refuse. It would be enough to tangle anyone's tongue and deprive them of a tactful turn of phrase.

I am better off without him—without hope of him, Sarah told herself firmly.

If Nicholas would only settle down to being uniformly chilly, superior and aloof, that would be so much easier to deal with. It was those sudden flashes of kindness and concern, like his insistence that she come here, that were her undoing. They kindled hope, like someone blowing on the last embers of a fire. It flickered into life for a brief moment, then died again when that puff of breath ceased.

The water felt cool suddenly. Sarah sat up. 'Millie!' she called. 'Come and help me wash my hair.'

Chapter Twenty

It seemed to Sarah after two weeks that she had lived in the Mount Street house for months. It felt like a refuge, like home when she returned after the difficult experiences that seemed inevitable, however carefully Nicholas shielded her.

There was the visit to Bow Street where she was required to identify Mr Axminster as Josiah Wilton. Several of the men who had worked for Parrish Shipping were present and one after another they identified him too. It had already been established who was responsible for the theft of the contents of her father's safe and the ships, so now the process of law swung into action to convict the man in custody of that crime.

Then, with great swiftness, came the trial. It was brief and, fortunately, she did not have to attend. Now Wilton was convicted, Nicholas had explained, the process of attaching his assets could begin.

'What will happen to him?' she asked. It seemed unreal to be discussing crime and punishment in the elegant comfort of Lady Grassington's drawing room.

'Transportation to Australia. A place they call Van Diemen's Land,' he told her. 'He will be confined in a prison hulk until the trial for the theft of Findlater's silver takes place. With Lockhart dead it will be a conspiracy to steal charge for both the silver and the *Gannet*. Apparently the mysterious Mr Brown has decided to throw himself on the mercy of the court and has turned King's Evidence. It remains to be seen whether what he has to say makes any difference to Wilton, adds to the length of his sentence. It might send him to the gallows if they can make a charge of conspiracy to murder stick to him.'

'I do not want him dead,' she said. 'There has been too much death. I hope he has a horrible time in the hulks and on the voyage and that they set him to work on something he hates when he gets there.'

Nicholas had nodded and told her that Rundell, Bridge & Rundell and the Duke of Findlater intended rewarding those responsible for recovering the stolen silverware. 'They will pay Captain Barlow's widow a pension and will give Captain Fawcett and his men a bounty, but you are the one who realised what was being stolen—most of it goes to you.' He named a sum that made her blink.

'But no! That is unfair. You sent for Captain Fawcett and his men.'

'Do you think I am in need of it?' he asked, all chilly and ducal again.

'No, of course not. But you have earned it.'

'I will not take it. It is yours.'

'Then Pendell and Millie deserve some of it. They were in danger and he was hurt and she fought back. And Charlie—he helped capture Wilton.'

'I will look after Pendell and Charlie, I promise. They will be rewarded properly.'

They haggled and argued and eventually he persuaded her to accept the money with a generous sum for Millie.

'Cor blimey, Miss Sarah,' Millie said, when told the news. 'What am I going to do with that?'

'You could set up a little business,' Sarah suggested.

'No. I can't think of anything I want to do. I

like being a lady's maid. Might get married one of these days: it'd be useful then. Not that I'd tell any man I'd got money, not beforehand,' she'd added cannily.

So Nicholas had arranged for it to be invested for her, all except a sum Millie asked for to buy a complete new wardrobe. 'Sunday best that'll have them staring when I go to church. That'll be capital. But I can get some out when I want it? Never know when I might get a scheme, after all. Don't want to rush things.'

They saw a lot of Nicholas at Mount Street and Sarah thought it attractive that he was such a good brother. But then, she was finding it harder and harder to identify any traits that did not make her love him more.

He called with any snippet of news about the case, never staying long, but taking the time when he could have dashed off a note. He took Sarah and Anna for drives in the park, or walked with them or simply sat, took tea, discussed any news that interested them. He never seemed to be with them for more than an hour, but Sarah knew she was becoming dangerously dependent on that almost daily contact.

Which is foolish. I was with him all the time from when I bumped into him on the dock.

But this was somehow different. Probably because the strain of being captives, or of hunting the criminals, was gone, she told herself.

Now, on a sunny morning, Sarah sat on the sofa and tried to explain to Anna that, as she had some money, she should be looking for lodgings of her own.

'But you haven't enough for your own house, have you?' the Countess said. 'You'd be in lodgings and surely they wouldn't be as comfortable as this.'

'Well, of course not. But I can hardly abuse your hospitality by living here like a cuckoo in your nest indefinitely,' Sarah protested.

'You are doing no such thing! I love the company.' Anna peered at her anxiously. 'You like being here, do you not?'

'Of course I do, but—'

'I have come to feel you are like a sister to me.'

'I would not presume to claim the same, but I value your friendship greatly,' Sarah admitted, flattered and flustered in equal parts.

If I were Anna's sister-in law... No, stop it.

'Presume, *pshaw.*' Anna waved the comment aside. 'May I confide in you?'

'Of course.'

'I am very concerned about Nicholas.'

'The Duke?' Sarah asked, playing for time.

'Yes. He is not happy. I had thought he was… settled. Content. But I realise now that is not enough for him. He has not been truly alive for a long time. Ever since—' She stopped abruptly.

'Ever since he damaged his leg?' Sarah prompted.

'Yes. Yes, then,' Anna said. 'Do you know what happened?'

'No. I did not like to ask.'

'It was when Papa was alive, and my brother Frederick, the Marquess of Farne, also. Nicholas was coming home to Severton from London and decided to ride the last stage. A little bridge over a stream in the woods collapsed, throwing his horse into the water. Nicholas was trapped beneath it, his thigh bone broken. The water was icy and it felt like an age, he said, for the horse to get itself to its feet again. It was a mercy he was not knocked unconscious. Thankfully, the horse had galloped on to the stables, but we do not know how long it took for the search party to find him.

'He was terribly ill and in great pain and we thought he would die. We never did discover why he had made the journey—he said he could not recall. The only happy outcome was that our neighbour, Marietta Langley, came to enquire and was such a support to Mama. Then she and Frederick, who had last seen her when she was just a girl and before he went off to university, fell in love and married.'

'That, sadly, did not last long, I believe?'

'No. Poor darling Freddie.' She hesitated. 'It was so difficult. Nicholas slowly recovered and spent some time at various spas and at the seaside resorts for his leg. He came home when Freddie died, of course, and he and Marietta...' Her voice trailed off and she seemed to be looking back through time. 'Nicholas was so cold to her, so distant. She was terribly upset. She was anyway, of course. I could never understand why he treated her like that. And then Papa died. Oh, it was a dreadful few years.'

'Perhaps it is both the loss of his brother and the injury that darkened his mood and he has never regained his spirits and being serious and reserved has become normal for him,' Sarah said. She thought that he had seemed well adjusted to his leg injury, treating it as a minor inconvenience, but that could simply be a smokescreen, she thought now. What if it pained him a great deal or his pride was wounded by the limitations it might impose?

'I had thought that the adventure you shared had lifted his spirits. When he came in that morning when he brought you, I glimpsed the Nicholas I remembered from his youth.'

'It was exciting, even while it was frightening and uncomfortable,' Sarah admitted. 'It would certainly be a change from the everyday life and duties of a duke.' They fell silent and Sarah found herself thinking back to that uncomfortable breakfast. With the sensation of someone probing an aching tooth with her tongue-tip, she said, 'I have met Lady Farne. At Lord Sutton's house. I thought then that there was some…tension between her and your brother.'

'Sadly, yes. I wish I could get to the bottom of it. But, that aside, I am wondering what I can do to bring some joy to Nicholas. I can hardly provide him with pirates and maidens in distress to enliven his days as a regular diversion, now can I?' She pulled a comical face.

'He did speak of looking for a bride in the coming Season,' Sarah said. If he had spoken so freely of it to her, it could hardly be something he intended to keep secret from his sister.

'He did? To *you*?' Anna seemed taken aback.

'You think it something he would not have confided to a stranger? We had spent a great deal of time in each other's company by then,' Sarah said defensively.

'No, no. You misunderstand. That is not what I meant. Oh, dear, men can be such—'

'His Grace has called, my lady.' The butler stood in the doorway. 'I ventured to say that I believed you to be At Home.'

'Oh, yes. Please show him in, Handley.'

Anna jumped up to kiss and be kissed while Handley asked whether he should bring the sherry—or perhaps His Grace would prefer the Madeira?—then Anna insisted that Nicholas sit on the sofa next to Sarah: 'So I can look at you, such a stranger that you are!'

Sarah moved a little along the sofa to make room and so that she could turn and look at Nicholas's face. He was smiling at his sister's teasing, but she thought he seemed serious beneath that and he was a little pale.

A sense of dread crept over her. There had been no message from him about the progress of her affairs for a few days and now, here he was, looking decidedly serious. Bad news, then.

She straightened her back, put up her chin and made herself breathe. She had the reward money. She had a friend in Anna, who would surely give her a reference. If she had to seek another position, then so be it. Surely she could find a superior one when she had the recommendation of a countess?

'Sarah?' Anna was looking at her oddly.

'Oh, I am so sorry. I was wool-gathering.'

'Nicholas was asking if you would care to go for a drive in the park. It is such a lovely day.'

He was going to break the news that her claims had failed and, man-like, was going to do it where she would not break down and weep, or upbraid him for letting her think success was a possibility, she thought grimly.

'How thoughtful.' She stood up, smile firmly fixed. 'I will go and find my bonnet: I will not be long.'

Nicholas was driving a curricle, a simple one without the high perch, and the pair harnessed to it were handsome, but not the showy greys who had enlivened their previous expeditions to the park. His tiger was not perched up behind, either, so he was not intending to walk once they arrived at the park, it seemed.

Sarah had expected they would go to Hyde Park, as usual, but Nicholas turned his horses down Park Lane, then into Piccadilly and, finally, into Green Park.

His usual flow of casual conversation appeared

to have deserted him and Sarah found that everything she thought of to say sounded artificial and strained, so she contented herself with keeping her parasol out of his way, looking at the passing scene and trying not to think too much about the fact that she was alone with him.

It was not until they had entered the park and the bays were trotting placidly southward along one of the grass drives that she glanced sideways as Nicholas's profile and saw how serious he looked, how set his jaw was.

Yes. He has come to tell me the case has failed, that I cannot get our ships back, that the money has all gone.

Her stomach swooped sickeningly and she tightened her hold on the side rail until her glove leather creaked.

I will be quite calm about it. I will not make a fuss and let Nicholas think he has somehow failed.

With an effort she relaxed her grip on the rail and schooled her expression into bland passivity. Whatever happened she was better off now, with the reward money and a friend in the Countess, than she had been before.

This is not a disaster.

Sarah was so concentrated on her thoughts

that it took her a moment or two to realise that Nicholas had reined in the bays in the shade of a group of young oak trees. He looped the reins around the whip handle and the horses stood obediently, not stirring when he shifted in his seat to face her.

'Sarah, there is something I must say to you.'

'It is quite all right. I guessed, just now, and I am braced for the worst.'

'For the worst?' He seemed taken aback. Then he took off his hat, stripped off his gloves, put them on the boards at his feet and ran both hands through his hair, a quite uncharacteristic gesture of—what? Frustration?

'It is bad news about the court case, is it not? You have come to tell me that my claims have failed or that the assets cannot be traced.' How very strange to be the one who was composed...

'No. That is not what I want to say. As far as I am aware everything is proceeding smoothly. There is nothing to worry about.'

'Oh. Then Wilton has escaped?'

'No!' His balled fist hit his knee and one of the horses tossed its head. 'Nothing bad has happened, Sarah. I do not anticipate anything bad occurring. It seems I am doomed to utter incompetence at this.'

'At what?' she demanded, rapidly becoming as frustrated as he appeared to be.

'At proposing marriage to you.'

'Oh.' With her lungs apparently empty of air there was nothing else she could say.

'Yes. Oh,' he said ruefully. 'Sarah, I made a mess of it last time. I did not understand my own mind, my own feelings, and as a result I insulted and hurt you. I was clumsy because what I thought I ought to feel was at odds with what I now realise I felt for you. I see now that I love you, that I would be honoured and humbled if you will consent to be my wife.'

Nick looked down at his own hands, knotted together because the urge to pull Sarah into his arms was so strong. He stared at them because he did not have the courage to look at her face as the silence stretched out.

'If you could forgive me. If you could love me,' he added.

From across the greensward he could hear the laughter and excited shrieks of children playing by the reservoir with their nursemaids, the chatter of jackdaws in the trees above them, the faint jingling of the harness as the pair shifted slightly in their traces, Sarah's breathing, uneven despite her stillness.

'When did you realise you…loved me?' she asked.

'When I suggested that you went to stay with Anna. I could have found you respectable lodgings very easily,' he confessed. 'I have a very efficient secretary. I caught myself wondering why Anna, and I realised it was because then I could call on you whenever I wanted and it would cause no comment. I could see you every day and perhaps you would come to see me as more than an arrogant duke with a limp and a short temper who was unable to make a civil proposal of marriage.'

'I see,' she murmured. 'I had wondered that you called so often when what you had to say could have been sent in a short note. I was grateful that you set my mind at ease personally.'

'Only grateful?' He found the strength to look at her.

Sarah looked back at him through wide, sherry-coloured eyes, her expression serious. 'Your leg is neither here nor there so far as my feelings are concerned, although I hope it does not pain you too much. Your temper appears to me to be no worse than mine.'

'My being a duke is therefore the handicap? Your pride and your sense of what is fitting keep telling you that the match is an impossibility.'

'If I loved you I would not care whether you were your butler or a royal duke—although I suppose the Royal Marriage Act might be a complication in the latter case.'

'Are you *laughing* at me?' Nick demanded, suddenly aware of a sparkle in Sarah's eyes that had not been there before.

Hell. The first time I am insulting. Now, apparently, I am laughable. Only this time I understand just what this pain in my heart is.

Chapter Twenty-One

Sarah snapped her parasol shut with some force, dropped it at her feet where it made a dent in his hat and seized his hands. 'Laughing at you? No, never that. At myself, perhaps. Nicholas, I have been in love with you for weeks. For ever, it seems.'

His hands unclenched slowly and he turned them so he could cup hers between them. The little movement that she made clutched at his heart. The pulse in her wrist beat against his, a secret, silent communication.

'You love me?' It was as though another man said those words, they seemed so impossible. 'You loved me when I proposed on board the *Gannet*?'

Sarah nodded. 'I do not think I would have been so angry with you, certainly not as hurt, if I had not loved you. Do you remember driving to Boston and discussing the draining of the Fens? That was when I realised that I loved you.'

'Drainage?'

'I think the very banality of it gave me the room in my thoughts to examine my feelings.' She wrinkled her nose in a comical grimace. 'I would much rather have discovered no such thing. Loving a duke seemed an impossible dream.'

'Loving anyone was not even a dream,' Nick heard himself say. 'If you had asked me I would have said that I do not believe in ghosts or unicorns or love.'

Sarah's smile deepened and she began to untie the ribbons of her bonnet. Then she took it off and set it, very deliberately, at her feet, straightened and looked at him. 'I was exceedingly shocked to discover how much I enjoyed kissing you, even before I realised that I loved you.'

'I had been wanting to taste your lips almost from the moment I saw you,' he admitted, leaning forward.

She swayed towards him and he released her hands, catching her in his arms as their lips met. The taste of her was so familiar, so dear and so deeply arousing that he groaned, pulled her closer, tighter. His entire body ached for her and yet he could have kissed her, just kissed her, like this, for ever. Her body was both yielding and demanding against him; her hands touching his nape, spearing into his hair, were soft, yet left trails of fire in their wake.

He wanted those hands on him, on his bare flesh. He wanted to look down on her, see her naked beneath him arching into his urgency, her—

The thud of hooves behind him and a loud female voice jerked him out of his erotic fantasy. 'Disgraceful! Stevens, go immediately and fetch a park keeper!'

Sarah jerked in his arms.

'Don't look back,' Nick said, unravelling the reins. 'Can you catch hold of our hats?' He sent the pair into a brisk trot away from the outraged rider behind them as Sarah managed to snatch up her bonnet and his tall hat.

She looked over her shoulder. 'She isn't following us.'

'Even so, I think I will drive around to Constitution Hill, put up the hood and mingle with the traffic. I have no intention of being denounced by the Dowager Marchioness of Warnham in the middle of Piccadilly.'

'Is that who it was?'

'Unmistakably. She is a leading member of the Society for the Suppression of Vice. I have no doubt we would have been horsewhipped if she had her way. Sarah, this was not how I had hoped my proposal to you would go. I had planned a dignified, sincere and restrained declaration in the tranquillity of the park, instead I virtually ravish you in public, in considerable discomfort, and then expose you to Lady Warnham at her worst.'

'I did not find it at all uncomfortable,' Sarah said demurely, fiddling with her bonnet ribbons. 'I enjoyed it excessively.' She tucked her hand under his left elbow and pressed close, making him want to preen like a peacock. 'Is it true? I am not dreaming, am I?'

'If you are, then we both share the same dream.' He brought the horses to a halt and handed her the reins while he put up the hood. 'There. Hopefully we will pass unnoticed if we encounter her. I have to confess that murderous pirates are one thing, the Dowager Lady Warnham is quite another. I am still trembling.'

'So am I,' Sarah murmured, her hand moving slightly against his ribs in a way that set his heart thudding. 'I thought it was desire.'

'Ah, Sarah.' A crossing sweeper darted out

and he forced his attention back on his horses and the crowded street. This was no place to be making love.

Sarah bent to retrieve her parasol, which she was unable to open now, and sat demurely beside him as he negotiated the streets leading north from Piccadilly.

She loves me. I love her.

It was a miracle. He had thought he would never love again. Had not wanted to love, if the truth be told, because he could not trust it. Marietta had said that she adored him, worshipped him, could not live without him, and he had believed her, only to be betrayed when he most needed her.

Cold talons of doubt gripped his gut for a second, then he told himself that if Sarah was as mercenary, as calculating, as Marietta, then she would have accepted his first proposal, however insulting it had been. She would have become the duchess his sister-in-law had yearned to be. That refusal, even though she loved him, was all the proof he needed that Sarah was true to him.

You should not require proof, he thought as they turned into Mount Street. *You love her, you should trust her implicitly. She is Sarah, not another woman.*

'You look very serious,' Sarah said, smiling at him as they drew to a halt.

'I feel it. I am about to introduce the woman who is to be my wife to my sister and I will have not a moment's peace from then until I put the ring on your finger. Ah, they have seen us.'

A footman was running down the steps to take the reins. 'Your tiger is in the kitchen, Your Grace. He has been sent for.'

The man came up the area steps as the footman spoke. 'Your Grace.'

'Take them home, John. I will walk.'

Nick handed Sarah down and followed her up the steps into the house.

Trust. From this moment I must never let that waver or I will be visiting Marietta's sins on Sarah's innocent head.

Despite Anna's friendship, despite her protestations that Sarah was like a sister to her, Sarah could feel the apprehension running through her happiness like a dark thread. She could hardly believe it herself—how could anyone else take this match seriously, let alone the loving sister of the man who had asked her to marry him?

But he loves me. Nicholas loves me. I must just hold on to that and nothing can hurt me. I love him, I believe in him and I trust him. We will be happy.

Anna was reading when they entered the drawing room. She looked up, smiled at them and then her mouth opened, just a fraction, and the sheets of writing paper in her hands fluttered unheeded to the carpet. 'What is it?' she asked. 'You both look so…'

'Sarah has done me the very great honour of agreeing to be my wife,' Nicholas said with some formality and was promptly knocked backwards into the door—fortunately just closed by the footman—as Anna hurled herself into his arms.

'Darlings!' She freed herself from Nicholas and hugged Sarah. 'Oh, I am so happy for you. I knew he was in love with you when he brought you here.'

'How?' Nicholas demanded, extracting Sarah from Anna's embrace and leading her to the sofa where he sat beside her, her hand in his.

'I am your sister. Of course I can tell.' Anna sat down in the chair opposite and beamed at Sarah. 'Usually young women gaze adoringly at Nicholas, because he is quite handsome— not that I'd tell him so, you understand—but you were so carefully not gazing, or adoring or even very impressed, it seemed. Not beyond expressing gratitude for the help he was giving you. So, naturally, I guessed you were in love with him too.'

'Does that make any sense to you, Sarah?' Nicholas asked her.

'Oh, yes, perfect sense.' She rested her cheek against his shoulder, marvelling that she could do that. 'But what about the rest of your family? Will they approve of me? I can hardly hope so.'

'Either they live in London or they are about to descend on it.' Anna gestured towards the scattered letters she had been reading when they had entered. 'Our sister Julia has decided to go to Brighton and writes that she has not a thing to wear and will arrive tomorrow for a week of intensive shopping. Apparently she has already written to her favourite *modiste* so she will have an orgy of fittings beside anything else. And Wellingfield and the children will be with her, so you can meet them.

'We are not a large family and most of our cousins and aunts and uncles and connections live nearby except our uncle Lord Horace Terrell, who is rooted in the country near Severton, the better to disapprove of every improvement Nicholas makes to the estates. He is one of the old guard, you know.' She pulled a comical face.

'Oh, dear. I expect he will not approve of me, then.'

'Uncle Horace would not approve of any wife Nicholas chose, so you must not take him personally.'

That was hardly reassuring, but the news that the family was not vast and the hope that Lady Wellingfield would be as kind as her sister Anna was some encouragement.

'Now, you will be married from here,' Anna announced. 'Unless you intend to marry in the chapel at Severton, Nicholas?'

'Severton,' he said firmly. 'Sarah has few relatives—'

'None,' she corrected.

'The chapel at Severton is small and can hold all our immediate family and close friends. I believe you will find it more comfortable than a large society wedding at the town house, or in a church. But you may prefer otherwise.'

'Whatever you think is best.' She had never expected to marry, not once they had been ruined, so she'd cherished no daydreams of an ideal wedding day. 'A small family chapel sounds very…comfortable.'

'Severton, then,' Anna said. 'Now, who to give you away?'

'There isn't anyone. I suppose I could give myself away. Or, would Lord Horace do it, do you think?'

'Now that is inspired,' Nicholas said warmly. 'He is very punctilious about me being Head of the Family—capital letters, of course—but he is also very much on his dignity as being the senior male representative. I will tell him it was all your idea, of course, and he cannot possibly disapprove after that.'

He and Anna settled down to planning. Anna started to make lists and they showered Sarah with questions, most of which she had no idea about.

After an hour she said, 'Frankly, I do not care whether we do it on a punt in the middle of the Fens wearing nothing but sackcloth, just so long as I can marry Nicholas.'

'You truly are the ideal woman,' he said, lifting her hand to his lips.

When they came to themselves five minutes later, Anna had crept from the room.

'Or she may have left with as much noise as a troop of cavalry,' Sarah said ruefully as she attempted to tidy her hair. 'How could we! Honestly.'

'If I cannot kiss my betrothed and rely upon

my sister to tactfully remove herself, it is a poor state of affairs,' Nicholas said. He stood up, much to her disappointment, and went to straighten his neck cloth in the mirror over the fireplace.

'I am still having trouble believing this is real,' Sarah confessed, admiring the view of his broad shoulders and narrow waist, the way his coat sat on his athletic frame. She wondered, not for the first time, how it would be to be with this man, naked.

'I would have thought that my sister armed with her interminable lists would have convinced you of the reality,' he said, turning with a smile that made her insides perform not unpleasant acrobatics.

'Have you ever been in love before?' Sarah asked. Surely he had, but she was determined not to be jealous. After all, if he had been, he would be married by now because nobody refused a duke, surely?

Except me, of course, or someone who was in love with another man, she thought, suddenly uneasy.

He leant one elbow on the mantelshelf, one booted foot on the fender and stared down at it. 'I have never loved,' he said abruptly. 'I did not have much belief in the emotion until I realised what I felt for you, to be honest. It seemed to me too sentimental, self-indulgent. A delusion.'

'I suppose, in your position, you must experience people claiming feelings for you that are motivated only by your title,' she ventured, starting to think it through aloud and not expecting more than a nod of agreement.

'Hell, yes,' Nicholas said violently. He pushed away from the fireplace and took one stride towards the door before he stopped. 'I apologise for my language. You touched a nerve, I'm afraid. Not something I should discuss. There are always people who want to grab at advantage and it is better not to think of them.'

'Of course,' Sarah agreed, smiling to cover her sudden apprehension. It sounded almost as though Nicholas had suffered some hurt, some disillusionment. But then, she reassured herself, he said he had never loved. Perhaps someone he had begun to admire betrayed her mercenary motives. Yes, that must have been what he meant.

'I must go. There is a great deal to do, because I am not willing to wait long for you, Sarah. Is a month enough?'

'About three weeks too long,' she admitted and surprised a laugh from him.

'I will leave you to Anna's tender mercies to plan your trousseau. I suggest you ask her lawyer to look after your interests and to meet with mine to discuss settlements. I will set my secretary on to the business of invitations and so forth—you will let me know who you wish to invite. We will accommodate them at Severton, of course.'

He broke off and shook his head at her. 'Do not look so bemused, my darling. After fighting off kidnappers and embezzlers a wedding should hold no terrors for you. Should I come over there and kiss the worry from your face?'

'No, because you know perfectly well what will happen if you do,' she said roundly. 'But, Nicholas... I will be a *duchess*.'

He grinned and was gone.

A month proved to be far too long and yet nowhere near long enough for everything that it seemed must be decided and done for a ducal wedding to take place.

Anna produced Mr Trentham, a small, fierce lawyer who reminded Sarah of a cross owl and who threw himself into protecting her interests with enthusiasm. She had tired of protesting that Nicholas was to be her husband, not her opponent, but he tut-tutted at her.

'A sound settlement prevents many future problems,' he insisted. 'Now, the question of children—'

She had argued with Anna about what her future sister-in-law thought essential for a trousseau as the reward money seemed to evaporate with one bill after another.

'Fiddlesticks. Give the bills to me. Nicholas will settle them.'

Sarah wanted to protest but, as Anna pointed out, she must dress according to her new status and Nicholas knew perfectly well that she did not have the resources to do so.

Then there were the jewels. Nicholas took her to his town house and, while she was still telling herself that she would, somehow, learn to be mistress of such elegance, dazzled her with an array of gems.

'These are all entailed, of course,' he said, sitting across the table laden with gemstones. 'Yours to wear until the next duke marries. But I will buy you your own, of course. Starting with this.'

And he had come around the table and knelt at

her feet to slip a great yellow stone on her finger. 'A yellow diamond. I thought it would be right with your sherry-brown eyes and it is.'

Their passionate embrace had ended up in a tangle on the table, until a tiara had dug into Sarah's ribs and she had sat up with a faint shriek, convinced they had squashed the priceless objects.

And so the time passed in a whirl of unreality and happiness until the day dawned when she followed Anna down the steps and into the carriage that would take them and their maids into Gloucestershire and to Severton Hall, a few miles beyond Gloucester. All Sarah's luggage except her overnight valise had gone ahead, the elaborate trousseau packed into trunks between endless sheets of tissue paper.

'We will stop overnight in Oxford,' Anna said, although they had already discussed the journey in detail. 'And then it will be another six hours to Severton. You will love it, I know.'

'I am sure I will,' Sarah assured her. In truth she was not concerned about her future home, she just wanted to see Nicholas again. He had gone on ahead the week before and for the hundredth time she had gone over their parting, trying to understand why it had left her feeling so uneasy.

'I hate leaving you,' he had murmured as they stood entwined, reluctant to break apart. 'My golden-brown darling.' He was playing with a lock of her hair that had come loose.

'Don't you prefer blondes?' she had asked, half teasing, half remembering something someone had said.

Nicholas had gone very still, his eyes cold. 'I do not think about blondes,' he said. And then the moment passed.

Now, as the carriage rattled over the cobbles in Shepherd's Bush leaving Kensington behind and heading for Ealing, she remembered.

...*dear Nicholas always chooses the prettiest of the highflyers for his* chère amies. *And always blondes.*

That had been Lady Farne and she had caressed her own golden curls as she had said it.

Chapter Twenty-Two

July 15th, Severton Hall, Gloucestershire

Someone must have been watching for them, because long before they arrived at the carriage sweep in front of the house Sarah saw Nicholas standing on the steps. She was breathless with seeing him again, watching as they drew closer and closer. And then he vanished from sight as the drive straightened.

Then she looked properly at the house and gasped. Soft golden stone sprawled in a way that made it clear that this had been a home for centuries and its inhabitants had simply added what they felt like, how they fancied. No rigorous Classical order here, she saw with relief.

'It is so large!'

'But very homely. You will soon feel comfortable here,' Anna assured her.

And then they reached the steps and there was

Nicholas and she could breathe again. He handed her out before the footman could reach the carriage door and, as she stood searching his face, she saw nothing but tenderness and love and happiness that she was there. Finally she could let go of the irrational anxieties that had been building like black clouds at the margins of her thoughts.

'Welcome to Severton,' he said. 'Welcome to your new home.'

Relief and travel weariness swept through her and she could only smile at him and cling to his hand as he turned to take her inside. There was an elderly butler who bowed and bade her welcome in a very avuncular manner. There were footmen smiling and an angular but cheerful-looking woman advancing down the length of the stone-flagged hallway to greet her, the bunch of keys at her waist marking her as the housekeeper.

'This is Mrs Patterson and Wolsey.'

The housekeeper curtseyed. 'Welcome, Miss Parrish.' She had a soft Scottish accent.

The butler bowed. 'Madam.' Anna must have entered behind them because he added, 'My lady.'

'Mrs Patterson will show you to your room,'

Nicholas said. 'Then when you are ready, there will be tea in the Chinese Drawing Room and you can meet the family.' He bent and whispered, 'They are nowhere near as frightening as a shipload of pirates.'

Taking courage, she released her grip on his hand and followed the housekeeper up to the next floor, trying to keep a sense of direction. They were going towards the back of the house, she thought.

'The duchess's suite, Miss Parrish.'

Sarah hesitated on the threshold. Perhaps Mrs Patterson was simply showing it to her. But no, there was Millie and another maid waiting for her.

'This is Hedges. She will assist your woman until she knows her way around.' The Scotswoman smiled. 'It can take a wee while. There will be a footman on the landing to show you the way down when you are ready, Miss Parrish. Is there anything else I can do for you just now?'

Sarah smiled at Millie and to the other maid, who was bobbing a curtsey. 'I think I will wash my face and hands and tidy my hair before I go down,' she said, trying to sound confident.

'The dressing room is through here, Miss Parrish, just off your bedchamber.'

The bedchamber was vast, but pretty in pale pinks and green with a delicate floral wallpaper and graceful furniture. The dressing room led to a bathroom with not only a large copper bath but, behind a screen, a water closet.

Trying to appear unconcerned at such luxury Sarah washed, let Millie tidy her hair and went out, resisting the temptation to hide up here and explore the sitting room with its comfortable-looking chairs and its bookcase and elegant writing desk.

A footman took her down, guided her to a pair of double doors at the front of the house and opened them.

'Miss Parrish, my lady.'

The room seemed full of people, but one, a matronly brunette, stood up and advanced, hand held out. From her resemblance to Anna, this would be Nicholas's other sister, Lady Wellingfield, who must be acting as Nicholas's hostess.

'My dear Miss Parrish. Welcome to Severton. My sister tells me that you had a smooth journey.'

'Very pleasant, Lady Wellingfield, and such beautiful countryside. This part of the country is all new to me.' Sarah shook hands, resisted the temptation to curtsey deeply and offered a silent *thank you* to Anna for insisting that she wore one of her new carriage dresses. At least she looked the part, even though she felt out of her depth.

Nicholas stepped forward and he and Lady Wellingfield began to introduce her around the room. 'My husband, Wellingfield. My son, Arthur, and my daughter, Catherine. Our uncle, Lord Horace Terrell.'

The older man stared at her from under beetling pepper-and-salt eyebrows and made a sound that might, she hoped, be approval. 'I'm to give you away, eh? What? Delighted, delighted.'

There were cousins and their offspring—she did not even try to commit them all to memory—and, finally, blonde, beautiful and exquisitely groomed, someone she recognised.

'Lady Farne.'

'You have met?' Lady Wellingfield said, sounding surprised.

'In passing,' Sarah said coolly.

'And this is Lord Gregory Huntington, my sister-in-law's betrothed.'

A tall, thin man in his mid-forties bowed over Sarah's hand. Beside her Nicholas made a soft sound, as though he had bitten back an exclamation.

'Suppose I should have consulted you, Severton,' Lord Gregory said. 'Head of the family and all that. But I only popped the question yesterday.'

'My congratulations, Huntington,' Nicholas said and shook his hand. 'And, Marietta, may I wish you all the happiness you deserve?'

The smile on Lady Farne's mouth froze. 'And I must wish you the same, Nicholas. You are to be congratulated, Miss Parrish.'

From the expression on Lady Wellingfield's face Sarah knew she was not imagining that she had just been insulted. Nobody congratulated the bride—that implied that she had made a calculating choice for gain.

'Thank you,' she said with great warmth and a smile.

There, that confounded you, didn't it? she thought as her hostess guided her to a chair next to her.

Nicholas sat on her other side. The ordeal by tea party was about to begin.

To Sarah's surprise it was not as difficult as she had feared. Everyone, with the exception of Lady Farne, was talkative, cheerful and friendly and she began to relax. Nobody appeared to find Nicholas's choice scandalous, nobody treated her as though she was beneath them. It might have been because they feared Nicholas's wrath, but she sensed it was genuine. They wanted him to be happy and they were prepared to like her.

Nicholas looked around at his extended family and released the breath he had not realised he had been holding. Sarah was magnificent. She was poised, friendly, absolutely correct in her manner and she looked beautiful. Yes, if one looked carefully one could see that she was nervous, but that would do her no harm in the eyes of his relatives and Uncle Horace was positively beaming.

The only unhappy person was Marietta and she was normally so brittle that nobody appeared to have noticed anything different. He hoped her forthcoming marriage would make her happy, because, despite everything, he could not wish her ill.

Sometimes, when he caught her looking at him, he wondered whether she was regretting not only missing her opportunity to be a duchess, but also her loss of him, for himself. Had she loved him and not realised it? Or was that just his self-esteem talking?

He told himself not to be seduced by the wish

that all her expressions of love had not been false, that she had been tempted and had succumbed to the lure of a great title rather than marriage to a man who she thought might be a helpless invalid. But whatever her feelings, they had not been strong enough. She had betrayed him, wounded him, when he was at his weakest and destroyed his faith in love. It had almost lost him Sarah, as well.

Whatever Marietta's feelings for him, she had secured herself an excellent marriage. Lord Gregory was the second son of a marquess and the possessor of a very significant fortune after generous bequests from two godfathers. His wife could fly as high as she pleased as a society hostess and would never have to count the cost.

That might sweeten her temper, he thought, catching her watching Sarah. The animosity made him uneasy.

Sarah went to her bedchamber that evening dizzy with wine, social strain and happiness. She liked Nicholas's family and they seemed to like her, or at least to be able to welcome her with complacency.

The household was not the rigidly grand and formal one that she had feared and she thought she had weathered all the social pitfalls safely. The servants appeared to approve of her and they, she knew, would be potentially her harshest critics.

'Well, Millie?' she asked as she sank down on the dressing table stool and removed, with great care, the pearl-and-diamond earrings that matched the necklace and brooch that Mrs Patterson had delivered before dinner with a note from Nicholas.

Millie tells me you will be wearing spring green this evening. I think these will complement it.

'Very well, Miss Sarah,' Millie said. 'I've a room twice the size of the one at Lady Grassington's even and it has a little sitting room and a dressing room. And when we sat down to dinner, they put me right at the top by Mr Wolsey and said I might as well go on as I would when you are married, miss. I don't rightly know if I'm on my head or my heels, I don't really. If my ma could see me now!'

She took the jewellery, placed it in its fitted case, then began to help Sarah undress. When she was in her nightgown and robe and in front of the mirror again, Millie began to unpin and let down her hair.

'And I saw Charlie in the kitchen. He'd brought in some vegetables for Cook and he looks grand, miss. Real roses in his cheeks and a big grin on his face and his hair cut and he's got a suit of working clothes like a proper little gardener and lovely boots too. Oh, miss, we're going to be so happy here.'

'I think so, Millie.' Sarah reached up and squeezed her hand.

I hope so.

She had been longing for her bed, but now she was in it, tucked up, comfortable, drowsily looking at the details of her lovely room in the lamplight, she found she could not sleep. Where was Nicholas? What was he thinking? Was he happy? Was he thinking of her?

She sat up, suddenly fully awake at the sound of a light tapping on wood. A door that she had hardly noticed in the far corner opened and there, silhouetted against candlelight, was Nicholas.

Of course, if this is the duchess's suite, then there will be a connecting door.

Her heart was doing most uncomfortable things and a hot, fluttery feeling had taken possession of her insides.

'You are awake,' Nicholas said and came in. 'Are you comfortable?'

No, she was not. He had been showing the most gentlemanly restraint in his lovemaking—disappointingly so, if she was honest—and Sarah had told herself firmly that she should be glad of it and wait for her wedding night. But now...

'Yes, thank you,' she said as demurely as she could. 'This is such a lovely room and I have everything I could want.'

Except you in this bed beside me.

'May I kiss you goodnight?' Nicholas came further into the room and, as the light from her own candles fell across him, she saw he was wearing a robe of crimson that glowed with the sheen of raw silk. His feet were bare and she could see a vee of skin at the neck. He looked male, slightly dangerous, utterly desirable.

'Please.' It came out as a breathless gasp, not the composed, sophisticated way she imagined a duchess should speak.

Nicholas stopped and she wondered whether she had sounded too eager.

'I have been trying, very hard, to behave as a gentleman should,' he said. There was a half-smile on his lips and a rueful note in the deep voice. 'When I think about you I ache to be with you. When I am with you, I want to touch you, to kiss you. And when I have you in my arms I do not want to stop at kisses. It occurs to me now that perhaps you have been thinking that whatever restraint I have been able to exert means that I do not desire you.'

'But you do?'

'Oh, yes.'

'Then I would rather you were not quite so gentlemanly, although that may result in me becoming very much less ladylike.'

'In two days we will be married. Some romantic fancy has me imagining carrying you across the threshold of this room on our wedding night and seeing you in all your beauty then.' The half-smile became a sensual curve of his lips that fixed her gaze and refused to let her look away. 'I think my self-restraint is sufficient to risk a kiss now,' those lips said, and she imagined them moving over her skin, from her mouth to her breast to…everywhere that tingled and throbbed and yearned for him.

'Yes,' Sarah murmured, and Nicholas knelt by the bedside, took her in his arms and kissed her, his mouth hot on hers as her lips parted and his tongue found hers in a sensual slide, a tantalising promise.

She curled her arms around his shoulders, pulling him down to her, needing to feel his strength, the weight of his body. Needing all of him.

He broke the kiss and she murmured a protest, then his lips were moving across her cheek, to her temple, into her hair, nuzzling against her ear, making her squirm, half laughing, half panting. Then down the tendons of her neck, licking now, nipping, and then he was still, poised above the opening of her modest nightgown, his breath warm and urgent on the swell of her breasts, on her cleavage just revealed above the ribbon ties.

Instinctively Sarah pushed aside the bedclothes, arching up to him, and he found her right nipple, licking and nipping through the thin cotton until he could tease the cresting peak with his lips and teeth before moving to the other, back and forth until she was panting out meaningless words, her hands clasped on his head, fingers locked into the thick hair.

And then he released her, pushed away from the bed and on to his feet.

Sarah heard the rasp of his breath, forced open heavy lids and saw him standing a few feet away, too far to touch, his back to her.

'That,' Nicholas said, his voice unsteady, 'was a near-run thing. I think, my love, that I best return to my bedchamber and leave you to your maidenly dreams.'

She was still quivering with reaction, but Sarah found that she was smiling. 'I think they will be most unruly and unbefitting to a respectable maiden,' she confessed.

'I dare not turn around, dare not look at you now, or my self-control will give up entirely, but may I say I am glad to hear it?'

'I love you,' she said, still smiling.

He was at the door, his hand on the panel. 'And I you.'

Sarah sat looking at the closed door, imagining Nicholas on the other side, shedding that gorgeous robe. He wore nothing beneath it, she was certain.

At last, with an effort of will, she reached out and snuffed the candles, lay down and tried to sleep.

The next day was too full of activity to brood on Nicholas's kisses. She had nothing to do, Anna and he assured her, everything was being taken care of, but various people had been delegated to show her around what would be her new home.

First there was Mrs Patterson. The housekeeper gave her a rapid tour of the family's side of the house. 'His Grace will show you everything in detail, of course. This is just so you do not become lost,' she explained. After five minutes Sarah was convinced that only a map and compass would help with that.

Then they went through the green baize door and into the servants' domain. Maids curtseyed, footmen bowed, Cook beamed from the midst of her bustling kitchen, a scene of organised chaos with all the wedding food preparations under way. Sarah's head spun with the onslaught of names and faces and the endless green-painted corridors.

After tea in the housekeeper's room she was handed over to the head gardener to be further confused and disorientated by parterres, a sunken rose garden, a pond garden, a wilderness, the vegetable gardens and forcing houses—and a glimpse of Charlie, weeding. He waved enthusiastically.

There was even a maze with, she was informed, a small temple at its centre.

'And now, Miss Parrish, I can show you the park,' the head gardener said.

'That would be delightful, but I am rather tired, Mr Gresham. There is so much to take in. I think I will just sit here in the shade by the entrance to the maze and admire the prospect across the pond of the house. Thank you so much for the tour,' she added firmly.

Fortunately he took the hint and went off, leaving Sarah to peace, disturbed only by the realisation of what she was committing herself to. Or she had thought she would be undisturbed until a flash of colour, the sound of women's voices, broke the stillness. Her immediate instinct was to retreat into the maze, then she thought she might be seen and that would offend whoever was approaching, so she stayed where she was.

Two of the cousins, whose names she could not recall, were strolling with Lady Farne, she realised as they stopped on the far side of the formal pond. She sat very still, hoping that the spray of the fountain hid her. The two cousins said something and turned away towards the house leaving Nicholas's sister-in-law on the far side of the pond.

It was pure instinct, but Sarah slid from the end of the bench and whisked into the entrance to the maze and down the first yew-lined turning she came to.

She stopped, a little out of breath and several turnings later, and told herself not to be a ninny. She did not like Lady Farne and the other woman did not like her, but there was no reason why they couldn't simply remain politely aloof. She had just decided it was time to retrace her steps before she lost herself when she heard the brush of skirts against the foliage and the sound of footfalls on the hard, dry ground.

With a panicked sense of being hunted, Sarah turned and fled deeper into the maze.

Chapter Twenty-Three

Sarah twisted and turned between the high yew hedges, forcing herself not to break into a run. She could see no logic in the layout of the maze, and it was complete chance that she found herself stepping out into a little clearing with a miniature temple at the centre of it.

There was only one entrance to the clearing, she realised, so she faced the choice of waiting there or plunging back into the maze. Really, the most dignified thing to do was to sit on the stone bench behind the little row of columns and pretend this is what she intended all along.

It took only a few minutes for Marietta Terrell to stroll into the centre of the maze. She looked cool, calm and perfectly turned out. Sarah was convinced that her own cheeks were scarlet, her nose was shiny and there were bits of yew hedge in her hair.

Behave like a duchess, she reminded herself. *Nicholas doesn't care what anyone thinks.*

'Do you know the key to the maze?' she asked brightly before the other woman could speak. 'I confess I just wandered around until I found myself here. What a charming spot on a hot day.'

'Oh, I have known it for ever,' Marietta said. She sat on the edge of a bench facing Sarah. 'My family are neighbours, you know.' She paused, her smile sad now. 'It might have been my home for ever.'

'Of course. Such a tragedy, the loss of your husband so young.'

'I mean that I so nearly married Nicholas. That accident was the tragedy.'

'You—you almost married *Nicholas*?'

'Oh, yes.' Marietta gazed down at her clasped hands. 'That is why he was coming here, you see. To tell the family about our love, our plans to marry.'

'So why didn't you?' Sarah demanded and could have bitten her tongue for the urgency of the question.

'We thought he was going to die, he was so ill. It was not important to tell the family of our plans, not then. Frederick was beside himself with grief and anxiety. I knew he had…

admired me, but I had not understood the depth of his feelings. I allowed myself to comfort him, to hold him in my arms. It was a terrible mistake. In his confused state his ardour overcame him...' Her voice trailed off.

'Are you saying that he raped you?' Sarah demanded.

'He... No, there was no force. The comfort we gave each other in our grief overwhelmed us. When we came to ourselves and realised what we had done, Frederick said that in honour he must wed me.'

'Neither of you thought to discuss this with Nicholas, I suppose? You didn't think to tell Frederick that you were in love with his brother?'

I feel sick, but I will not let her see what she is doing to me.

'We thought he was dying. And when he was no longer in danger he told me that he would be lame, that he could not ask me to marry him. He loved me so much you see. And so I married Frederick. But Nicholas, alas, has never forgotten, never loved another. He loves me still.'

'Until now,' Sarah said crisply. Was it possible for a heart to break? She had always thought it a poetic fancy, now she felt real pain when she breathed, but she was going to fight.

'Oh, my dear Miss Parrish. He compromised you, did he not? All those frightful adventures at sea. He is a gentleman, of course he offered for you. And he desires you, I am sure. You are pretty enough and, I have no doubt, willing too.'

'You—' Sarah closed her lips tight on the word. Oh, yes, she had been willing. 'Why, exactly, are you telling me all this?'

'So you understand him. So you will not hurt him further by speaking of me or by reproaching him if he does not show you the devotion you no doubt feel you deserve. He will always be the gentleman, my Nicholas. He will try and hide it from you. But it is me that he loves and always will.'

'You do not think that your affianced husband might be somewhat disturbed by the revelation that you love Nicholas?'

'Oh, but no longer. My goodness, of course not!' Her trill of laughter was mocking. 'As a brother, of course, but all that died a long time ago. Frederick was so very like him, after all. Only he was a man and not an idealistic youth.'

'I expect I must thank you for your frankness,' Sarah said. How she was keeping the smile on her stiff lips she had no idea.

The other woman got up. 'I will leave you to

regain your countenance. You are sadly flushed, my dear.' She strolled out of the clearing. 'I do hope you can find your way out,' she called back. And laughed.

Sarah sat and concentrated on breathing until she could get her emotions under some kind of control.

The disloyal, miserable... He almost died. He thought he would be lame for life... An idealistic youth. Then, *He loved me so much. He still does.*

She found the tears were streaming down her face. Tears for herself, tears for that young man, idealistically in love, freeing Marietta from marriage to him because he thought he would be unfit for her. Tears for lost love.

And then the memory came of Nicholas in London, standing before the cold grate in Anna's drawing room saying, *I have never loved.* Lying to her, because she had known from that strained breakfast at Lord Sutton's house that there was something between Marietta and him.

She had betrayed her own feelings too clearly, she thought drearily. He had felt honour-bound to offer again and he knew that she would not accept anything but an apparently heartfelt proposal. A protestation of love.

So now what should she do? Freeing him

would not give him Marietta because he could not marry her. She got up and re-entered the maze. It was an apt path to be treading when her thoughts were so confused. Perhaps she could stay in its green sanctuary for ever…

Voices. She stopped in her tracks because one of the speakers, unmistakable even though she could not hear the words, was Nicholas.

They were ahead of her, so she walked on quietly, listening. The other voice was Marietta's. Sarah stopped. Whatever they were saying she did not want to hear it.

Silence fell and she moved again, taking each turning without thought, and found herself at the entrance. Marietta was running away, past the pond, towards the house. As Sarah watched Nicholas appeared from the side of the maze and she stepped back into the shadows.

His hat was in his hand and his hair looked disordered, as though someone had run their fingers into it. He put up the other hand and tugged his neck cloth straight and stared after Marietta. Sarah stared at his profile and saw an expression of raw emotion that she had never seen on his face before, and could not read now. Then he turned abruptly and strode off towards the park.

A little stream ran into the pool. Sarah heard

its bubbling as she emerged from her hiding place and she knelt, dipped her handkerchief in it and cleaned the tear-tracks from her face, sat beside it until she felt calm enough to walk back to the house.

Somehow she managed to avoid Nicholas until the family gathered in the drawing room before dinner. She put on another of her new gowns and the diamonds that Millie produced and recited a mental lecture about self-respect and dignity, then she sailed downstairs, head up and battle in her heart.

Marietta, stunning in palest gold and amber, gave her a sweet, pitying smile, but—wisely—kept her distance.

Nicholas greeted her with outstretched hands and then lifted hers to his lips. 'You look magnificent tonight,' he murmured.

'I love you,' she whispered back, gazing deeply into his blue eyes.

'And I you.' There was no hesitation, no flicker or blink, just total focus on her.

'Now, remind me who everyone is. I must make certain I offend none of your family by getting them muddled. There's your uncle Lord

Horace, and next to him your cousin Cynthia? Yes. Then next to her is Wilfred.'

She worked around the room, glancing up at him each time as though to check that she had each name correct.

'And then Marietta, your sister-in-law.'

Yes, there it was, the tense jaw, the flicker of an eyelid. The small exhalation of breath.

She carried on around the room and he showed no other sign that anything was wrong, applauding her memory and correcting her few errors. But she knew him too well to have mistaken those signs: Marietta had a powerful effect on him.

The night before she had sat on Nicholas's right hand at table, but tonight she was partnered by Lord Horace, who appeared to have taken a liking to her. As they were seated at the other end of the table she was able to look at Nicholas without him noticing.

Sarah ate and talked and laughed and all the time watched Nicholas and tried to examine her own feelings. These were more important than thoughts, she decided.

She loved Nicholas and nothing Marietta had said had changed that. And if she loved him, then she must trust him, or the love was not real.

The idea made her stop, her soup spoon halfway to her lips, and she had to put it down again.

He tells me he loves me. If I trust him, then I trust him to tell me the truth.

She felt immeasurably lighter. Yes, she still had to get to the bottom of Marietta's tale because she could not believe that Frederick had seduced the woman his brother intended to marry, not knowing about the betrothal—but the dark, nagging misery had gone, replaced by apprehension that she might not get this right.

If that was true. Has she lied about everything? Just who did the seducing?

One more day before our wedding day. Twenty-four hours to get this right for the rest of our lives.

Nick sat at his dressing table and pared his nails, taking great pains over it because that stopped him looking at the connecting door to Sarah's bedchamber.

He tried telling himself that it was ridiculous, at his age, to feel like this. He was as happy and as besotted as he had been when he had fallen for Marietta, and yet he recognised the difference. This was bone-deep, soul-deep contentment. This was love and it was going to last their lifetime.

A soft sound had him looking up into the glass and the paring knife fell from his hand.

Sarah was standing in the doorway in a white robe, her hair loose about her shoulders. He got to his feet, every sense alert.

'May I come in? I need to talk with you.'

She was not smiling and he could feel her tension across ten feet of space. There was a cold knot in his stomach and a chill down his spine.

'Of course,' he said evenly. 'Come and sit here.' He led the way to where a pair of deep leather chairs stood either side of the fireplace.

Sarah curled up in one, tucking the hem of her robe around her bare feet. He took the other and waited. It seemed she was having trouble framing the words and the cold knot became ice.

'I would like to speak about Marietta,' Sarah said suddenly.

Hell and a thousand damnations.

'Yes?'

'Were you going to marry her?'

'Yes.'

'But your family did not know?'

'They did not.'

How does she know this?

'You were injured riding here to tell them, but you never did because you were so ill.' She saw he was about to speak and added, 'Anna told me how your horse fell from the bridge and trapped you in the stream.'

'Yes.' That was all he could think of to say.

'So why did you not marry her? Why did she marry your brother instead?' Again Sarah hesitated. 'I should tell you that I have heard her explanation.'

'She told me that she could not marry me in my condition,' he said before he had time to think of some way of glossing over the humiliation and the pain. 'They thought my leg was going to be far more serious than it proved. They might have had to amputate it. One can appreciate her point of view.'

'And so she married the heir to the dukedom.' Those big sherry-coloured eyes regarded him seriously.

He had to ask, but the words were difficult to articulate. 'What did she say?'

'That *you* gave *her* up because you could not bear to inflict yourself on her. That your brother, seeking comfort for his distress about you, and not knowing of the betrothal, seduced her and insisted on marrying her. That she loved you and that you love her still.'

'Where did she tell you all this? When?'

'She found me in the maze this afternoon and greatly enjoyed spinning her poisonous little web. She left and I followed her out. I saw you, although you did not see me. She had kissed you, I think.'

Her face was fully lit by the branch of candles on his dressing table. He could see how white she was and that tears were standing in her eyes. 'Yes,' he said. Then, 'I see.'

'May I have a handkerchief, please?'

'Of course,' Nick said, as though his world was not disintegrating about his ears. He went to the dresser, found one and handed it to her, careful not to touch her fingers as he did so.

Sarah wiped her eyes, then blew her nose prosaically. 'I think that she kissed you, not that you kissed her. She is lying, I realise that. Twisting the truth about all of it.'

'You do? Why? How?'

'Because I trust you, of course. I love you. You told me you had never loved. You said it as part of a declaration to me, so I know it is the truth. I believe that you might have been infatuated with her when you were much younger, that you believed you loved her and that you came here to tell your family.'

'Yes,' Nick said, too shaken to do more than

stare at her. 'You trust me without question? You do not ask me if it is true, or to explain, you simply trust me because you love me.'

'Of course.'

'I owe you the truth. When she told me how she felt about my injuries, and that she could not marry me because I would be an invalid for the rest of my days, she wept very prettily. I think my infatuation lasted until I heard the news a few days later that she would marry Frederick. It was not a great success, that marriage. If he had lived I think there might well have been a scandal.'

'She twisted and turned the truth because she wanted to be a duchess. And I think that, when she realised she never could, she also discovered that she had loved you, in her way. It is strange, how often someone who has done something despicable turns on the person they have wounded,' Sarah mused. 'Self-defence, I suppose.'

She stood up before he could move and came to curl up in his armchair with him, her head on his chest, her hair tickling his chin. 'I almost didn't tell you all this. I did not do so because I wanted explanations. But I wanted you to know how I feel about you and I do not want secrets between us.'

Nick closed his arms around her and held her tight, her heart beating against his, the scent of her, flowers and woman, filling his nostrils, and found he had no words, no sensual desire, nothing except joy so deep that he thought he was struck dumb by it.

Sarah did not seem to need words, nor even kisses. She settled against him and he felt her lips curl into a smile against the bare skin where his robe lay open just below his throat.

At last he stirred, rose to his feet with her in his arms and carried her through to her own bed.

'Tomorrow,' he said, and bent to kiss her goodnight.

'Tomorrow, it begins,' she murmured, already half asleep.

Chapter Twenty-Four

The chapel at Severton Hall was small and ancient and it possessed a spare beauty and serenity that the decorations of white flowers and green swags served to enhance, not conceal. There was no stained glass, so that the light from the little windows fell in bright, dazzling patches on the worn stone of the floor and caught the wingtips of the cherubim on the memorial to Nicholas's grandfather, the fifth duke.

There were fifty guests seated, with some crushing of the ladies' finery, in the carved oak pews and the gallery above. Millie had a seat in the gallery, at Sarah's insistence.

Sarah stood behind the entrance screen while Anna, in her role as attendant, twitched and smoothed at her skirts of cream silk with the antique lace borrowed from Anna at neck and cuffs and gold-and-amber ribbons twisted at the hem. Her something blue were very dashing garters and the something new gleamed like wine on her ring finger.

Lord Horace cleared his throat and tugged at his waistcoat. 'Stop fussing the girl. You look very well, my dear. Very well indeed. Off we go, eh?'

Sarah smiled at him through her veil and nodded and they began to pace, out from the shadow of the screen, down over the ledger stones of Terrells laid to their rest beneath. She caught a glimpse of a name and a crest here and there and hoped they would approve of their descendant's choice of bride.

When she dared to raise her eyes, there was Nicholas waiting for her, Lord Sutton at his side. Lord Sutton was beaming while Nicholas wore the stark expression she knew now hid his deepest feelings. He was white to his lips and the realisation of his nerves gave her confidence.

They reached the altar steps and Sarah turned and handed her bouquet to the skinny figure in its brand-new suit of clothes, hair brushed into shining order, face scrubbed pink.

'I've got it, Miss Sarah,' Charlie said, hoarse with nerves, and a ripple of laughter ran around the chapel.

And then she turned back to face Mr Percy, the family chaplain. He smiled at her and she looked at Nicholas, drew a deep steadying breath and knew that she was going to be able to speak her vows without a tremor because this was the man she had waited for all her life, the man she could trust with her heart, her love and, she dearly hoped, their children.

'Dearly beloved, we are gathered together here,' Mr Percy began. Sarah blinked away one happy tear and waited to make the most momentous promise of her life.

'Where are we going?' It was the middle of the afternoon. The voices of the wedding guests, well fed and happily full of champagne from the wedding breakfast, floated out after them as Nicholas took Sarah's hand and ran with her from the front door, around the side of the house and into the gardens.

'It occurs to me that I must carry you over the threshold,' he said as they arrived at a small door set into the house wall behind the shelter of a vast rosebush.

'But the front door—' She broke off as Nicholas kissed her with all the pent-up passion of a bridegroom who has spent the past few hours making polite conversation with everyone from the local squire to the bishop.

'But this is so much more private,' he said when he broke the kiss and opened the door onto a stone staircase.

He lifted her in his arms, walked in—'Mind your head!'—and kicked it closed behind them. She had a moment of fleeting worry about his leg with the stairs, and the burden of a wife who was not, she thought ruefully, exactly dainty, but Nicholas seemed to have no trouble managing wife or stairs.

'This is exceedingly romantic,' she murmured against his neck.

'Good,' he said and did sound a trifle breathless, which made her laugh as they entered Nicholas's suite.

'Pendell.'

The valet, who had been setting a vase of flowers on the table, jumped. 'Your Grace!'

'Be off with you down to join your colleagues and their party. I will not need you again today, although a cold supper left on the table outside might be welcome. If anyone asks, you have no idea where I might be.'

'Your Grace, of course.' Pendell effaced himself as Nicholas walked through to the bedchamber and put Sarah on her feet by the big bed.

'One moment while I lock all the doors. I have no desire to be interrupted, not until tomorrow, at least.'

Sarah watched him, as he kicked off his shoes and struggled out of his tight coat as he went. By the time he had locked the connecting door to her suite he was down to his shirtsleeves.

'Do you mind—in broad daylight, I mean?' he said, as he pulled his shirt over his head. 'I should have thought. Shall I draw the curtains?'

'Oh, no,' Sarah said. 'Please, no. I very much want to look at you.'

That brought the colour up over his cheekbones and she felt herself blush in response as he murmured, 'That is mutual.'

He removed her gown, patient with the fiddly bows and hooks, and lifted it and her petticoats off with care. She looked over her shoulder as he worked on the lacing of her corset, fascinated by the concentration on his face as he wrestled with the knots. Then that fell away leaving her in her shift and her stockings and, all of a sudden, very shy indeed.

Nicholas seemed to understand because he kept his hands quite still on her shoulders. 'Easier we both do the rest at the same time?' She nodded and he smiled as his hands went to the fastenings of his formal black silk breeches. 'One, two...'

It made her laugh, as she supposed he intended, and she grasped the hem of her shift and pulled it over her head. When she dropped it, it fell on top of his breeches and she looked up to find him watching her face.

'You are exactly as I imagined you would be,' he said and drew her to him. He was very aroused, but his hands were gentle as he held her against him, letting her become used to the sensation of their naked bodies.

He was hard with muscle and there was the unexpected roughness of body hair and the hot demand of the thrust against her belly and yet the gentleness of his touch and the softness of his breath against her cheek.

Nicholas must have lifted her, because she was lying on the bed and he was above her, his weight on his arms as he looked down into her eyes. It seemed natural to open to him, to hold him between her thighs where he fitted so perfectly, that she forgot to feel apprehensive and felt all her shyness melt away.

He kissed her, lowering his body over hers

until they were tight together, breathed together, and she lost track of where her own flesh and his began. But there was more and she was impatient now, as bold as he was careful, and she nudged upward against that heat and hardness.

'Yes?'

'Yes.' She kept her eyes open, watched his face, lost in the wonder of this. It felt shockingly intimate, but not as painful as she had thought it might be, but still… She shifted, trying to ease the stretch and the ache and suddenly there was the pain but Nicholas was part of her. That pang was already fading as their bodies found their rhythm, one rhythm, because now they were one body, and her eyes drifted shut as Nicholas's mouth closed over hers and his movements became more urgent. The sensations building within her became more desperate and she heard him say, 'I love you, I love you,' and then she was lost in him.

Nicholas somehow found the energy to roll to the side, bringing Sarah with him to lie limply against his shoulder. One of her hands came up and made small circles on his chest as though reassuring herself that he was still there and not moving any more.

'All well?' he murmured.

'All very well. May we do that again?'

'In a while.' He ran his hand down the sweet curve of her from shoulder to thigh and back. 'Let me lie here and get over the shock of realising that you are finally mine.'

She wriggled and sat up, her legs curled under her, her weight on one arm, and made a leisurely survey of his body. *'Well.'* He thought it was approval. He hoped.

'I so nearly did not find you,' he said after a while. 'It makes me go cold to think how very nearly.'

'Destiny?' Sarah leaned over and kissed him. 'I could wish it did not use such drastic measures as threatened murder and ransom to achieve its ends. But we are free now.'

'I am not,' Nicholas said, catching her and pulling her down. 'You are holding me to ransom and I am never going to be able to buy my way free. Never.'

* * * * *

Author Note

All the places named along the Suffolk, Norfolk and Lincolnshire coast are real places, although the residents described are not based on any real people—especially not the villains!

You can walk through the Horsey Gap to the beach today, with a convenient car park and no risk of plunging into drainage dykes or marshes.

The New Inn at Saltfleet, in Lincolnshire, was a pioneer of the seaside break. As early as 1673 local gentry came regularly to eat fresh fish and enjoy the sea air, and by the middle of the eighteenth century the landlord had built an entire new wing to accommodate those wishing to bathe. It is still there and still catering to holidaymakers—these days as the centre of a caravan park.

The jewellers Rundell & Bridge had several

changes of name over time, becoming Rundell, Bridge & Rundell in 1804, and Rundell, Bridge & Co in 1834.

LET'S TALK
Romance

For exclusive extracts, competitions
and special offers, find us online:

f facebook.com/millsandboon

⊙ @millsandboonuk

🐦 @millsandboon

Or get in touch on 0844 844 1351*

For all the latest titles coming soon,
visit millsandboon.co.uk/nextmonth

Want even more
ROMANCE?

Join our bookclub today!

'Mills & Boon books, the perfect way to escape for an hour or so.'

Miss W. Dyer

'Excellent service, promptly delivered and very good subscription choices.'

Miss A. Pearson

'You get fantastic special offers and the chance to get books before they hit the shops'

Mrs V. Hall

**Visit millsandbook.co.uk/Bookclub
and save on brand new books.**

MILLS & BOON